In My Mother's Footsteps

CHERYL WATERS

1st edition, 2021

Edited by Nicola Lovick

ISBN 978-1-80049-806-8 (paperback)

ISBN 978-1-80049-805-1 (Kindle)

Designed by Yummy Book Covers

Typeset in Droid Serif, 10.5pt

ACKNOWLEDGEMENTS

You need support, encouragement and honesty from those around you. I was very lucky to have four amazing women with me, and to them all I say thank you!

Rosemary Robertson, you have encouraged me every step of the way.

From reading my first awful draft, highlighting my plot inconsistencies and proof reading the final copy. No mean feat!

For giving me support when I could "see it far enough" as they say, and for expressing your enjoyment of what you read!

Rosie Whitely, you read my manuscript in its raw form, fed back and constantly encouraged me on.

We had many a coffee over the years that included the words; "that would be good in your book one day...".

Thanks for believing in me, and perhaps giving me some ideas to write about!

Karen Darke, you chose the fictional town names for Cheshire, where we both grew up.

Our friendship has come a long way from eating your

mum's homemade pancakes in our maths class!

Kathy Foster, you are a lifelong friend and confidant.

Your enthusiasm for my writing and all that it has entailed spurred me on!

I am also forever grateful to these two ladies.

Designer Enni Tuomisalo of 'Yummy Book Covers'. From just one Brief, she produced the book cover I had always envisaged for the story, and also the interior design and formatting of my book.

Editor Nicola Lovick for pushing me out of my comfort zone, encouraging me and guiding me as I found my way. I considered all her suggestions and watched my story grow as a result.

Thankyou both for your help and support as I navigated my way into the world of publishing,

Lastly, and by no means least, thank you Phil. For helping me to follow yet another dream, for fixing the errors, wiping the tears and giving the hugs.

My husband, my best friend, toughest critic and soul mate.

With a special thank you to Peter Robertson who had had to listen to all the tribulation every Friday evening, for the past eighteen months, in the "Covid Arms" on Internet Street!

Finally, dear reader, a very special thank you to you, for choosing to pick up my book.

I hope you enjoy reading it, as much as I have writing it.

Cheryl Waters

IN MY MOTHER'S
FOOTSTEPS

Chapter 1

Claire sat perched on the edge of the bath in her small bathroom. Just how many times she had done this in the past five years she couldn't remember. Clutching the white stick in her hand, she couldn't bring herself to look. Sean, her husband, should be sitting here with her. What if this was the moment, what if this was when they finally found out they were going to be parents. He had been called to a meeting, or so he said. Claire knew Sean was fed up with the pressure the fertility treatment was putting on their lives.

Sighing, she shifted her numb bum further into the corner of the bath ledge. The IVF treatment had been so expensive. They were now on their last chance, funds depleted, energy gone. She knew that even if they had the resources to continue, neither of them could stand the disappointment of yet another negative test. Claire glanced at her watch. Time was up. In her mind she was planning how she would tell Sean they were to be parents. A grand unveiling of the news. The excitement they would share of finally knowing they were to have their long-awaited baby. He would hold her tenderly in his arms, caressing her tummy. Claire was aware her heartbeat had quickened. Nervously, she turned the stick over. She could feel her hand trembling and her chest ached. She couldn't bear to look. She squeezed her eyes shut. Then, with a deep breath, she opened them again.

There was just one thin blue line, the test was negative. Claire shook the stick. It had to be wrong. This couldn't be happening to them again. This was supposed to be it, their turn. Maybe she hadn't left it long enough. She dumped the test on the sink, then yanked open the bathroom cabinet to look for another stick. Damn it, had she run out? She threw everything out of the bathroom cabinet. Pills, lotions and potions spilled onto the bathroom floor. The anger was rising; she wanted to scream, but nothing would come. Finally, she slid to the bathroom floor and sobbed.

The past few months had been awful. She was a travel journalist working for a large newspaper in Manchester. Although she enjoyed writing articles, she had felt restless in her role there. The only thing that kept her working there were the people she shared the office with. That and financial reasons, of course.

Then, four weeks ago, after a long battle with dementia, her mother had passed away. Claire's world had once again been turned upside down. Her mum had been everything to her, the one she could confide in, share her ups and downs with. Her comfort when life was too much, especially with all the treatment they had been going through. Now, here she was again on this fruitless path.

Claire just couldn't get off the roller coaster. She had to keep going. It had put a strain on her marriage to Sean, Claire knew. Regardless, she had continued on relentlessly. Pulling herself up from the bathroom floor, she slowly picked up the strewn contents of the medicine cabinet. As if in autopilot she carefully placed them one by one back on the shelf where they belonged. Splashing her face with cold water, she glanced at her reflection in the bathroom mirror. Her face was drawn, dark circles under her eyes. This had to stop. She had to get off this carousel.

Sighing, she dabbed her face dry. Walking through to the bedroom, she changed into her running clothes. A good run would sort her out. Normally, Claire would run with her neighbour, Jacqueline. Not today though, Jacqueline was away out for the day. Having lunch with her sister, she had told Claire over the garden fence this morning. Sighing again as she tied the laces on her trainers, Claire reached for her headphones off the hall table, placing them on her head. Scrolling through her phone, she selected some uplifting sounds of the 80s. That would help her get into her pace.

Stepping outside, she pulled the door shut behind her. It was a beautiful spring day. Claire knew she had to embrace this, lift her spirits. A good run would start the healing process, as it had done many times over the past five years.

This time it had to be different. *I have to pull myself together*, thought Claire pulling the garden gate shut behind her. The village was quiet for a Tuesday. Mrs Barlow from across the road waved as she saw Claire set off. Claire waved back. Jogging down the main street of the village, a couple of workmen at the side of the road whistled as she went past. Claire couldn't help smiling. That felt good, she thought as she turned the corner away from the village green. Claire knew she needed to avoid being there this morning. Mothers and babies would be gathered around the swings after dropping the older children at school.

She pounded on. She could do this, she could keep going. 'I can do this, I can do this' she kept repeating, almost in beat with the music. As she reached the edge of the village, she slowed. Her body didn't want to carry her any further; it was like a battery had run out. The tears came streaming down her face as she slumped on the bench. She sobbed, sobbing for every negative test she had ever done. Sobbing for the baby she would never have.

When, finally, the tears subsided, Claire pulled herself to her feet. She suddenly felt idiotic, sat there at the side of the road. Luckily, no one had come past. Claire didn't think she could've coped with the humiliation of being a bubbling wreck in front of a stranger. She decided it would be a good idea to walk back to the village. Maybe running wasn't a good idea. She tried, after all. Her body was telling her to slow down, to rest.

By the time she reached the village she was feeling a little more in control, pleased that she could finally hold it all together. Maybe that good cry had been exactly what she needed. Turning the corner back on to the main street, Claire stopped at the Magnificent Mr Mole Cafe. Pushing open the glass door, she walked inside. It was fairly empty, just an elderly couple lingering over a shared tea cake.

Jean, who ran it, greeted her with a smile. 'Claire, lovely to see you. What can I get you today?'

Claire smiled back. She could do this. 'I'll have a latte please, Jean,' she said, taking some coins from the small pocket in her running shorts and putting them on the counter. 'To take away, please.'

'No problem.'

The aroma of coffee felt like an injection into Claire's senses. *Just what she needed.* The milk machine frothed away in the background, making it impossible to continue the conversation, not that she felt up to it, so she sat at one of the little tables.

'There you go, my dear,' said Jean, placing the cardboard cup in front of Claire.

'Thanks, Jean,' said Claire.

Saying goodbye, Claire stepped back out on to the high street. She knew a quiet spot where she could go to enjoy the coffee, away from the play park. Claire was relieved to see the bench under the large, gnarled oak tree was free.

Its branches, adorned with lime-green spring leaves, gave a little shade from the warm morning sun. Claire sipped her coffee.

The street was getting busy. It was your quintessential village main street. The butchers already had a queue outside, its red and white awning sheltering the villagers waiting in the queue. The postman whizzed by in his electric van, waving to Claire. She waved back. Everyone knew everyone in Butteroak. Claire liked that, though. It gave a sense of belonging. And that was a feeling she desperately needed just now.

Coffee finished, she tossed the cardboard cup in the recycling bin to the side of the tree. Crossing the road, she found herself outside the florist shop. A carnival of colours flowed out onto the street. Flowers of every form and hue lined the pavement. In a bucket to the side of the roses, Claire spotted her favourite; freesias. Their beautiful purples, pinks and yellows always uplifted her. Reaching down for a bunch, she picked them up and inhaled the glorious, heady scent. Why not? It was about time she treated herself to something nice. Now that the fertility treatment was over, there would be opportunities to enjoy some little luxuries in life.

The heavy aroma of lilies hit her as she pushed open the door. Marlene, in the middle of serving an elderly lady, smiled, acknowledging Claire. Waving back, she gestured she would have a look around whilst waiting. She was distractedly browsing the house plant section when she glanced out of the window. There, on the road opposite, was Sean. He was talking to Jacqueline. *That's strange*, thought Claire. She was sure that Sean had said he was at a meeting. It must have been postponed or cancelled. She bent and picked up a small bunch of roses to go with the freesias. Standing back up, she looked out of the window again. This time she stood, frozen to the spot. Sean was looking down at Jacqueline as she looked up at him, laughing. He bent to quickly kiss her on the lips. Claire felt sick to the pit of her stomach and her knees seemed to buckle as she watched them slowly pull apart, Sean tucking a lock of hair behind Jacqueline's ear.

Dropping the flowers, she turned for the door.

'Claire?' called Marlene as the door closed behind her. 'Are you OK?'

She was going to be sick. She staggered to the side of the shop. Resting her forehead against the cold brick wall, the world swam around her: Sean, Jacqueline, Sean, Jacqueline, Sean, Jacqueline, almost in the same rhythm as her erratic heartbeat. She felt tears, hot and salty, sliding down her blushed cheeks as suddenly things came back to her.

The broken door handle Jacqueline wanted fixing, the computer breakdown she had called him for, the problem in the loft with the TV aerial. *How could I have been so stupid?* She was shaking. She took a deep breath. Then another. She had to get home, get away from here. How could they? Her best friend, her neighbour, her husband. God, it hurt. An almost-physical pain.

Once home, she ran up the stairs. She ripped off her running clothes. Frantically, she pulled on her jeans and a t-shirt that was hanging on the wardrobe door. Running back down the stairs, she grabbed her car keys from the hall table. She needed to get away. Away from the house. Away from the pain that was ripping through her.

Jumping in her car, Claire just drove. How should she handle this? Should she confront him? Leave a note? Throw him out? So many questions whirling round and round in her head. After driving for what felt like for ever, Claire could see a pub ahead. The Dusty Miller. A typical Cheshire pub.

Pulling into the car park, she pulled herself together. *Goodness, she looked awful*, she thought, looking in the driver's mirror. Licking a tissue, she dabbed under her eyes, wiping away smudges of mascara. Rummaging in her handbag, she pulled out her lipstick and applied a delicate coral colour to her lips. Claire opened the car door and stepped out. The fresh spring air washed over her as she scrunched her way across the gravel in her pumps.

The whiteness of the pub glared in the spring sunshine. Pushing open the heavy wooden door, Claire walked into the pub lounge. It was a large room with an old-fashioned bar tucked to the left and an open fire. Only a handful of people sat around chatting at the small tables, laughing and smiling as they drank. The aroma of beer filled the air. It was that slightly stale smell you got in pubs.

'What can I get for you, love?' asked the friendly landlord.

'Gin and tonic, please. Make it a large one, please.'

Claire felt like a bottle of gin. She had hardly drank over the past few years because of the fertility treatment. For now, it would have to be just the one; she had to drive back. Fumbling in her handbag for her wallet, she realised tears were slipping down her face again. She rummaged again for tissues. Her bag fell to the floor, contents spilling out. The man at the table across from her jumped up and started collecting the contents of Claire's handbag from off the floor. Claire, down on all fours, came face to face with him.

'Here you go,' he said, handing her the tissues from her bag.

Claire blushed, suddenly feeling very embarrassed. 'Thank you,' she said, taking them from him.

The gentleman stood up, offering his hand to Claire to pull her up, which she accepted. 'Are you OK?'

Claire realised he still had her hand in his. He realised too, letting it go.

Claire sat down on the chair. 'Thank you, I'm fine, just had a bit of a bad day, that's all,' she replied, trying but failing to smile.

'No problem,' he said, returning to his seat across from her. 'Can I help with anything?'

'No, no thank you, I'll be fine,' Claire replied weakly, trying to return the smile. He nodded and Claire turned away. She needed to be alone, to think.

The gentleman bid her a pleasant afternoon and went back to looking at the brochures laid out on his table. Deep in thought, she nursed the glass in front of her. The coldness of the ice inside it matched the feeling inside her. Jacqueline, how could she? They were running, coffee and wine buddies. The thoughts were going round and round in her head. Claire knew she needed to go home to face Sean. There was no other option. She felt so betrayed; she had thought her marriage was stronger than this. They had been together for twenty years, childhood sweethearts. It was always Sean and Claire, Claire and Sean.

Finally, sinking the last of her G&T, Claire regained her composure. She left the table, saying goodbye to the landlord as she stepped outside into the spring air, shivered as it hit her.

Unlocking her car, the gentleman from the pub appeared, walking towards his car. For a moment he stopped and hesitated as if he was going to say something, but he lifted his hand to wave, then he was off.

Chapter 2

Sean turned his car onto the driveway, next to Claire's. Pulling on the handbrake, he sighed. He knew today was the day that Claire was due to take the pregnancy test. Now he was feeling terrible because he had chosen to see Jacqueline rather than be there to support Claire. What type of man was he leaving his wife to do this alone? Sean knew what type of man he was. He was tired, exhausted, bereft of any emotions where the infertility treatment was concerned. There was only so much a man could take. Their life savings were depleted. Their relationship revolved around the right time of the month, the most fertile time of the month.

Then came the test-taking, the disappointment, the heartache, watching Claire crumble yet again. Having a baby meant everything to Claire. Sean knew that, but he couldn't do it anymore. He didn't enjoy lying to Claire; he felt bad for wanting to be with Jacqueline. Sneaking away for afternoons with his neighbour. They had even been in the house next door when Claire had been in their home. Sean's chest felt tight just thinking about it, almost as if someone was sitting on him. He knew this had to stop, he just didn't know how.

'Hi, just me!' he called as he placed his car keys next to Claire's on the hall table. There was no reply. Maybe she was in the garden, he thought as he climbed the stairs to change out of this work clothes. Pushing open the bathroom door, he spotted the pregnancy test stick straight away, on the side of the sink. Once again, that overwhelming sense of pressure crushed his chest. He bent down to pick up the stick and saw that it was negative. He was overwhelmed with guilt knowing that Claire had gone through this again, alone, whilst he had been lying in Jacqueline's arms.

Switching on the bathroom taps, he splashed his face with ice-cold water. Sitting on the edge of the bath, he tried to get his thoughts together. They were out of money, out of energy, and out of their marriage. Sean wanted out. He loved Jacqueline, he wanted to be with Jacqueline. The news that Jacqueline had delivered to him this afternoon had confirmed all of that.

Making his way downstairs, he could see Claire sat in the lounge, TV off. She was sat still, staring out of the lounge window. As she heard his footsteps on the stairs, she turned to look at him. Her face was drawn and he could see she had been crying. Any normal husband would have rushed to her side, taking her in their arms. Any normal husband wouldn't have avoided being with her today, he told himself as he stood rooted to the bottom step.

'Sean, we need to talk,' said Claire quietly.

Sean nodded. Walking into the lounge, he sat down opposite Claire. He couldn't bring himself to touch her. What sort of man was he? The same question kept going through his head.

'How was your meeting today' she asked quietly, praying that he could be honest with her. Surely he owed her that. She looked him in the eye.

He looked back into her's. 'I didn't go to a meeting today, Claire,' he said, waiting for the explosion. It didn't come.

Instead, Claire replied, 'I know you didn't.' Sean was worried now. Why was she being so calm? Where were the floods of tears that came with every negative test? He looked pensively at her.

As he finally went to speak – someone had to fill the silence – Claire interrupted. 'You weren't in a meeting because you were with Jacqueline today, weren't you?'

Sean just looked at her, then he nodded. There was no point denying it all now. Claire had obviously found out.

Maybe this would make it easier for him. 'How long has this been going on, Sean?' Sean didn't answer.

Then Claire, raising her voice, yelled, 'How long, Sean?

How long have you been seeing our neighbour, my friend?' She was angry, so angry. He looked pathetic, sat there not saying anything, like a dog with its tail between his legs.

'Just over a year,' he replied, not looking at her.

Claire jumped up from the chair. 'Get out!' she yelled. 'Get out of this house!' Her eyes blazed, and her hand was shaking as she pointed to the door.

Sean tried to speak, his mouth dry. *This was awful.*

'Get out!' she screamed again.

Standing up, he tried to reach out to her to calm her.

Brusquely, she turned away from him. 'Go,' she said in a quieter voice.

Sean felt terrible. He tried to speak, to explain, but, as tears streamed down her face, she just looked at him and repeated, 'Go, please just go.'

With a click of the front door, he was gone. Claire stood watching as he cut across the front garden to Jacqueline's house. The bastard couldn't even have spared her that.

Sean didn't show his face for a couple of days. Claire couldn't face work, she phoned in sick. Besides all of that, she had just found out that her mother's house had sold within two days of going on the market. Now she had that to deal with that as well. She went about the house in autopilot. Knowing Sean was tucked up next door with Jacqueline cut through her like a knife.

We need to talk, she texted.

Can you come round this evening? About 7?

Yes.

Taking a deep breath, she put her phone down and looked for a pad of paper. What next? They couldn't come back from this. Sean had destroyed every ounce of trust she had in their relationship.

Having asked her recently divorced friend for a recommendation, she called the solicitor, arranging an appointment for Friday morning.

Claire felt empty, void of any emotion. Even the tears would no longer come.

That was enough for now. Tired to her very bones, she climbed into bed and slept.

At 7pm sharp, Sean tapped on the door. Claire was relieved he hadn't used his key.

Opening the door, she stepped back, without a word, letting Sean walk through to the lounge. They sat, opposite sides of the room, looking at each other.

'Do you want a drink?' Claire asked, getting up to pouring herself a glass of wine. She'd restricted herself to a small one before his arrival so she could do what she needed to do.

'A scotch, please.'

'I'm sorry, Claire. I shouldn't have treated you in this way.'

Claire nodded, stiffly. 'I think we both know that our relationship is over.'

He nodded.

Claire continued. 'We'll have to sell the house, but until then I'd need to stay here and you can stay with Jacqueline.'

He nodded again. He would agree with whatever she

wanted, he owed her that much.

They talked about putting the house on the market, using the same chain of estate agents that were handling her mother's house sale and dividing what little money they had left.

This feels so mechanical, thought Claire as she slowly ticked things off the list. No trace remained of the couple that used to talk and dance into the early hours.

He certainly wasn't resisting her. He had no right to, even if he wanted to.

Eventually he said, 'Claire, I have something that I need to tell you.'

It was now Claire's turn to just nod. He sat upright in the armchair by the designer gas fire, its fake flame flickering away. Slowly, he turned the glass of scotch in his hand. The evening light caught the crystal, sending prisms of light along the wall.

He had to say this. Taking a deep breath and looking her in the eyes, he said, 'Claire, I'm sorry, there is no easy way to tell you this, but I need you to hear it from me. He took another gulp of whisky before continuing. This was going to destroy Claire. He didn't want to see her face, but it had to be done, he had to say it. 'Claire, I am so sorry. I know this is going to be incredibly painful for you, but Jacqueline is four months' pregnant.'

Claire stared at him in horror. The pain tore through her chest and she couldn't breathe. She couldn't believe that after *everything*, he could still inflict such pain on her. Sean reached out to touch her arm, looking genuinely sorry. He wished he hadn't had to tell her. His heart was breaking, too. Claire pulled away with anger, running from the room.

Lying down on her bed, she sobbed her heart out. She had vaguely heard the door shut as Sean had let himself out. Now Claire knew the door was shut on their relationship for good. It hurt, it hurt so much. Despite knowing that there was no future for her and Sean, it still filled Claire with pain. They had been part of each other's lives for so long, it was only natural.

It seemed like she went round in a state of shock for days. The For Sale sign had gone up in the front garden that week. Claire had seen the neighbours looking, nodding and talking, it felt like whenever she appeared the talking had stopped. *How many of them had known?* thought Claire. Still, it didn't matter what everyone else thought now. Waking up on Saturday, five days after Sean had delivered his bombshell,

Claire finally felt a little more like her old self. From now on, Claire was going to do what she wanted to do. She was broken, but she was going to put herself together again. There were decisions to be made. On top of everything else, she still had her mum's house to empty. Normally Sean would have been with her, supporting her. This would be the first step in getting on and doing things for herself. She didn't need a man in her life.

Picking up the phone, she dialled the agent for her mum's house. They informed her the new owners had a date of 31st May, just six weeks' time. Was Claire OK with this, they asked. Claire agreed she needed to keep going, keep focused. Clearing out her mum's house would be the first step in her recovery. Putting down the phone, she felt quite pleased with herself. *Step one of the new me*, she thought proudly.

Slowly, she ticked a few things off the to do list. Claire hoped their house would sell quickly. Picking up her car keys, she decided there was no time like the present to clear out her mum's house. It would take a while to go through everything. Feeling a little more positive, Claire decided it would be good to focus on memories of her mum rather than the remnants of her marriage.

Chapter 3

In life, it was inevitable the time would come. Everyone passed on eventually. It didn't make it any easier. Claire had seen her mum go from a lovely, lively lady with her beautiful brown eyes, grey hair and smile, to this person Claire hardly knew, living inside her mum's body.

Dementia was an awful disease. You saw the person you loved, but it was just their shell; they were no longer the person they used to be. It was the days that her mum didn't recognise her, that Claire found those the hardest. Her mum had always been so active; riding her bicycle every day for many years. Gloria had always loved helping friends and neighbours; to think that was only three years ago was almost inconceivable.

The disease had crept up on her, slowly at first; it was all the silly little things, even Claire thought then that it was absentmindedness. Then, gradually, it got worse. Their local taxi driver had found her wandering the streets at midnight in her nightdress. That was the final straw. Claire had known then that she had to do something quick to protect her mum.

That was when moving her to Pine Trees happened. It had proved such a wonderful, safe place for her mother. They had given her so much care and attention. Although she had deteriorated in some ways, in many she had also flourished under their care. It had been a wonderful choice.

In the last few months of her life, as the disease really got its claws into her mother, Gloria had started to mention Chateau Le Grand Fontaine. Claire knew that her mum had worked there as an au pair. She had, in fact, met her father there. Hearing her mention it after all this time had intrigued Claire. When questioned, Gloria would just stare wistfully out of the window. Nothing else would then be said, leaving only unanswered questions.

When Claire's father, Maurice, had died of a heart attack five years ago, it had hit Gloria hard. She never let it show, continuing to throw herself into all her activities. Gloria had played bowls at the local club for twenty-five years. She was in the Red Cross and the WRVS. She enjoyed working in the canteen at the local hospital. It kept her busy; the customers loved her cheerful outlook. Gloria seemed to put everyone at ease. Right to the end, Gloria had been the life and soul of the party.

Claire remembered, with fondness, the night Gloria and Sean's mum had sat in a corner at one of their BBQs making their way through a bottle of Advocaat and lemonade. The two of them had laughed hysterically. They had even knocked a glass of wine all over Claire's brand-new carpet; fortunately it had been white wine, so it had been easy to clear up. They were both in a sorry state the next day, vowing to never drink again.

Then, finally, when the dementia had been noticeable, Gloria had to leave her job. It was a sad day for all; they had given her a wonderful leaving party.

It would not be easy, but Mum's house had to be sorted. For the next week, Claire went back and to between her mum's and home. It was hard clearing out the belongings of someone you loved. Claire had smiled, laughed and cried as she sorted through everything; everything seemed to have memories attached.

Today was the day she was going to tackle the attic. Letting herself in the front door once more, Claire thought how much she loved this house. It had been the heart of the family for many years. It made Claire smile, remembering Christmas, Easter egg hunts, birthdays and family Sunday lunches around the large oak table. That table that had been the feature of the kitchen. Every room she walked into came alive with voices from the past.

As Claire climbed the steps to the attic, she noticed, outside in the garden, a little robin perched on the garden seat. It wasn't the first time this week he had been sat there. Her elderly neighbour, Mary, had once commented that after the death of a person you could always see a robin in the garden keeping watch over you. Claire had laughed it off. The little bird hopped onto the bird table, pecking at the nuts she'd been putting out. The morning sun hit the smattering of dew in the garden, making it sparkle.

Coffee, thought Claire, I forgot my coffee. Making her way back down to the kitchen, she picked up her mug from the kitchen table. Glancing around and smiling, she remembered afternoons with her mum sat here, near the Aga, listening to tales of what had been happening at the WRVS and the bowling club. Gloria had always made Claire laugh; they had identical senses of humour.

Claire smiled to herself again as she started her ascent back up the stairs to the attic. Shivering, she turned on the light, pulling her worn, old cardigan tighter around her. *There doesn't seem to be much up here*, she thought. A couple of old chairs, a gramophone player. Claire didn't remember this being in their house.

Then, on a shelf, she spotted a purple velvet box with a little brass lock. Claire thought she would be better off taking this back downstairs. Tucking the box under her arm, she was careful to keep it the right way up, so nothing fell out. Carefully, she made her way back down the loft stairs, pulling the door shut behind her. Claire was too tired to go through the purple box this afternoon. She would save it for a rainy day when things had settled down. Claire popped the box in the back of the car, then closed the door. She walked back up the garden path for one last look at her mum's adored house and garden, following the gravel path to the back of the house.

The wisteria was coming into bud, sending out a beautiful perfume. The magnificent magnolia tree added a splash of spring colour to the garden. She could see her mum sat in the deckchair with a glass of Pimm's in her bowling outfit, smiling. Then at the garden table in her summer frock, cutting a slice of Victoria sponge she had made that morning. She could see her pegging out her washing on the line that ran from the garden shed to the garage. The little pink pegs still sat loyally on the line.

Taking a deep breath in, she felt like she was inhaling these memories to hold them in her heart for ever. Pushing open the glass back door, she wandered into the now-empty house, empty of material items, but still full of love for her mum. To Claire, it was like she was still there. She could smell her mum's rosewater perfume, she could smell the freshly laundered clothes, the Sunday lunch. Claire could see her mum setting out the pale-blue flowered tea-set on the kitchen table.

The house was empty now. The feelings, however, would live on in her memories for ever. She pulled the front door shut, wiping tears from her eyes, her heart heavy. With one last glance back, Claire walked down the front path to the gate. Turning again, for the last time, she took in the whitewashed cottage, its beautiful, thatched roof and pretty garden gate. Claire hoped the new owners would make as many happy memories as she held in her heart for this lovely home. *Nothing would take these memories from her*, she thought as she put the car into gear and drove home.

That evening, Claire sat with a couple of family photograph albums, flicking through the pages of childhood memories.

Many of their summers had been spent holidaying in France. Both Gloria and Maurice had loved it there. They were both fluent in French, which had always amazed Claire. Sipping her glass of red wine, Claire smiled at the memories. They all looked so happy.

A thought suddenly came into Claire's mind. That was just what she needed, a holiday! Why not? There were plenty of reasons why not. The house was up for sale; they needed to divvy up their belongings. There was paperwork to see to.

The more Claire sat and thought, the more the idea seemed very appealing. Work would be an obstacle, or would it? She was owed some time plus plenty of holiday still to use. Her boss was understanding. Susan knew what Claire was going through, and she had been very supportive. It probably wouldn't take much to convince her to give Claire some time off whilst she came to terms with all this. Plus, Claire could write from anywhere, so maybe a mix of holiday and some remote working until she could work out what to do with her life. It certainly beat sitting around with Sean and Jacqueline next door.

There was no way Claire could handle seeing their baby when it arrived. That would destroy her. Thinking it over a little more, she decided to email her boss, requesting some extended leave. No time like the present; she would only get cold feet if she left it.

And now, she had a holiday to plan. She knew in her heart that if her boss didn't agree to her taking the time off, that she'd leave. She would see Orion first. They had met whilst both working in London many years ago. Claire had since written an article on Orion's restaurant; he had loved it. He and his partner were always trying to get Claire to come over, but she had known that Orion didn't particularly like Sean, which made it a little difficult. She emailed him. Yawning, Claire knew she had to give in at last and go to bed. *What a productive evening*, she thought as she shut the laptop lid.

Her boss not only agreed that Claire could take some extended leave, but also suggested she could write a feature on the Limousin region of France. Apparently it was an up and-coming region for the Brits settling there. There was no reason at all why she couldn't work from France. If it went well, there would be some other articles to come her way. Claire had agreed. Orion had been delighted that Claire was considering a visit. Feeling very upbeat for the first time in many weeks, Claire started sorting things out. Her first call this morning was to Sean. He answered the phone on the

3rd ring.

'Hi, it's me,' said Claire.

'Hi, are you OK?' asked Sean apprehensively.

'I'm fine. I need you to come round this weekend to help me sort out who is having what from the house,' Claire informed him very matter of factly.

'But we haven't sold yet,' Sean said, rather surprised. He also knew he was in no position to argue with her.

'I'm taking a break for a while. I don't want to have to come back and face clearing out the house,' she said.

'Oh. OK,' replied Sean. 'I'll be round first thing in the morning then, we can make a start,' he offered.

'Thank you,' replied Claire, then clicked the phone shut. She wouldn't be giving him any niceties. They just had to get on with the job in hand.

Claire went on to her laptop, looking up flights to Paris from Manchester. There was one next Tuesday, so, messaging Orion, she asked if that would be OK. The reply came back almost immediately, telling her that would be perfect. Delighted, Claire picked up her phone. Next, to arrange the storage for her stuff. It was straightforward; it didn't have to be done immediately. They could come and collect it once a sale was agreed. Claire couldn't quite believe she had achieved all this in only a couple of days. It had been a blessing finding those photograph albums.

Saturday morning, Claire was up as the sun rose. She felt quite invigorated. Quickly showering, she then dressed. Sean would be around at 9am to start the process of who was having what. There was no way she was letting Sean off lightly. Picking up the two packs of sticker Post-Its, she popped them in her pocket. Green for Sean, pink for Claire. Opening the back door, Claire let the cool morning breeze in. Spring had sprung. May was coming in, bringing a little warmth with it. The birds chirped in their small back garden as a cat slunk along the fence, eyeing them up. Claire breathed in the air. Fresh air, fresh start, she thought to herself.

Aware of the front door opening, she went back into the kitchen and came face to face with Sean.

'Morning,' she said, trying to sound amicable, which was more than she felt.

'Morning,' he replied, reaching for a mug from the cupboard to pour some coffee.

Claire watched, slightly irritated at his familiarity.

'Where do you want to start' he asked, looking around the kitchen. He, too, was slightly irritated with Claire. Why this had to be done this weekend, he didn't know. Surely they could have waited until they actually sold the house. Slowly they made their way around, room by room. Placing either a green sticky note or a pink sticky note on the major items. 'You can have all the kitchen stuff, there is nothing I need,' said Sean. He wasn't enjoying this one bit. Still, he knew he only had himself to blame. One by one, each item was marked up. Claire seemed distant, but then what did he expect? He was very conscious of all that she had been through recently. And he could hardly expect her to throw her arms round him, after all that he had put her through.

Finally finished, they sat having a coffee. Sean looked at Claire. 'I am so sorry you know, the last thing I wanted to do was hurt you.'

He sounded sorry, but Claire didn't care. She remained silent.

'Jacqueline is really sorry too. We both know the hurt we have caused. She misses you.'

Claire looked at him with cold eyes. Standing up, she walked into the kitchen. Sean sat looking around the room. It didn't feel like home anymore; the soul had been taken out. There would be no more cosy evenings here with Claire curled up watching Netflix. No more games of Scrabble with a few glasses of wine. No more lying by the fire listening to nineties music. There would just be no more, no more Claire and Sean. Sean thought back to the day they had bought the house a few weeks before their wedding. They had saved so hard to get the deposit. On their wedding night Sean had carried Claire, laughing, over the doorstep, kissing her as he put her down. It was all they had both ever dreamed of.

Claire stood looking out of the kitchen window with similar thoughts. She wanted Sean to come through and tell her it was all a bad dream. She wanted to go back to the pregnancy test, hold it in her hands and discover she was actually pregnant. Would he have still loved her then, probably not. They had both been so caught up in their fertility attempts that they had let their world crumble around them. Each had been lost in their own feelings, but very different feelings from each other. Claire knew she had carried on trying to have a baby, regardless, whilst her marriage withered. She had to take some responsibility. It certainly didn't excuse Sean from sleeping with her neighbour and friend, though.

That she would never forgive.

Sean stood watching Claire looking out of the window. He wondered just when he had actually stopped loving her, if indeed he had. What he had with Jacqueline was different, but then no two loves are ever the same. He wanted to reach out to her, to hold her, to tell her again that he was sorry, but he couldn't do it. Turning, he placed his keys on the hall table. He walked out of the house without a backward glance. Claire stood, tears streaming down her face, tears for the love they had lost, their home that was destroyed and the baby that was never to be.

Chapter 4

Claire walked into the busy arrivals hall at Charles de Gaulle Airport. Glancing around, she looked for the baggage carousel. There was a whir of the motor as the belt started. Claire walked over to the allocated carousel. Slowly, the bags climbed the escalator to the baggage hall. Claire almost missed her bag, but in the nick of time she lunged forward, grabbing her burgundy tattered suitcase, then her black one. That was pretty much her life in there now, she thought as she hauled them off.

At the customs desk, she handed over her passport to the official behind the glass panel. What a depressing job, she thought. The surly looking French douane handed her back her passport with no acknowledgment. Tucking her passport back into the side pocket of her bag, she glanced around for directions to the car hire desk. To her right there was a large sign pointing straight ahead. She suddenly realised she felt almost liberated, free. She felt alive and, for the first time in a month, good! The tiredness and stress just seemed to lift from her shoulders. There was almost a skip in her step. She hadn't felt like that in a long time.

Claire joined the small queue along with a man who had the look of a suave businessman. He stood talking on his mobile, gesticulating and talking in what sounded like Italian. An elderly couple smiled at her. They spoke in what Claire thought was German. There was also a young couple kissing and cuddling as they stood waiting their turn.

Stepping up to the desk, 'Claire Fitzgerald', she announced. Claire handed over her paperwork to an agent named Fabien behind the desk, or so his badge said. Claire had treated herself to a Fiat 500. She had always fancied one, but, sadly, had never had enough money to buy one, so this was a real treat. He nodded, then in his lilted French accent he asked for her driving licence. Claire initially had the car for a month but Fabien informed her it would only take a phone call to extend. His English certainly put her French to shame. Signing the papers, she then passed them back. Finally, with a smile, she took the keys that were offered. Fabien explained which floor of the carpark and in which bay she would find the car. Wishing each other a good day, Claire walked away from the desk.

Following his instructions had been easy. There, in front of her, was the baby-blue Fiat with cream interior. She couldn't have wished for anything better. Not quite the romantic 2

CV, but it was certainly a little charmer; Claire was going to enjoy the ride. Loading her luggage into the back, Claire laughed. The suitcases only just fitted. Unlocking the door, she slid onto the cool cream leather; it smelled new. Glancing at the clock, she could see it had in fact only done 5,000 km. Settling herself in, she made herself familiar with where indicators and lights etc were. Claire was suddenly feeling excited. Her new adventure was about to begin. It was quite a way down to Orion and Maude's, so Claire had decided that she would stay her first night with a business contact she had made a few years ago when working on a travel supplement, Lilian.

Heading out of Paris was a nightmare: her sat nav took her around the Périphérique. It was a Monday, so incredibly busy. Motorcyclists wove in and out of the lane, horns beeping and hazard lights flashing. Lorries thundered by, their fumes flowing through the car ventilation system. Cars went from lane to lane and her head was hurting. Claire gripped the steering wheel, trying to fight back the tears; she was feeling incredibly vulnerable and her head hurt with concentration.

Slowly the road opened up, and the traffic became lighter. Claire sighed in relief. Flicking her indicator, she took the next exit. A calmness came back to her, the tension easing. This was a much quieter road. Tall popular trees proudly lined the route. Releasing her death grip on the steering wheel, Claire turned up the radio. To her surprise, it was a Leo Sayer track. Claire sang along as she drove. If someone asked her to name a French singer, she would have difficulty coming up with one. Oh yes, Vanessa Paradis. Then, thinking a bit more, she remembered Joe le Taxi. How sad was that, she thought. Then she laughed. It felt good to let go!

The late afternoon sun was hazy across the open country-side: Peroncey was, at last, in the distance. Le Grand Pont de Somme would be her base for tonight. This B&B was owned by Lilian and Tristan. Claire had first 'met' Lilian when she put together a supplement on holidaying in France, which was about ten years ago now. Claire and Lilian had never met face to face, but they had spoken many times on the phone. Lilian was delighted when Claire had called about staying. The Fiat slipped into the side road. On the left, by the swinging sign, was The Grand Pont de Somme. Behind, Claire could see the bridge from which the B&B took its name. In what was now the early evening sun, the building stood, almost slightly Gothic, very different to the architecture Claire knew she would see as she travelled further south.

Turning off the engine, just for a moment, Claire sat, closing her eyes and taking a deep breath. Then, opening the door, the smell of freshly cut grass enveloped her and a waft of baking followed. It was such a relief.

Wham! Claire was startled out of her warm, fuzzy feeling by a bundle of grey hair that came bounding up to her, wagging his tail. The dog was running round in circles. Ah, this must be Garcon, she thought.

'Bonjour, Garcon.' She laughed, ruffling his silky fur. Glancing up, Claire saw a very elegant young woman approaching.

Wiping her hands on her apron, she called out to Claire. 'Bonjour, I am so pleased to see you.'

Lilian, with blonde curly hair and an infectious smile, greeted her warmly, kissing each cheek. 'Hello, how was your journey?'

Claire smiled and told her about her baptism into French roads, driving around the Périphérique. It made them both laugh.

Lilian linked arms with Claire. 'Come!' she exclaimed.

The pair wandered up the paved path past the beautiful hydrangea bushes. Their delicate pale-pink and blue colours glowed in the late afternoon sun. These were her mum's favourite flowers. Pushing open the red back door, adorned with rambling roses, there was a sweet scent in the evening air. *Wow, what a kitchen*, thought Claire. It was everything a French kitchen should be. Beautiful floor tiles, black and white, and adorable little curtains hung from the oak counter tops. The delicious smell she had noticed as she had arrived now had her taste buds tingling.

'Oh, something smells delicious, Lilian,' said Claire.

Lilian smiled. 'It is the lapin for this evening. Have you ever eaten lapin?' For a moment, Claire wasn't too sure how to answer, but she had to embrace this.

'No, Lilian,' she replied hesitantly, despite herself. 'No, I haven't but I will try anything.' Claire hoped that she could actually eat it!

Suddenly, a tall shadow appeared in the doorway, followed by the man himself. 'Ah, Tristan, come, this is Claire,' said Lilian, proudly introducing her quite-handsome husband to her friend. With a confident stride and a warm smile, he took Claire's hand and kissed her on both cheeks. A wave of aftershave engulfed her. *Why were French men always so suave*, mused Claire.

'You are very welcome in our home; it is a pleasure to have you to stay. Now, has my dear Lilian offered you a drink?' Tristan's dark hazel eyes looked at Claire as he raised a quizzical eyebrow.

'No, not yet, Tristan, I am going to show her to her room first,' taking Claire by the hand as she replied. 'We will take a drink in the last light of the garden. First though, I will show you where you are to sleep.'

The pair walked out in the cool, tiled hallway, where an elegant oak staircase dominated the grand entrance. Claire had come through the back entrance, but, even approaching from this angle it didn't take away from the grandeur. Climbing the winding stairs to the second floor, they stopped at a beautiful oak door. Lilian turned the large brass knob, leading Claire into the Lady Eloise suite. The soft peach hues of both the room and the evening sky enveloped one in a soft cotton wool ball. Claire felt as if she wanted the bed to swallow her up, letting her sleep for days. Lilian proudly showed off the stunning en-suite shower room with a beautiful glass shower that could easily fit three people. The large copper bath tub gleamed from the little spotlights in the ceiling, a modern twist to a traditional room. Claire couldn't wait to luxuriate in it, she thought, running her hand along the cold copper bath edge. Lilian pointed out towels, toiletries, tea and coffee.

'Dinner at 9 and an apéritif at 8.30pm, but for now relax, enjoy, and we will see you later.' Lilian turned away with a waft of lavender perfume and a smile, leaving Claire to sort herself out. She felt overwhelmed with tiredness. What a long way she had come in a day. The damp, dreary morning of Manchester airport seemed a lifetime ago. Slipping off her shoes, she fell back on the goose down eiderdown, pillows cushioning her. All she wanted to do was close her eyes. Sighing, she knew she really had to get washed and changed. Then there was the challenge of eating her first-ever rabbit.

The three of them enjoyed a wonderful evening, laughing and chatting as old friends. Claire watched their chemistry; they made such an enchanting couple. Wine flowed throughout the evening. The rabbit, to Claire's surprise, was actually delicious. It almost tasted like chicken, the sauce to die for. They finished the cheeses, each one superb, then came her favourite; Crème brûlée.

It was a very relaxed and tired Claire that climbed the stairs to bed that night. It was all she could do to clean her teeth. Removing her makeup, Claire unpacked her night clothes. She went to pull out her laptop but stopped herself. That can all wait. Tonight is, she sighed, tonight is for me.

Drawing back the soft cotton sheet under the feather eider-down, Claire climbed into the large oak bed. The mattress wrapped around her body protectively and her head sunk slowly into the soft cotton pillows. She yawned, then, reaching over, switched off the bedside light.

It was the sound of a dog barking that stirred her. Claire opened her eyes. For a minute, she couldn't think where she was. The floral smell of the fresh bed linen wafted over her as her bleary eyes tried to focus. Stretching, she remembered. Throwing back the covers, she walked over to the window. Pulling back the chintz curtains, she opened the leaded-glass window with a creak. The bird song was beautiful.

Down in the garden, she could see Garcon leaping around while Tristan was pulling up vegetables. Goodness, thought Claire, what is the time? Picking up her iPhone, she looked at the screen. Oh, goodness, 10:00am! Claire realised she had slept for ten hours. She hadn't done that for years. She laughed. Feeling slightly guilty that she had overslept, she really hoped that she hadn't put them out for breakfast.

Claire hurriedly splashed her face and brushed her teeth, pulling a comb through her straight, blonde hair. Twisting the hair round, she fastened it in a half-hearted bun on the back of her neck. Opening her case, she pulled out clean underwear, a crisp cotton shirt and leggings, then slipped them on. A quick touch of lipstick and a spray of scent. She was ready to embrace the new day. Glancing in the mirror, she couldn't help noticing her trim figure. There was one good thing, at least, to have come out of the last few months: the weight loss would do her no harm at all. With a last pat at her hair, she turned and left the room. Pulling the door shut behind her, she headed for the stairs. The smell of fresh croissants made her suddenly feel very hungry.

As she took the stairs, she couldn't help being in awe again of this magnificent staircase. Running her hands over the smooth oak, she thought the carved bannister rods were beautiful. So much detail. There were some lovely pictures decorating the walls, showing country scenes which she assumed were of the area. Lilian was singing away in French in the kitchen as she entered.

'Ahh, Claire, my love, you must have slept well. Coffee?' inquired Lilian, turning to the copper coffee pot steaming on the stove.

'Music to my ears,' replied Claire.

Lilian affectionately rubbed Claire's arm 'This morning, after breakfast, we will go to the market. I am sure you will enjoy it,' Lilian said. 'It will be lovely for me to show you around.' She smiled, handing Claire a coffee.

Claire loved her friend's enthusiasm, her eagerness to please her. 'That would be wonderful, Lilian,' she replied. 'I love a good market.'

'Now, come with me. You can have your breakfast in the garden,' said Lilian.

Claire stepped outside into the warm late May morning air Lilian had set up a beautiful table under the magnificent magnolia tree. Claire looked at the stunning view; fields stretched far into the distance. Not a sound except for tweeting birds disturbed the morning ambiance. Kissing her gently on each cheek, Lilian left Claire to her breakfast. The coffee hit just the right spot, the butter croissants literally melting in her mouth. Flakes of pastry fell on the plate as she smeared homemade strawberry jam across them. *Maybe my newly svelte waistline won't last very long*, mused Claire. The fresh blueberries were delicious, tangy in her mouth. The local yogurt was creamy and cold.

Sitting back with her coffee, she wondered if she should check her emails. Scanning through them, there was one from her exercise class, one from the bank, the usual Next and Marks and Spencer emails. Of course there had to be one to spoil the moment, Sean! He was asking if she had received the draft of the divorce petition from the solicitor and could she respond quickly; he wanted to get things moving. No pleasantries, she noted, but they were way past that point now.

Sadly, Claire put her phone away. She could see their relationship had run its course. Claire realised now that they had actually fallen out of love some time ago. She couldn't pinpoint when, but it had certainly died, slowly. Sighing, she took a long, deep breath, then went back to drinking her coffee. Right, she said to herself, today is the day of new beginnings. Pushing back the chair, it scraped noisily on the gravel.

She almost felt guilty for disturbing the peace. Time to find Lilian. The market was calling.

Walking around the market with her friend, Claire wasn't disappointed. What a wonderful place. Such vivid colours and smells that filled her senses. There was the sweetness of ruby-red strawberries. The powerful aroma of sweaty feet as she passed the cheese stall. The sun had shone all morning and Claire had taken in every sight, sound and smell. She enjoyed every minute.

An hour later, after a lovely stroll around the market, Lilian had suggested the perfect people watching spot for lunch at a tiny bistro tucked into the corner of the market-place. Everyone had greeted them with the upmost friend-liness, kissing Lilian on the cheek and exchanging smiles and sometimes kisses with Claire. It was so stereotypically French. By the time they returned to La Pont de la Somme, it was already 3pm. Sadly, Claire had to prepare to leave this wonderful haven.

Chapter 5

Lilian had to see to some guests that had just arrived. Claire, returning to her room, packed her suitcase. Glancing out of the window at the garden below, she felt an overwhelming sense of sadness to be saying goodbye to her new friends. She knew she had to move on, to stand on her own two feet.

Picking up her suitcase, then her handbag, she made her way down the stairs. Tristan was just coming up to help her. 'Here, Claire, let me. You shouldn't be carrying a heavy suitcase like that down the stairs,' he said, leaping up the next two steps to take the suitcase from her.

Claire smiled. She wouldn't argue. Lilian was waiting in the kitchen. A gorgeous aroma of freshly baked bread filled the room. To Claire, it summed up the perfect life they had here. For a moment, she felt just a little envious. Lilian put down her cup, wiping her hands on her apron as she did so. Then, walking over to Claire, she wrapped her arms around her. 'You have to come back, we need more time,' said Lilian, kissing Claire on the cheek. Claire hugged her back. It was such a comfortable feeling. Tristan was waiting out by the car. 'Thank you both so much. You would not believe how much I needed that,' said Claire, giving them both another hug. With tears in her eyes, she climbed into her little blue Fiat. Then, with one last wave from the car window, Claire was off.

It would be a couple of hours' drive down to the Loire Valley. Claire was really looking forward to seeing Maude and Orion. They had met many years ago when Orion had his restaurant in London. They had a gorgeous little girl who Claire had only seen in photos. Orion had given up on London life, moving back to his home country to open a B&B in a beautiful old wine merchant's house. They had spent many months doing up their stunning home. Claire was now excited to see it. She had written a brilliant piece for his restaurant in London; it had amazed him, especially the overwhelming response he had received. But those were the days when advertising in papers used to work, she mused, waiting for the traffic lights to change colour.

Claire had decided she would keep to the smaller roads on this trip, no autoroutes. She was going to see the real France, not whizz by it all at 130km an hour down a straight motorway with some French driver sitting up her backside! She had a map and a sat nav and she was going to use them both. The country roads were quiet in the late afternoon. As she drove, she thought how flat the landscape was around here was. It was amazing how quiet the towns were. Some looked almost shut up, she thought as she passed through them.

Claire could feel herself smiling. Turning up the music, she breezed along the country roads. Popular trees lined the route. Napoleon must have been a busy man getting them all planted to give his troops shade on their long marches. The villages, so sleepy, just what did everyone does in these places; even on such a beautiful day there was no one around.

As she approached the Loire, the sun was dropping. Claire, looking ahead, gasped. In the golden hues of the evening sun, a hot-air balloon came into sight, appearing from nowhere. Then another, then another. Claire couldn't resist pulling to the side to watch them make their descent. She wasn't sure she was brave enough to take a ride in one, but it looked amazing. The blast of the fire filled the evening air. Everywhere lit up as flames shot high, then silently the balloons drifted out of sight down into the field. She sat for a moment, enjoying the silence.

Starting up the engine again, she continued on. Glancing at the dashboard, the sat nav said 3km to Orion's. Taking the next left, as instructed, she drove along the lane. 'You have reached your destination,' said the sat nav. There, sure enough, on the left was a very impressive maison de maitre, surrounded by outbuildings, dominated by enormous iron gates that made you feel you had arrived at a grand chateau. Window boxes, amass with geraniums, spilled from the windows of La Coeur de Vichy. There was no mistake she was arriving, Claire thought, as her car crunched noisily across the gravelled courtyard to a parking place. She turned off the engine. Claire looked around her. *Wow, it's just beautiful*, she thought. A figure appeared on the pathway

'Here she comes!' exclaimed Orion. 'My dear Claire.'

Coming towards her was the handsome, if not slightly built, Orion. He strode confidently down the gravel path; he had such presence. There was hardly any time to shut the car door before Orion had her in a firm embrace, planting enthusiastic kisses on both cheeks. Behind came Maude.

'Oh my dear Claire, it's been so long! It's so lovely to see you!' Clasping her face in her hands, Maude also exchanged kisses with Claire. 'Orion, fetch Claire's suitcases. Come, Claire, I have the wine chilling, you must tell me all.'

Leading the way up the path, Claire took in the beautifully landscaped gardens. A lot of care and attention been paid to this beautiful place. They made their way across the courtyard, entering through the double-glazed doors into a magnificent kitchen. Sure enough, three wine glasses stood poised, alongside some little aperitifs of saucisson and cheese. Maude picked up the plate, offering it to Claire. She popped one in her mouth. The tangy saucisson had quite a kick to it but the mild creamy cheese soothed the palate.

Claire hadn't realised just how hungry she was. 'That was delicious,' said Claire. Maude handed her another. Claire couldn't resist. Orion arrived in the kitchen; he had already dropped her suitcase in her bedroom. Turning now to Claire, he handed her an enormous glass of chilled wine. 'Our very own sauvignon,' he informed her proudly. Claire inhaled its lemony aroma. Taking a sip, the glass was ice cold to touch. The wine caressed her throat with its honey hues. It had been a long day. It didn't take more than a few sips for Claire to start to feel relaxed.

'Mama, Mama!' Appearing in the doorway was the beautiful Lisette. 'Come and meet Claire. She is an old friend of Mama and Papa from Angleterre.'

The little girl glanced shyly at Claire. 'Claire will stay with us for a few days so you will have time to get to know her. For now though, it is bedtime. Papa will read you a story,' said Maude, giving her daughter a cuddle.

Lisette looked at Claire through her tangled curls, smiling. 'Bonjour, Claire,' she said, in her soft voice.

Claire ruffled her curls. 'Bonjour, Lisette. I am looking forward to you telling me all about your beautiful home.' 'But first, bed,' said Maude.

Lisette walked off, begrudgingly, to bed. 'I wish I could spend time with you,' she said to her father as he took her hand. Claire then heard her whisper, 'I like Claire' as they climbed the stairs to her bedroom.

Claire and Maude both laughed. 'Come, Claire, I will take you to the Madame Vichy suite. It will be your room for as long as you need. I have just spent the winter redecorating it,' Maude told her proudly. 'I think you will love it'. The long spiral staircase twirled up through the centre of the house to the attic. Maude pushed open the door to reveal a room that looked like it had stepped out of a chateau; sumptuous reds and golds against the warm walnut floor. Ancient furniture graced the room; a huge armchair that Claire really just wanted to sink into. She was going to enjoy an evening alone here. Orion and Maude had a prior engagement with their accountant that night.

Orion appeared in the doorway with a tray. 'That is our little angel asleep,' he informed the two women. 'She is looking forward to getting to know you, Claire,' said Orion.

Maude, taking the tray from her husband, handed it to Claire. 'Here is your supper.' She smiled. They had filled the tray with a platter of cold meats, cheeses, and breads. Maude laid it down on the little table by the comfy chair, placing a carafe of red wine alongside. 'I do hope there will be enough here for you,' Maude said, looking at Claire. 'I feel so bad that you won't have a hot meal tonight.'

Claire patted Maud's hand. 'Believe me, Maude, I have been so looking forward to this all day. See that beautiful bath there,' said Claire, pointing to the enormous tub. 'I am going to take my wine and lie there for a good hour.'

They both chuckled. 'OK, OK,' said Maude. 'As long as you are sure.'

Kissing Claire on both cheeks, she turned to her husband, 'Come, Orion, let's leave Claire to relax.' Orion also kissed Claire before they both turned and left the room, pulling the large oak door closed behind them. 'Bon Soirée,' they called in unison.

Claire reached for her suitcase, lifted it up on to the rack, laid it down, then unzipped it. Right, first, unpacking, she thought. Carefully, she took out each item of clothing. Finding a suitable hanger or drawer for them, she put them away. She marvelled at what a vast dressing room it was compared to her two-door wardrobe she had left back home.

Packing done, she zipped the suitcase shut, popping it up on the top shelf of the dressing room. Right, time for a bath, she thought. Walking into the luxurious bathroom, Claire turned the gleaming chrome taps on. The water gushed into the brilliant-white bathtub. Reaching up to the shelf, she took a squirt of bubble bath. The aroma of lavender filled the room as the windows slowly steamed up.

While the bath ran, she unpacked her laptop, then lay her cosy PJs on the rather large-looking bed. Picking up her wine, she headed back into the steamy bathroom. Slipping into the hot suds, the aroma of lavender filled her nostrils, her hairline already damp from the steam; she felt ready to melt. The warm water enveloped her tired body and mind. She closed her eyes. Claire, slipping deeper into the tub, felt the soothing water caress her neck.

The wine was the perfect accompaniment to her bath but made her feel ever so sleepy. She pulled herself reluctantly to her feet, then, stepping out of the bathtub, enveloped herself in the soft white, fluffy towel. Slipping on the elegant towelling bath robe, Claire smiled at the monogrammed gold letters of the B&B.

Nice touch, she thought, slipping on the matching slippers. Back in the bedroom, she reached over to pick up her laptop. Then checked herself. It was not a good idea to read emails after such a relaxing bath. The world could wait. The last thing she wanted was to be reading any correspondence from Sean. Being here, in France, the world felt totally different. Sean and all her sadnesses were a lifetime ago, and that is where they will stay for tonight, she thought, tucking the laptop back in its case. Claire walked over to the bed and pulled on her PJs, then tucked herself back into the sumptuous robe. Sitting back down in the lovely chair, she pulled the cloth off the supper tray. She could almost feel herself dribbling, looking at all the wonderful meats and cheeses laid out before her. First things first, she thought. Picking up the decanter, she poured herself another glass of lovely wine. Claire heard a car pulling into the drive. That must be their accountant arriving, she thought. Then, feeling exhausted, Claire looked at the clock. It was already 9pm. Picking up her book, she headed for the bed. She was asleep in minutes; so much for book reading.

The next morning, Claire was awake bright and early. She could hear Lisette chattering in the garden. Sighing, she realised she really must look at her laptop before joining them for breakfast. It was 7:30am, so she had time. Climbing out of bed, she stretched. A shower first was probably the best idea before tackling the emails. Shower done; Claire was certainly feeling refreshed.

Drying her hair, she then pulled it back into a ponytail. Settling down at the little desk, Claire opened her laptop. She went through her emails. There was nothing too important. She wanted to take a quick look at her bank account before she finished. She was pleased to see that the account was looking relatively healthy. The money was also due to come in from the sale of her mother's house in the next few days. Claire had been pleasantly surprised when Sean had told her he wouldn't be taking any of it from her. Claire had been expecting a battle on her hands. Maybe he had a conscience after all. Looking at her watch, she realised she had better get downstairs for some breakfast.

Chapter 6

Breakfast was a convivial affair in Maude's kitchen. The aroma of dark-roasted coffee greeted her, along with Maude's smile. The table was laid with a gorgeous daisy tablecloth adorned with plain white crockery. Bless her, thought Claire as she leaned over to smell the freshly cut yellow roses that Maude had placed on the table. Outside, the sunlight shone in the backyard. The pool looked like it had tiny pieces of glass scattered all over; they twinkled in the morning sunshine. Lisette was away to school, so the house was quiet. Maude greeted with a kiss on each cheek.

'I have a few things I need to do this morning. Will you be OK on your own for a little' she asked. 'No problem at all, Maude, I have some paperwork that I need to finish anyway for mum's house sale,' Claire said, taking the coffee that Maude offered her. 'I would like to head out to have a look around the area, maybe have lunch somewhere.'

As they sat at the table, coffee cups in hands, they chatted amicably, catching up on all the news since their last meeting. Claire loaded a teaspoon with homemade jam, spreading it over a croissant, sighing as she did so. She would be the size of a house at the end of this trip. Orion arrived just as they were clearing the dishes. He kissed Maude, then Claire.

'What are your plans today, Claire,' Orion enquired, taking a cup down from the shelf and pouring himself some fresh coffee. He gestured to Claire with the pot. Claire shook her head.

Maude went to get on with her laundry, smiling delightedly to see the two friends back together again. Claire and Orion chatted for a while, then Orion bid her a good day. Work called. Claire climbed the spiral staircase back to her room.

Having looked through the leaflets she had picked up downstairs, Claire decided it would be an excellent start to her day to visit Chenoceau. This chateau always intrigued her, particularly its history. It also looked stunning. She was suddenly felt very content at her plan all coming together. However, she knew she needed to look to the future. Orion and Maude were happy for Claire to stay as long as she needed, but Claire didn't want to outstay her welcome. Certainly, a few days here would be good for the soul, she thought. There were a few chateaux she wanted to visit, along with the towns of Amboise or Blois. There was also the lovely house of Close de Luce, which was the last home of Leonardo da Vinci. Claire had also wondered about going to Reims.

Maybe the memories of that holiday with Sean would be too raw, however.

They'd had a wonderful trip. Claire even remembered a beautiful vineyard they stopped off at. In the grounds was a gorgeous little auberge where they ate a delicious lunch. On the menu there was char-grilled chicken breast, served in a champagne sauce; a gourmet delight. Even to this day she still said it was the best chicken she had ever eaten, washed down of course with a glass of the local champagne!

Claire realised she was spending far too much time reminiscing. The trouble was that everywhere Claire wanted to go held memories. It made her realise that this was going to be a hard trip emotionally, but she was determined it would be an enjoyable one.

Later, on Orion's recommendation, Claire set off for Amboise. As she drove along the side of the Loire river, she marvelled at how wide it was. There was an abundance of herons and swans going about their business on the sandbanks. Claire could see Amboise up ahead, its majestic castle sitting proudly above the town, surrounded by a jigsaw of rooftops and crooked chimneys. Crossing the bridge, Claire looked up at the flags flying from the castle ramparts. So regal. Spotting the car park by the river, she turned into a space.

Leaving the car, Claire made her way across the main road. The sun was glowing, the sky azure blue, June was just starting. Claire removed her light-grey cardigan. She tucked it around her waist; pleased she thought to put her light linen shirt on that morning. As she crossed the street, she could hear an accordion playing. There was a jolly man who looked in his element as he pushed in and out on the concertina's bellows. He smiled at Claire as she dropped a euro into his cap.

The shops were beautiful; little individual shops selling lovely products lined either side of the street. The aroma of fresh soaps filled the air, its stall spilling out on to the street, a pastel rainbow. The wonderful aroma of lavender and lemons engulfed her. She looked to see if she could find a rosewater-scented one. Yes there was, on the top shelf. Reaching out, she popped it into her basket. The lady then wrapped it in cellophane, adding a pretty little bow to the beautiful wrapping. Claire thought she would take it back for Maude.

Claire visited Chateau de Amboise, then went for lunch in one of the quaint little restaurants that lined the cobbled street. The magnificent chateau stood on the hill in front of her. Claire was in her element as she sipped her glass of wine. The little restaurant, like many others along the street, busy. There were so many languages being spoken around her. She could pick up Italian, Spanish and German. Everyone appeared so relaxed. Couples in deep conversation, an elderly gentleman reading his paper, the two young Italian girls chatting away, continually glancing at their phones.

Claire felt the need to glance at hers. Nothing urgent to attend to, and she felt relieved as she tucked it back into her handbag. That afternoon she explored Clos de Luce. The garden of red 'Leonardo' roses was a delight. From the cafe, the view across to the town and the chateau was stunning.

Later, feeling accomplished, she pulled her car into the car park back at Orion and Maude's. Claire could hear Lisette splashing around in the pool. That might be just what she needed after being in the heat all day. It didn't take her long to get changed. Claire waved to Lisette as she approached the pool.

'Claire!' called Lisette, waving her little hands and laughing as Orion splashed her.

'Ah, Claire, you are coming to join us,' laughed Orion.

'Come and tell me all about your day.'

Claire spent the next hour in the pool. She laughed, as she played with Lisette; the little girl was a delight. In between throwing a ball, she filled Orion in on her day's exploration. That evening, they gathered around the large oak table in the kitchen. Maude prepared a fantastic meal of fillet steak with frites and vegetables.

Proudly, Orion showed Claire the red vintage that they would have to accompany the meal. He pulled the cork out of the bottle with expertise, pouring Claire a glass. Orion showed her how to inhale the wine's aroma first, rolling the liquid around in the glass. Then he told her to 'take a sip', to feel it in your mouth. Savour the flavours. Claire felt ostentatious in doing so. It wasn't her, but for Orion she would give it a go. Not quite getting the tasting right, Claire almost choked on her wine, which made Orion roar with laughter.

'Not too fast, Claire,' he scolded her. 'Are you so desperate for a glass of wine?' he laughed, patting her shoulder.

Claire loved hearing about the renovation work that Orion and Maude had carried out in their beautiful home. Orion had handed her a lovely photo book to look through. 'Wow! That is very impressive,' she remarked, flicking through the glossy pages. 'What a labour of love.' Their talk soon turned to Claire and Sean. Claire knew, deep down, they had never liked him; they had put up with him for her sake. Sean always knew everything, quite often coming across big-headed. However, Orion, always the perfect gentleman, had tolerated him. He hadn't wanted to jeopardise his friendship with Claire.

They moved outside, the sweet smell of grass and roses filling the night air. Contentedly, they sat chatting. 'I am truly sorry that things didn't work out for you, Claire,' said Orion, patting her hand.

Claire shrugged. 'Some things are just not meant to be,' she sighed with a faint smile.

'It must have been an incredible shock finding out that he was seeing your next-door neighbour,' said Maude, standing up to collect the plates. 'It was, but that wasn't the worst part.'

Maude and Orion looked at her expectantly, and Maude sat back down. Claire was quiet. 'You don't have to tell us if it is too difficult,' said Maude gently, seeing the tears fill Claire's eyes.

'It's OK, I have to talk about it sometime,' she said. 'Sean and Jacqueline are going to have a baby,' Claire said, her voice almost a whisper. Both Maude and Orion looked shocked.

'Oh, Claire,' said Maude, putting her arms around her. 'How awful.'

Claire looked at them, tears filling her eyes. 'It hurts so much,' she sobbed. Maude held her and Orion went to find some tissues. He felt slightly uncomfortable; this was women's territory! He hated to see Claire so distraught, though. If he could get his hands on that Sean, he knew what he would do. Returning with the tissues, he handed them to Claire. After a few minutes, she regained her composure.

Maude excused herself to clear the table. Claire's offer of help got a definite 'no!' from them both. 'Sit here, Claire, enjoy the evening, I will be much quicker on my own.'

'OK,' conceded Claire. For the next few moments, Claire and Orion sat in silence. A million stars twinkled, filling the night sky above them. The full moon cast a white veil of light across the garden. Claire took in the beauty of it all, enjoying the amicable silence.

Orion reached for her hand and said to her, 'It will all be OK, Claire, you will see. All will be well.'

Claire squeezed his hand back. 'I know it will, Orion, thank you.' She smiled. 'Thank you for a wonderful evening, for allowing me to stay in your beautiful home.'

As darkness fell, Claire bid them good night.

Morning broke, the birds sang. Somehow it always seemed more special abroad. Claire wasn't sure why. After all, the birds tweeted each morning at home, the same sun still rose, yet here you noticed every movement, every sound.

Throwing back the bedding, Claire walked to the large French windows. Opening them, she reached out to release the shutters, fastening them back against the already warm brick wall. The sounds drifted up from the kitchen where Lisette was playing. Morning dew glittered on the green grass. It lit up the cobweb slung across the ancient pine tree in front of the house. In the distance was Orion, raking the gravel ready for the arrival of their next guests. Suddenly, as if sensing he was being watched, he stood up and turned and waved to Claire. Claire waved back. What a beautiful morning. She smiled, turning her attentions back to getting ready.

Pulling the bedroom door shut behind her, Claire stepped onto the oak spiral staircase. The large oak staircase with its ornate iron railings winding down the three floors. Claire ran her hands over the cold iron as she made her way to the breakfast room. An American couple were pouring over a map of the region, raising their heads with a 'bonjour' as Claire entered the room.

'Bonjour.' She smiled back.

'Ah, you're English,' the American man said.

'Yes I am, is it so obvious?' smiled Claire.

He laughed. 'It's funny, isn't it?' he said. 'You can speak in your best French anywhere and they know you're English or, like us, American. Then, offering his hand to her, he said, 'Arthur.'

Claire took his hand.

'This is my wife Veronica. We are doing a whistle-stop tour of Europe,' he explained. 'We couldn't resist a few days here.' He laughed. Claire noticed his eyes twinkling with affection towards his wife.

Veronica smiled, holding out her hand to Claire too.

Just then, Maude appeared from the kitchen. 'Bonjour, how did you sleep?'

'The room and the bed are just divine; I haven't slept so well for ages! I think it also had something to do with that delicious supper.' Claire smiled.

The Americans went back to their map. Claire settled herself at the table across the room, picking up a map herself. Orion appeared in the breakfast room, speaking first to the Americans. They asked him a couple of questions. Claire noticed how he answered them; the passion for his region so obvious. It was lovely to see him so happy and content. This differed from the conveyor belt of stress and tension she had seen him on when he was running his own restaurant in London. Making his way across to Claire, he smiled, 'Good morning, madame.'

'Good morning.' She laughed.

Orion kissed her on each cheek. 'So, my friend, what have you planned today?' he asked, looking down at the map she had open on her table.

He also bent over the map, pointing out places he thought she should see.

Maude appeared. 'Claire, will you join us for dinner tonight, we would love your company?' 'That would be lovely.'

'Eight?'

Dinner with Orion and Maude would be the perfect end to a day of sightseeing. Her day took her to Blois this time, another chateau. Its beautiful and unique stone staircase, which spiralled up the outside of the chateau, was amazing. Claire stood on the flagged-stone floor of the courtyard, staring up at it. She wandered around the vast rooms listening to the audio commentary playing in her ears. She loved the history of it all.

Lunch was a delight in the restaurant across from the chateau. It was a shame she had to keep to soft drinks; she would have loved to have tried one of the many wines that they offered. After lunch she had taken a walk along the esplanade of the river. Driving back that evening she felt content, a feeling she hadn't felt in a long time.

Claire joined them for dinner, as arranged, at 8pm. Later, settled outside, Claire, suddenly remembering, decided to take the opportunity to ask Orion if he had heard of Chateau Le Grand Fontaine. He hadn't but would make enquiries.

'Why do you ask?'

'My mother, in her last few months, kept mentioning this chateau. I know she met my dad there.'

'Dementia is so unkind, Claire.' Claire nodded.

'I know, and I think I am reading far too much into it but thought I would run it by you.'

Orion smiled at her. 'I am pleased you did. I will certainly look into it for you.'

Claire nodded. 'Thank you, what would I do without such good friends?'

Orion smiled at her. 'It works both ways; I am sure you would be there for me.'

Claire agreed. She certainly would be there for either of them. Then, yawning, she said, 'Time for bed, I think.'

Tomorrow is another day. Tomorrow she would get moving on the next step of her life.

Chapter 7

Claire woke, with renewed determination. She knew she would have to move on from here. Maude and Orion were fabulous, but Claire needed to gain some independence. Step out on her own. Make some decisions. Mulling it all over last night, she knew she was ready to move on. Ultimately, she needed to get to La Creuse region to find a cottage to rent. With this in mind, she had asked Maude and Orion over breakfast if they knew anywhere.

'I'll certainly make some enquiries for you, Claire,' said Orion supportively. 'I have a cousin there who has a cottage. He may be able to help,' he offered kindly. 'You know you don't have to move on,' he said kindly.

'I know.' She smiled. 'You have both been so incredibly kind having me to stay,' she said, picking up one of the delicious-looking croissants laid out on the table. 'I need to look at my life. Work out what I want to do from here. I can't do that when I am so beautifully cocooned by my wonderful friends.'

Maude and Orion laughed too. They enjoyed having her with them, but they also knew she was doing the right thing. 'Well, we will always be here if you need us. Remember that' said Maude, topping up Claire's coffee.

Orion then made his excuses; he had work to tend to in his office. Maude had to change a couple of rooms over, ready for guests. 'Can I help you,' offered Claire, finishing her coffee. 'That's kind of you, but I have Agnes in with me today so you just enjoy yourself,' said Maude giving her a hug.

Claire went to brush her teeth. There were another couple of chateaux that she wanted to take in today. She might as well see as much of the area as possible, she thought to herself. As she came back down the stairs, Orion came to meet her in the hallway. 'Look,' said Orion, handing her a piece of paper. 'My cousin down in the La Creuse has a cottage for rent. He is happy for you to go and have a look.'

Claire took the piece of paper, tucking it into her bag. 'Oh lovely, thank you, Orion. I will call him later.'

Now it was time for one last day visiting this beautiful region. There were another couple of chateaux to see. She loved this area of France; it would be an interesting one to write about one day.

Claire headed off to Chateau Chaumont, it was only just up the road from where she was staying. Each year the chateau held a flower festival. Claire wandered around the grounds.

The displays were stunning. So much so that she spent far longer than she had expected walking around them. It made her think of her mother. Gloria had loved her garden, whiling away many an hour amongst her plants. Pruning, cutting, replanting. Claire smiled, thinking of her mum with her gardener's apron, her old, faithful straw hat carefully placed on her head. Her mum would want her to smile when she thought of her.

Claire looked around her. The place was busy. Everyone was admiring the flowers, stopping to smell them, to take photographs. Children ran around squealing with delight at the water gardens. There was such a feeling of connection for Claire with life in France. It would be lovely to see more. Thinking back to her holidays with her parents, Claire wondered if she should do a little a tour? Take a trip back down memory lane, visit some of their holiday haunts. The more she thought about it, the better it sounded. It gave her such a positive vibe as she continued her walk around the grounds.

Later, back at the B&B, Claire took out her road map of France. It was a huge country but some places she could remember were certainly within her reach. Looking in more detail on the map, she found the town where Orion's cousin lived: La Terraine. It was certainly central on the map. A good place to base herself and explore. It would also mean if Susan had any other writing assignments for her, on France, she would be ideally placed to get to them. Pondering a little more, she looked to see where the Jura was.

That was one place she would head to from here. She could remember the rolling mountains. Azure lakes with an abundance of walking trails. Jotting these all down in her note book made her feel she was getting somewhere. It was a step forward. It certainly helped her forget about the last couple of months. Claire looked again at where La Terraine was. She noticed the city of Limoges was quite close too. If she remembered rightly, it was famous for its porcelain. She would enjoy a day wandering around the shops there. Thinking back now, she could remember her mum's blue and white tea service. Claire was pretty sure it had come from Limoges.

Looking at her notebook, she had quite a list. It was certainly an outline of a route she could take. Decision made, Claire couldn't wait to share her plan with Maude and Orion. She was looking forward to spending time with them over dinner again tonight. Talking of which, thought Claire, she had better jump in the shower.

Dressed in one of her few summer dresses, Claire made her way down to dinner. There was a wonderful aroma coming from the kitchen. Peeking round the door, Claire said,

'Yum, Maude, something smells amazing.'

Maude, removing a wisp of hair from her face, smiled at Claire 'I have made you escalope de veau in a mushroom sauce' she said proudly.

'Where is Lisette?' asked Claire. 'It's very quiet?'

Maude laughed. 'It certainly is, she is spending the night with her grandparents.'

At that moment, Orion came through the door. 'Ah, Claire, how was your day?' he asked, reaching into the fridge for a bottle of wine. 'It was amazing,' she replied. 'The gardens at Chateau Chaumont are out of this world.'

Orion handed her a glass of chilled wine.

Claire, as she had been taught by Orion, lifted the glass to her nose, swilling the contents for a few seconds before letting the wine infuse her mouth with its zest of lemon and oak. 'Ah, my dear Claire, you have learned well,' laughed Orion.

Maude turned to the pair of them. 'Right, you two, shooo! Out you go. I want to finish dinner and you're getting in my way.'

Orion and Claire laughed as they went out through the door. 'You don't argue with Maude.' He smiled. They sat down at the table in the courtyard. Maude had put a beautiful cream linen cloth on the table, crisp and bright. In the centre of the table was an arrangement of freshly cut roses and lupins. Claire bent over to smell them. 'So, what have you decided to do, then?' asked Orion, pulling out a chair for Claire to sit on.

'Well, I think I will take myself on a little tour. I would like to revisit some of my childhood holiday spots, then I will contact your cousin in La Creuse and see what the cottage is like.'

Claire sipped her wine, then continued, 'La Terraine seems to be very central. I could base myself there for a month or even longer whilst I get my thoughts together.'

'That sounds an excellent idea,' Orion replied. 'You can do this, you will be fine, I know you will.'

Claire smiled at him, wishing she had the same confidence in herself that Orion seemed to have in her. Maude appeared with the first two plates. 'Oh my, that smells amazing,' said Claire, as Maude popped the plate down in front of her. Maude joined them with her plate. Orion reached for his wine glass, holding it in the air, 'To friends and to new beginnings.' He smiled and the three of them chinked their glasses. Claire knew she was very lucky to have such amazing friends.

After dinner, Orion fetched his road map from the hallway. Laying it out on the table, he and Claire leaned over it, looking at the places she could remember. It was decided that she would spend one last day with them tomorrow, then set off on her grand tour. Going up to bed that night, Claire felt happier than she had felt in a long time. Sean was miles away. It still hurt. Somehow, though, she was pushing the thoughts to the back of her mind. It was the first time in twenty years she had put herself and her feelings first. It felt good.

The next morning, Claire was up and about early. She could hear Maude hoovering in the bedrooms. Looking out of the window, she saw Orion drive off towards town. It was going to be another warm day; there was a stillness to the air. The birds tweeted their morning song and there was a cat licking its paws on the grass in front of the house. He looked incredibly content, thought Claire. France seemed to have that effect on people.

Turning back to the room, Claire knew she was going to miss being here. It was a haven for her. Comfort, privacy and two lovely friends. Picking up her laptop, she placed it on the small table, making herself comfortable. Not that she wanted to go back to the real world; however she had to read her emails sometime. While the laptop warmed up, Claire popped a capsule in the coffee machine. It was still early, only 8am. She had time to do this before breakfast. Maude hadn't had guests last night, but Claire knew she had rooms to get ready for tomorrow, so she didn't want to get in the way.

Looking through her emails, she spotted one from her boss. Claire opened it. Susan was filling her in on what was happening in the office. It made Claire smile with the office politics. Susan was looking forward to her piece on La Creuse. Claire dropped a quick note back, telling Susan she planned to start in about two weeks' time. Finishing her emails, she gathered up her clothes. Maude had kindly offered to do some washing for her before she left. It would be good to have some fresh clothes for the next stage of her journey.

The hard bit now was saying goodbye to Maude and Orion tomorrow morning. They had welcomed her so lovingly into their beautiful home. Maybe today she should look for a little gift for them. Something to say thank you. Goodness knows what she would buy.

Down at breakfast, Maude had set up a little table for one. There was a note on the plate to say that Orion had had to go out for the day. Maude said, Claire would find her in one of the rooms if she needed her. Claire thought it would be nice that they didn't have guests again tonight. At least she could thank them and say goodbye over dinner so as not to prolong it the next morning. There was a lovely gift shop that Claire had remembered on the high street, so she decided to head back into town. Maybe she would find something for Maude and Orion there. She wouldn't insult them by buying wine, but maybe two crystal wine glasses would be nice, she mused, as she looked in the window.

Stepping inside was like walking into an Aladdin's cave. The shop sold everything you could imagine you would need in a kitchen. The lady behind the desk was incredibly helpful and showed Claire to the large display of crystal at the back of the shop. After browsing for ten minutes, changing her mind more than once, she finally selected two beautiful white wine glasses. The shop assistant assured her they were a good choice as she carefully laid them in the velvet box.

'Are they a gift?' she asked, as she fastened the bow around the box. 'Yes, they are,' smiled Claire.

'Lucky people, then,' smiled the lady.

Back at the B&B, Claire placed the box carefully in her room before taking a bath. Who knew when she might get to luxuriate in bubbles again; she was going to make the most of this. Afterwards, Claire dressed for dinner. As they all sat around the table later that evening, Claire watched the chemistry between Maude and Orion. It happened; she thought. Love can last. They were proof of that. She felt a little sad, thinking of Sean. Wondering how he felt now that Claire was out of his life. He was probably too wrapped up with Jacqueline having the baby. She was suddenly jolted back to the now, by: 'Claire, are you OK, you look very sad.' Maude sounded concerned.

'I am fine, honestly, just thinking back to a few things, it's never good,' sighed Claire.

'More wine?' asked Orion, picking up the bottle. Claire placed her hand over the glass. 'I had better not, I am driving tomorrow!'

Now it was Maude's and Orion's turn to look sad. 'We will miss you,' said Maude, placing an arm around Claire's shoulder.

'I'll miss you too.' Then, reaching down to her side, she pulled up the box she had hidden under the chair next to her. Handing the box to Maude, she said, 'This is just a little something to say thank you to you both for looking after me.'

Maude looked surprised and Orion exclaimed, 'Claire, you didn't have to do that!'

'I know,' said Claire, 'but I can't tell you how good it has been for me staying here with you. I feel like a new woman.' She laughed.

Maude opened the box. Carefully, she lifted out one of the

crystal glasses, turning it in the light from the chandelier. Prisms of the rainbow glowed from the glass. 'Thank you so much, they are beautiful,' exclaimed Maude, placing the glass on the table and hugging Claire.

Orion joined in. 'Don't leave me out,' he laughed. The three stood there hugging. Claire felt so secure and happy. Tomorrow would be the start of her new life, but she knew she would always have Maude and Orion to come back to.

When she woke the next morning, she felt sad. It was time to go. To step out on her own, leaving behind the comfort and security of her friends and their beautiful home.

Lisette had come to see her before she left for school. 'I am very sad you are leaving us, Claire,' said Lisette. Claire crouched down to the little girl, who then threw her arms around Claire. Kissing her tenderly on the forehead, Claire held her close. She smelled like fresh soap, her silky curls brushing Claire's cheek as she nestled into her. Lisette drew back, handing Claire a pebble. 'This is my favourite lucky stone,' she told Claire. 'It's magic. You can have it to take with you.'

Claire smiled. Taking the pebble from Lisette, she said, 'Thank you, I will treasure this for ever.' Lisette seemed content to know that Claire would be safe with her pebble. Maude said she would be back in five minutes; she would just walk Lisette to the end of the drive, her friend was picking her up this morning. This gave Claire a moment alone with Orion. He placed both his hands on her shoulders. Looking her in the eyes, he said, 'If you ever need us, we are here, just a phone call away. Please don't hesitate.'

Claire could feel her eyes filling with tears. Orion pulled her to him in a bear hug, squeezing her tight. Claire laughed as she gasped for breath. Maude appeared back and she gave Claire a hug. Her eyes were brimming too.

'What a pair we are,' laughed Claire, wiping her eyes.

Climbing into her car, she started the engine.

'To new beginnings,' said Orion.

'New beginnings,' laughed Claire as she pulled away off their drive. With one last wave from the window, Claire knew she was on her own now!

Chapter 8

Having left the comfort of her friends in the Loire, Claire had made her way across to near Dijon. Sampling, of course, the delicious mustard that must have been in almost every shop she had visited in the bustling town. Finally, she had success-fully located the B&B at Montbard that she had remembered from twenty years ago. It was, of course, under new owner-ship, run by quite a shy couple who were from north of Paris originally. They told Claire they were loving their new life in this beautiful region. The B&B wasn't as she remembered it. All the same, they had made her very welcome.

After this, Claire decided, it was not always good to go back to places in your memories. Sometimes it was just bet-ter to remember them as a special moment in time. From Dijon she had travelled on, slightly east, to the stunning Jura region. Fresh mountain air was just what she had needed. When she reached Lons-le Saunier, Claire couldn't help but smile fondly as she drove past the Laughing Cow factory. To her surprise, it was still going strong. It had been there when she had visited as a child. Claire had adored the lovely creamy cheese. She smiled as she remembered spreading it on fresh, warm toast. From the Jura, Claire had crossed to the Auvergne, stopping in a farm a couple of kilometres from Moulin. Once again, another retired couple. It must be something about retiring that gave you the inclination to run a B&B in France.

At this one, Claire thought they had the perfect setup. It was a beautiful, almost chateau-like, country house. They had also converted one of the outbuildings into four lovely bedrooms around a central room. This gave them the option of making it into a self-catering unit if required. Perfect if a large family or group of friends came to stay. There were magnificent horses on the farm and even the smell of horse manure added to the ambiance. The rooms, at the front, looked out over the farm pond. The rooms were so comfortable and Claire had enjoyed the whole ambiance of the place.

Monsieur had good friends in Ireland, so they had enjoyed a very amicable chat over breakfast. Of course Le Rugby was mentioned. Like many places in France, he was a stopping off point. Guests stayed mostly for one night, especially for people en-route to Geneva. They were also only about an hour and a half from Mâcon, well known for its wine. He had recommended to Claire that she visit the centre of Moulin. You must go to the Cafe de Bourgogne, he had exclaimed.

Claire had taken his advice. What a stunning restaurant, all decked out in art deco mirrors everywhere. They played on your eyes, making you think the restaurant was actually bigger than it was. The food had been delicious, the staff so welcoming. It was places like this B&B and its local restaurant that epitomised France for Claire.

Then had come the difficult bit; should she head south or west? Where would have the most interest, she mused? South was further into the stunning Auvergne region, down towards Clermont Ferrand. Then she knew from there she was getting into touristy areas. What Claire really wanted to experience was an 'off the beaten track' feeling. The back lanes of France. The forgotten villages, monuments, rivers, lakes and places less frequented that could give so much enjoyment without crowds. Claire didn't want a hotel that was just giving an overnight stop to get to the south with its bulging mass tourism beaches. Although, to be fair, they had their place.

She loved nothing better than walking on a sandy beach in bare feet, watching the sand slip through her toes. To feel the cool lap of the salt water on her baked feet. It made her sigh to think of it. She must get in a trip to the beach at some point. She so deserved a treat!

Finally, she decided; she would head south. Her travels took her to a beautiful village called Saint Nectaire, famous for its superb creamy textured cheese. Claire had slipped in a visit to the cheese cave. This had been fascinating, especially to see rows and rows and rows of cheeses lined up maturing in the cold caves. The highlight had been the cafe serving a local dish of potatoes and sausage smothered in that same cheese. It had been an explosion of pure calories, but worth every mouthful. The walk afterwards had been a necessity; Claire was determined she would not return home overweight.

As much as she loved the area, she decided her waistline could only stand a night in this cheese heaven. That was when she decided she would go west, towards the city of Limoges. It would be better to take the motorway this time, she thought. It would speed up the route. She was conscious that she had to start writing in a few days' time. There was still so much to do before then; finding a place to live being one of them. Limoges was a small city compared to cities she knew back home, thinking of London and Manchester. Claire had fitted in a trip to the Musee de Porcelaine, which, to her surprise, had been really interesting. Later she had walked around the old town. The cathedral was beautiful. She had enjoyed a delicious lunch in one restaurant in the old town. Its timber-framed buildings were a step back in time. It made Claire wonder what would have been happening a century ago in these narrow winding streets.

Finally, deciding to head into La Creuse countryside, she wasn't disappointed. It was a glorious region with rolling green hills, lakes, and streams at every turn. This was where Orion's cousin lived; a small medieval town called La Terraine. Claire was going to stop for the night in a small village called Cindré. Pulling into the driveway of the B&B, Claire had to smile at the sign hanging in the driveway. 'The Rabbit with the Green Wellies'. Such a charming building. Apparently, according to the guidebook she had looked it, its previous life had been a railway hotel. Kirsty and Malcolm were wonderful hosts. It all seemed to come so naturally to them. The meal Kirsty had prepared would rival any top chef.

Claire was feeling a little awkward that night as she sat around a table of nine. There were four couples and herself. She needn't have worried. A few minutes into the meal and she was feeling quite at home. Everyone included her. Thankfully, the main conversation was in English. Claire knew, though, that she would have to work on her French. The Dutch couple were delightful; Claire had enjoyed chatting with Marijke. Later, sitting alone in the garden with her glass of wine, Claire realised just how relaxed she was now feeling. The decision to make this trip had been the best she had ever made. Later, as she lay in bed, she was quite excited. Tomorrow she was going to view a cottage where, hopefully, she could put down her bags for a while.

The next morning, she bid farewell to her fellow guests. Driving along the back roads to La Terraine, Claire was taking in all the scenery. Some houses she passed made her smile. An estate agent would certainly class them as 'with potential'. It was a shame really to see these beautiful homes neglected although, to her surprise, some were still actually lived in. You wouldn't think it looking at them from the outside. It was like time had stood still in this area. Claire couldn't wait to find out more about it.

La Terraine had a lovely sense of history about it. People were going about their business, greeting and kissing their friends as they met. Walking past the library, Claire looked at its beautiful mansard roof. In front of the library stood an enormous tree, its leaves were huge. Hanging from them it had what looked large beans; Claire had never seen one like that before. She wondered what it was called. Looking at her watch, she felt ready for a morning coffee. The pretty little cafe, opposite the large tree, had tables that spilled out on to the street. Little clusters of people sat around drinking coffee, chatting away to each other. Inside, three very local-looking men propped up the bar with their morning glass of wine. They turned to look at her as she walked in.

Claire glanced at her watch again: it was only 10:45, a little early for wine! Placing her order at the bar, she walked outside on to the terrace. There was a table for one, nestled in the shade against the clematis that was blossoming. It sent out a heavenly scent. Across from the cafe, Claire marvelled again at the beautiful tree with its large leaves wafting across the water fountain. Someone had thought it funny to add some washing up liquid to the fountain. It made her smile watching the bubbles as they spilled on to the street. The lady appeared from the cafe, handing Claire her coffee. She inhaled the aroma as she turned her head towards the warm sunbeams, adjusting her sunglasses on her head to shield her eyes.

There were a great deal of English voices around her. It had surprised her on this trip just how many British people lived in France. She was beginning to understand why. There was the tiniest cinema she had ever seen opposite the cafe. Along the main street, that led away to the left, a queue of cars lined up behind a van that had stopped in the middle of the narrow street. No one seemed to care. If that had been in the UK, they would all be sitting there honking their horns.

Claire thought this cafe was an amazing place to sit people watching. It looked like there were some interesting shops too. So, finishing her coffee, she decided to take a stroll down the main street. It had been a while since Claire had treated herself to something nice. In later months, back in the UK, she had fallen into wearing jogging bottoms and t-shirts. Claire realised she had probably let herself go a little. Maybe Sean had got fed up with seeing her like that. However, it certainly didn't give him an excuse to go off with their neighbour. Claire felt annoyed with herself for thinking about it.

Across the street she noticed a little shoe shop. Wandering over to look in the window, a pair of sandals caught her eye. Pushing open the heavy glass door, Claire entered. After a quick conversation with Madam, she was able to try them on in her size. Looking down at her feet, she wiggled her toes in the shoes. Must get those toenails sorted, she thought to herself. She loved the sandals, though. Handing them back to Madam, Claire nodded, showing that she would like to buy them. They were a pretty tan leather with delicate pearl beading. They would be perfect; a pleasant change from wearing trainers, which were getting far too warm in this heat. Madam thanked her.

Claire left the shop, delighted with her purchase. Stepping back onto the main street, Claire looked in the window of what appeared to be some kind of supermarket/hardware shop. A little old lady sat on a stool at the till. It could almost have been 1940. Then, as she turned the corner, she found herself outside a clothes shop. On first glance, it looked quite fuddy-duddy! However, on stepping inside, she found, to her surprise, that they had quite a nice selection. Searching through the rails, Claire found a lovely cotton dress. She picked it up, holding it against herself. As she looked in the mirror, Claire realised just how frumpy she looked in her jeans and t-shirt. It was such a long time since she had treated herself to something pretty. Turning to Madame, who was watching her with a smile, she said, 'Can I try it on?'

'Bien sûr, of course,' smiled Madame.

Claire took the dress into the cubicle and slipped out of her jeans and t-shirt. Pulling the dress over her head, then smoothing it down, she turned to look in the small mirror. Deciding she needed a bigger mirror, she pulled back the cubicle curtain. In front of her was the large mirror. Staring into it, Claire thought how pretty the dress looked on her. The cream background with the coral-coloured flowers were a perfect combination on her. Madame turned to the rail behind her, handing Claire a little cardigan in the coral colour that brought out the flower detail on the dress. Claire smiled as she took the cardigan. 'How pretty,' she said. The dress and cardigan fitted perfectly. Claire was thrilled. 'Would you mind if I kept it on?' she asked hesitantly.

'Of course you can,' beamed Madame. 'You look so pretty.'

Claire blushed a little. Slipping off her trainers, she pulled the new sandals from the bag and slipped them on, too. Doing a little twirl, Madame clapped her hands in delight. Laughing, Claire handed over her card. Madame wished her a good day as she left the shop. Back on the street, Claire thought how much she was enjoying herself. It was turning into a wonderful day; a long-overdue, well-deserved treat.

The church clock showed that it was just about to turn twelve. Then, as if on cue, her stomach rumbled. The shops were about to close, so Claire decided it was time to head off for some lunch. In front of her loomed a medieval tower with an entrance underneath. It was obviously part of the old town walls, she thought, as she walked into the shade of its large turret. On the other side of the tower, the road brought her to a beautiful part of the town. All around the church stood old-timbered buildings, the tabac, the pharmacy, a beauty salon, ahead the stone steps leading up out of the town. Bright-red geraniums spilled out of the boxes over the walls.

The map on her phone confirmed she was heading in the right direction for a restaurant. The marketplace was quiet, but, Claire would bet, on a Saturday, it would be a hive of activity. Standing for a moment, Claire looked back at the tower from the other side with its beautiful arch. People were heading to their cars, no doubt all heading off for lunch somewhere. Further up the incline, the buildings shadowed Claire from the heat. Ahead, she could see the restaurant. It looked busy. Claire hoped, being a table for one, she would get a table.

Luckily, because of the beautiful weather, their back terrace was open. Claire was enthusiastically welcomed. The maître d' was a kind man; dark-haired, not over tall, but with dark, twinkly eyes. He showed her to a small table by the water fountain. As she sat down, a bee buzzed by. He swotted it away from her.

'A drink?' he asked her, smiling pleasantly.

'Yes please, I'll have a Kir Royale and some table water,' she said, as she smiled back at him.

'No problem,' he said, handing her the menu. Carefully, in his broken English, he explained what was on the menu du jour. Leaving her to decide, he left to fetch her a drink. Claire, placing the menu back on the table, had decided on the menu du jour. She loved fish. Hake in a lemon sauce with rice and vegetables sounded delicious. On his return, Claire took the drink from him. 'I'll take the menu du jour, please,' she said, handing the menu back to him.

'Thanks a lot,' he replied in his best English.

As she sipped her Kir, the pleasant bubbles tickled her

tongue; the cassis flavour was so refreshing on this warm day. The starter was served buffet style. There was an excellent selection of charcuterie, salads, rice and pate. Claire tucked in; the shopping had obviously made her hungry. The fish, as she had predicted, was delicious.

Claire loved to see how busy this local business was. As she looked around her, she noticed a man sat on his own in the corner, he somehow seemed familiar? Claire, looking again, wondered where on earth she knew him from. As her delicious chocolate dessert appeared on her table, however, he was forgotten. The dessert was far more interesting than any strange man. Finishing her meal with a coffee, she felt rather full. How on earth did people manage to go back to work after a meal like that, she wondered. All she felt like doing now was sleeping! Paying her bill at the till, she thanked the proprietor. He walked her to the door, bidding her a good afternoon. Claire stepped outside back on to the warm street.

Suddenly she heard a voice. 'Excuse me. Excuse me.'

It took Claire a moment to a) realise that this was an English voice and b) that they were trying to get her attention. Lifting her sunglasses on to the top of her head, Claire squinted in the brightness.

'Sorry,' he said. 'Sorry, I don't mean to bother you, but do you remember me?' he asked hesitantly. Claire looked intently for what seemed like minutes but was in fact only seconds. Then, suddenly, it dawned on her; it was the man she'd seen in the restaurant. Still, for the life of her, Claire couldn't remember from where else she knew him. He smiled. 'We met briefly, do you remember, in the Dusty Miller in Butteroak?' He was looking a little embarrassed. 'It was the day you were upset,' he said. He looked at her as she tried to think, then the realisation dawned on her: of course it was him, the kind man.

'Yes, yes I do,' exclaimed Claire 'Goodness me, fancy meeting you here, are you on holiday?' Claire asked.

'No, no, I'm not. I'm actually working; however one benefit is being able to have lunch in a lovely restaurant like this,' he said, pointing back to where they had both just left. Claire took in his features. Dark hair with splashes of grey. Tall and certainly not unattractive. She was relieved she had finally remembered his face. Claire smiled at him. 'You were very kind that day.' Then, holding out her hand, 'I'm Claire, pleased to meet you.'

He took her hand. Shaking it, he said, 'Adam. I work for a large wine estate here in France and I was delivering some wine to Sebastian in the restaurant,' he explained.

They chatted on for another five minutes. 'Well, it was lovely to see you again, Adam,' said Claire.

'Enjoy the rest of your trip,' he replied, smiling at her.

They both turned to head in opposite directions. 'Um, look,' Adam said, pausing. 'I am around for a week. Here is my card, and, well, if you fancy a coffee sometime, it would be nice to meet up. Some English conversation would be good,' he added with a laugh.

Claire took the card from him. 'Thank you,' she said. 'I may just do that.' They walked off in opposite directions. Well, that was a surprise, mused Claire, glancing at the card.

Adam Johnstone. Wine Consultant. Claire tucked the card into her diary.

Chapter 9

Looking at her watch, Claire realised she had ten minutes to get to the church, where she had arranged to meet Orion's cousin. Turning down the steps, she arrived with seconds to spare. There was a man of about sixty standing there. He was dressed in overalls with greying hair. As Claire approached, he smiled and waved at her. 'My cousin described you well,' he laughed, holding out a hand to her. 'Claude,' he said.

'Lovely to meet you, Claude,' said Claire, returning the smile.

'Where have you parked your car?' he asked.

'In the car park behind the library,' she said, pointing roughly toward where she thought it was. 'Ah, that's good, so am I. Let's go and show you the cottage.'

They talked as they walked. Claude told her a little about the area. It was very agricultural, he explained. Generations of families had farmed the infamous Limousin cattle of the region for centuries. Many of the youngsters had left for the cities, but the old ones had stayed on to tend the land and cows. Back at the car park they climbed into their respective cars and Claire followed him out of the car park. They set off for the tiny village of Jeux. It was only about twenty minutes from the town. Claire thought that was a significant advantage. She wanted to be in the countryside, but also to have all the amenities close to hand. This town certainly gave her that. They followed the lanes along through the beautiful countryside.

Suddenly, as the road came out of the woodlands, before her was a magnificent lake. 'Oh, wow!' exclaimed Claire, out loud. The sunlight glittered on the water like tiny little dappled diamonds. The sky was such a striking blue, the grass almost pea green. Along its banks sat many anglers. Claire had never understood what made them sit there, hour after hour, trying to catch a fish, to only throw it back in again. She guessed for many men it was an escape from nagging wives; a night away with a few beers, enjoying the company of like-minded men.

Claire noticed a small pizza restaurant. That would be a lovely place to spend an evening, she thought to herself. Claude didn't hang around as they sped along the tiny lanes. Then, taking a sharp left, they wound around a few more corners before Claire finally spotted the little sign for Jeux. How beautiful, she thought as they pulled up at the crossroads. On the right was a village pond, to her left there were just a few houses dotted about. Nobody was on top of each other.

Claire liked that. In France, everyone seemed to have lots of personal space. It was very rare that you came across a large housing estate, especially in La Creuse. It did always amaze her, though, just how many run-down and derelict houses there were. She wondered why. As she got out of the car, she asked Claude the same question. 'Well, the law in France, where property is concerned, states that it will always go to the children. It was then normal for the children not to agree on what to do with the property.' He smiled. 'Because of that it would then, invariably, sit there empty, rotting away whilst the children fought amongst themselves,' Claude explained. 'Such a shame,' said Claire.

Claude pointed out a cottage to their right. It had-ruby red shutters; Claire loved the little hearts carved into them. The front door shutter was also in the same colour. The small front garden, a little overgrown, didn't worry Claire, though. 'Wow,' she said to herself. It really had something about it. Grinning, she turned to Claude, 'How lovely is this?' whispered Claire in disbelief.

Claude laughed. Leading Claire around the back of the property, Claude put the key into the lock of the small barn door that was embedded in a much larger barn door. He pushed it open, then stepped inside, gesturing to Claire to follow him. The barn was empty, but it would give her plenty of storage space, she thought. Claude switched on the electrics on the barn wall. They then had to duck under a beam to reach the door into the main house. To their left was a downstairs bathroom, straight ahead, a toilet. It all looked pretty neat.

Then as they turned right into the principal room, Claire was overcome, her delight obvious. 'Oh, look at this,' she exclaimed to Claude. 'So pretty.' The major feature of the room was the big old fireplace with its charred walls. Two large, comfy-looking sofas sat either side of the fireplace, a lovely red rug added a splash of colour to the room. To the right was a wall press type of cupboard that looked ancient. It was perfect for the style of cottage. On the other side of the room was the tiny kitchen area with a huge breakfast table. Claire could just imagine sitting there with her morning coffee. She could feel herself grinning like a Cheshire cat as she took it all in.

Claude went around, opening the windows. Then he reached out, doing the same to the shutters. Next, he opened the old front door. The light flooded in. It was then that Claire knew; she was in love with this cottage. It was perfect. In her mind she had moved in. Next, they climbed the oak staircase up to the first floor. There was a small bathroom. Claude had gone ahead into the master bedroom, pushing open the large picture window, then tying back the shutters. Entering the room, it literally took Claire's breath away. The immense window gave a delightful view down the village lane. She could see the village pond in the distance. This room would be wonderful first thing in the morning with the sunrise. Her heart was beating fast. She couldn't take the silly smile off her face. There was a large, old, French, ornately carved wooden bed that dominated the room.

No bedding. Two little tables either side and a large oak wardrobe. That was all you could really fit into the room. Claire looked around her, taking it all in. It was at that moment she knew she was home! Turning to Claude, she asked, 'How much is a month's rent?' Crossing her fingers behind her back, she waited for his answer.

'How does €500 sound?' Claire was amazed. It was perfect. It wouldn't cost her much to buy some nice bedding. She would need to stock up on a few other bits and pieces as well.

Suddenly, on impulse, Claire asked, 'Could I take it for six months?' Claude, looking a little surprised, said, 'Oh, Orion said you only wanted somewhere for a holiday.'

Claire laughed. 'Well I did, but I've just made the decision that I am not going back to the UK yet.'

Claude looked surprised. It was nothing to the surprise that Claire felt. Where on earth had that idea come from? She wasn't turning back now, though. The deal was done. They shook hands.

To her surprise, Claude handed over the keys to her there and then. 'Strike while the iron is hot,' he laughed. 'Is that not what you English say?'

'It is indeed,' she laughed, taking the key from him. They discussed a few more formalities. Claire told Claude she would draw out the cash for him the next day. He waved his hand in the air. 'No rush.' Then he was off.

Claire had to sit down for a minute, she couldn't quite believe she had just taken on this little cottage for six months.
Never had she made such a quick decision. Sitting herself
down on the sofa, she took in the smaller details. Pretty little
lace curtains adorned the windows. It was minimal, but pretty. Everything seemed in fairly good condition and it felt so
homely. Claire knew this was the right thing to do. Tonight
she would stay at the B&B she had booked, then tomorrow
she could move into the cottage.

Going out to her car, Claire fetched in her belongings. Two
suitcases and two boxes; they were all she had brought with
her. The boxes had her favourite photos, especially the ones
with her mum and dad. Sean had sent them on to Orion for
her. Opening the box, she pulled out the carefully wrapped
photo frames. Her mum and dad smiled back at her. Carefully, she placed the two photo frames on the mantlepiece. It
made her feel content to have her parents with her. Inside
the box was also a wedding photo. Claire looked sadly at the
photo of her and Sean. Beaming on their wedding day. Why
on earth he had thought she would want that, she didn't
know! She tucked the photo back in the box, pushing the
memories of Sean aside. Nothing was going to spoil the excitement of having six months in this beautiful cottage.

Claire took another walk around. Upstairs in the spare
bedroom she found a couple of cushions that would look
perfect on the sofa, so, picking them up, she took them back

downstairs with her. She was right; the mustard shade added a touch of brightness to the room. The whitewashed walls were plain. There were no fripperies anywhere, but Claire knew that would allow her to add her own touch. Sitting down on the sofa, she tried to let it all sink in. She was still a little amazed that she had taken it for six months, but why not? why not indeed.

Going back to her two boxes, she opened the second one. Pulling out her mum's purple box, she suddenly remembered she hadn't opened it. As she stroked the faded velvet, it made her think of her mum. Maybe tonight wasn't the night to open it. She would have to do it soon though. It was strange that her mum had hidden it away. For now, though, it would have to wait.

Turning round, she picked up the first of her suitcases and lugged it upstairs to the master bedroom, then the second. There would be time to unpack these tomorrow, she thought, placing them next to the wardrobe. Looking in the bathroom, she realised she would have to buy towels and the bed linen. It would be good to make a little list. Claire had seen a large supermarket in the town; she was sure she could get most things there. She loved a good supermarket shop. Here, in France, you could get everything you needed from the hypermarché. A good shopping spree to cheer her up, just like she had enjoyed this morning in the town.

As she was walking towards the table, she dropped her diary. Bending down, she picked up the receipts and the notes that had fallen out. It made her smile to see Adam's business card. She tucked everything back, standing still for a moment, looking at the card. What harm could it do? It was only a coffee. Adam seemed so easy to get along with when they had spoken earlier today outside the restaurant. They were both away from their homeland; they would both appreciate some conversation in their native language.

Opening a bottle of white wine she poured herself a glass. Then taking a swig of wine for courage, Claire reached for her mobile phone, tapping in the number. On the third ring she was almost about to hang up in fear when a voice said, 'Adam Johnstone speaking.'

Claire almost put the phone down, but the voice in her head said: go for it. 'Hello, this is Claire, we met earlier.'

'Claire, lovely to hear from you,' Adam exclaimed. 'How has your day been?'

'Rather more exciting than I planned! I have just rented a little cottage in Jeux, just outside La Terraine, for a while,' she said.

Adam was interested to hear all about it and the conversation flowed easily. As Claire would be in town tomorrow and he was still in the area, they agreed that they would see each other at the little cafe. He knew the one she meant. Putting down the phone, Claire was not just amazed but very proud of herself. Two big decisions in one day. She was quite liking the new Claire, she thought, as she raised her glass of wine in a toast to herself.

Leaving the cottage she had checked into the B&B. A simple place, but it was all she needed for one night. The room was sparsely decorated, certainly not to the standard of Orion's B&B. She arranged to have something to eat in the bar before retiring to her room. Picking up her laptop and opening it, she noticed one from Orion. She smiled at his warm greeting. But then something in particular really jumped out at her. Oh, goodness, Claire thought, he has some information on Le Grand Fontaine:

I have done some local research. There appears to be a Chateau Le Grand Fontaine based in the Auvergne region of France, which is not that far from where you are now. Is that right? It is about 20 kms from Moulin, the principal town. I believe it belongs to the Le Fontaine Family; they go back many hundreds of years. The old Marquis is still alive, I believe.

Orion had ended the email by wishing her success with the research and, if he could help further, just to let him know. Claire was amazed: so, Mathieu Le Fontaine was still alive then. She wondered if he would remember her mother. Curiosity was certainly getting the better of her. Wouldn't it be lovely to see where her parents first met? Switching off the computer, she settled into bed. Tomorrow she would move into her new cottage. Tomorrow, her new life would begin.

Chapter 10

Adam was sitting at the little table outside the cafe when Claire arrived. She had already made some purchases and had dropped them back off at the car. Strolling through the archway, she had exited onto the main street. The large Indian bean tree, as she had discovered it was called, looked majestic, its leaves shading the ornate fountain underneath.

Adam was a little apprehensive, but Claire was a breath of fresh air that he needed. Work was busy just now; the family business that he worked for had a huge wine fair coming up, so preparations were all-consuming. As a favour to his employer, he had also been trying to help their uncle trace a woman he had once known. He hadn't been given too much detail, but the day he met Claire at The Dusty Miller, he had been following up a lead in Cheshire. He felt like he'd come to a dead end, which was just as well given how busy his job had become.

He spotted Claire across the road and waved. Claire waved back. Adam thought again how pretty she looked, her blonde hair caressing her shoulders. She had on a beautiful coral-coloured dress that showed off her tan. He thought how lucky he was to have bumped into her again. He wasn't sure why she was here, alone, in France, but maybe she would open up to him at some point.

'Claire, it really is lovely to see you,' said Adam, getting to his feet, awkwardly holding out his hand to her. What he really wanted to do was kiss her. Claire had taken his hand just as awkwardly.

Claire couldn't remember the last time that she had been on a date with a man. Not that this was a date, of course, just two people having coffee together. He was already sitting at the cafe when she got there.

'How are you? Thank you for coming.'

'I am good, thanks, and you? Thank you for inviting me,' he said, pulling out a chair for her to sit down on. Claire smiled as she took the seat next to him. The waitress appeared, asking what she could get them. They both ordered a cappuccino.

Adam turned back to Claire. 'So! Tell me about your cottage!'

Claire couldn't stop smiling as she described to Adam how pretty it was. 'Tonight will be my first night,' she said, feeling quite proud of her achievements. 'It sounds lovely,' said Adam.

'Maybe next time I am back this way, we could meet for lunch or something?'

He hoped that wasn't too presumptuous of him. Adam just knew he would like to see her again. To his surprise, Claire agreed. 'I would really like that.'

He had such a lovely demeanour about him; so likeable. She had to admit she did also fancy him a little; she felt herself blush just thinking about it.

Three coffees later, Adam, looking at his watch, said he was sorry but he would have to get back to work.

Claire, looking at her watch, exclaimed, 'Goodness me! Noon already. I'll never get the cottage ready for my first night at this rate, will I?'

They both laughed. Adam offered to walk her to her car, but Claire declined. There was another shop she wanted to go to before she left town.

'Thank you so much for a lovely couple of hours,' she said, looking up at him.

'It was my pleasure.' He smiled.

'I hope to see you again soon.' Claire smiled back at him.

Claire felt like she was walking on air. It had been so lovely to see Adam again. She really liked him. However, she was not in the right place for a relationship. Things were too raw from Sean just now. Still, she certainly hoped they could be friends.

As Adam climbed into his car, he had to smile to himself; he had thoroughly enjoyed Claire's company. Maybe it was time to move on and let another woman into his life.

Walking on down the high street, Claire found the little hardware shop that she had been searching for. All she needed were a couple of nails, and a hammer, so she could put some pictures up in the cottage. Finding exactly what she wanted, she paid, then stepped back out on to the street.

A magnificent church was just opposite and Claire thought she would look inside. Climbing the three steps to the enormous oak doors, she stepped in. The coolness of the interior was like stepping into a fridge. It was a welcome respite from the afternoon sun. The place was empty. Claire noticed they had some candles on the side and a donations box. Reaching for her purse, she took out a €2 coin and popped it in the box. Reaching across, she choose two candles, one for Mum and one for Dad. She held them to an already lit candle and a small flame burst out. Claire placed them both carefully on the display. 'Miss you, Mum, miss you, Dad,' she whispered.

Claire sat for a moment, took some time to reflect on where she was and where she was going. The calmness of the church put her at ease. In just a short time she had lost her mother, lost her husband, and made a rash decision to spend six months in France. *You're doing well*, she thought to herself. It was a more confident, stronger woman that walked back on to the street. Claire felt she could conquer anything that life chose to throw at her just now. That said, she certainly hoped there wouldn't be any more sadness.

Back at the car, she added the bag containing the nails and hammer to the pile of other purchases and left the car park. Turning off the ring road, she took the back lanes home. Yes, home, she thought to herself. Passing the large lake, Claire had to stop to take a photo. There was not a cloud in the sky, the water sparkled in the afternoon sun. There were pretty wild flowers dotted along the edge of the lake and, occasionally, a fish leaping out of the water. At the water's edge, Claire slipped off her shoes, letting the cool water refresh her hot feet. How perfect was this? To think, for the next six months, this would be right on her doorstep.

Back at the cottage, Claire hauled her purchases indoors, propping the front door open so that she could come to and fro easily. It didn't take her long to make up the bed. The pretty white linen looked crisp against the oak. Opening another bag, she pulled out the ochre throw that she had bought in the fabric shop. Carefully, she arranged it on the bed. It all looked really lovely. So pretty, so feminine.

She heard a knock at the front door. Going down the stairs, she called out hello. Standing at the door was an elderly lady. The lady explained she lived next door and handed Claire a box of eggs as a welcome gift. Claire was touched and invited her in. Her name was Anette, and she had lived in the village since she was two years old. Popping the kettle on Claire offered her a coffee.

They spent a good hour chatting in their Franglais, Anette telling her stories of what the hamlet had been like as a child, how her children played in the farm garden, and had swum in the stream that ran along the bottom of the lane. It sounded very much like Claire's childhood days of paddling in rivers, climbing trees, fishing for tiddlers. Claire smiled at the memories. Her parents wouldn't see her from breakfast through to the next mealtime: no mobile phones, no laptops, certainly no PlayStation.

As she left, Anette told Claire to call round anytime. Claire thanked her. How lovely was that.

Claire was bone-weary. *Wine o'clock*, she thought to herself. Opening the fridge door, she spied the quiche she had bought for tonight's dinner. Taking that out, along with a bottle of rosé, she reached for a glass. With her quiche and salad, Claire made her way out into the little side garden. The glorious colours of the evenings here never ceased to impress her in this part of the world. The sun, wrapped in the wonderful hues of vivid oranges and reds, cast a warm glow over the whole of the house, dappling the garden in peach hues. *So pretty*, she sighed to herself.

Quiche finished, she poured herself another glass of wine. Her first night in her new cottage. Claire had a moment of overwhelming sadness. Here she was in a pretty little cottage in the evening sunshine, alone for the first time in twenty years. Sean had loved France.

Claire swiped away a tear. Time to call it a day. She had achieved so much in such a short space of time; it was emotionally draining. Lying in bed, she thought back to Adam and the lovely time they had spent drinking coffee this morning. He was certainly easy to get along with and he made her laugh. It was strange how relaxed she had felt in his company after only a short time. There was a lunch to look forward to; at least she hoped he would be back in touch.

Sleep still wouldn't come, she couldn't get comfortable. She threw off the sheet. It was so humid, even for mid-July! The windows were thrown open, but it was still airless. Claire could hear a rumble of thunder from afar. A good storm would clear the air. As the storm grew closer, Claire had to get up from the bed to go to the toilet. She was suddenly feeling very vulnerable alone in this cottage. Quickly, she climbed back into bed as a bright flash of lightning lit up the room. There was a loud bang, but it wasn't thunder. Claire threw the sheets over her head. It took her a few seconds to realise that it was the shutters that had come loose.

Climbing out of bed, she stuck her head out the window and reached for the loose shutter. Rain began to fall, slowly at first; already the air began to feel fresher. The rain, heavier now, rattled onto the roof. Another flash. Claire, diving back under the sheets, counted the space until the thunder rumbled again. This time it was further away. Slowly, as the storm subsided, she drifted off to sleep.

Waking the next morning, Claire felt like she had not slept at all. Her head ached. She rolled over to look at the clock on her bedside table. 7:30am, only about three hours' sleep. She groaned, pulling the covers up around her neck. Trying to get back to sleep, she tossed and turned again. It was like she had had a double espresso.

Finally, giving in, she got up. Standing at the window, she looked out at the dawn with its dewy grass. There was that distinctive smell of a summer morning and the chirping of the birds filled the air. Claire grinned, it was hard to contain her excitement! With her dressing gown tied tightly around her, she went to the bathroom.

Down in the kitchen, she stepped onto the cold, tiled floor. It was a little chillier than normal this morning. *Maybe that's because she was tired*, she thought as she made a coffee. Sitting herself on the sofa, she pulled her knees up underneath her. She was feeling very unsettled, a little anxious. Last night had really taken it out of her. *But*, she thought, *I survived*. Looking at the photo of her parents on the mantelpiece, she knew they would be so proud of her. Claire hoped she could find out a little more about where they met. It pained her to think that she had never taken an interest in their life before her. If only she could speak to them both now.

Chapter 11

The last few days had been such a whirlwind. A new home, meeting Adam, the decision to rent for six months. What had she been thinking! Today she was going to take it easy. Claire set about doing some little bits and pieces around the place. Working out how to use the washing machine had been a good place to start; at least she would have some clean clothes. Unpacking both suitcases made her feel a little more settled. It was still strange getting used to life as a single person and not having someone else to bounce things off.

The storm had cleared the air last night and it was cooler today. Claire didn't feel in the mood for reading. As she placed her book back on the sideboard, her mother's box caught her eye. Maybe it was time to look inside. Picking it up, she decided to take it to the outside table. Touching the lid made her hesitate slightly. She thought of her life with her parents, Gloria and Maurice. It had been wonderful.

Claire had no idea what she would find, but she knew staring at it wouldn't help her. Just look, she told herself. She knew she wouldn't satisfy her curiosity until she had looked.

Picking up the box, she knocked a little attic dust off it. Carefully, she lifted off the purple velvet lid. Taking out the top envelope, there was her birth certificate and her parents' marriage certificate, both carefully folded in half. She slipped them back into the envelope, placing them to one side on the table. There were some old family photos she recognised, some of her mother's parents. She had been very young when they had passed away. Claire had fond memories of a trip to see them in the beautiful Yorkshire countryside. She knew her mother always felt like she hadn't done well enough for them in life. They never told her they were proud of her, or proud of what she had achieved. Claire they had idolised. She had very fond memories of being totally spoilt. Claire remembered the secret sugar sandwiches her nan used to give her; laden in butter and dipped in sugar.

Taking a sip of her wine, she shivered a little. Maybe it was better to continue this indoors. Collecting her plate and glass, she carefully wedged the box under her arm. As she got to the kitchen table, Claire put down the plate and glass just as the box slipped from under her arm. With a crash, it landed, its contents strewn all over the floor! Claire, annoyed with herself, hoped there was nothing breakable. Sitting on the cool tiled kitchen floor, she pulled the remnants of the box close to her. It was then that a letter caught her eye.

On closer inspection, she noticed it was addressed to her, in her mother's handwriting. She placed it to one side, carefully putting each piece back in the box. There was a picture of two lovely young children. Intrigued, Claire turned over the photo, written on the back. It read Thierry and Elodie, Chateau Le Grand Fontaine 1982. The children looked merry; they were playing beside a large lake. The next photo was also of the same children, this time in a beautiful nursery setting, the same inscription on the back.

Claire recalled her mother had mentioned being an au pair at Le Grand Fontaine. It had been during one of the muddled conversations they had had before Gloria died. The next photo was of a very handsome man, quite tall, with a lovely physique. He was dressed in tennis shorts and holding a racket in his hand. He had a warm smile and looked quite suave; she thought. Turning this photo over, it just said Mathieu Le Fontaine September 1983. The next photo showed the chateau. *Wow!* thought Claire, that really is stunning. In fact, majestic. On the back it was inscribed with Chateau Le Grand Fontaine 1983. So this must have been where her mother had spent the summer as an au pair, where she had met her father. There were a few more bits and pieces, including a beautiful notepad. Inside there was a pressed red rose. Claire wondered about the significance of the rose.

Gently, she pressed it back inside the front page of the notebook. Turning over the next few pages, Claire saw what looked like a to-do list. Like mother, like daughter. She smiled fondly.

There had been some event that had taken place at the chateau at the end of September 1983. From the notes, her mother had obviously played a part in its organisation. It sounded a very grand affair; she noticed the name Liselle Le Fontaine. Claire got out her own notepad, noting down the name. It would come in handy for some research at a later date. It was fascinating. She wanted to know more about the family. Knowing the chateau wasn't actually that far from where she now lived, enticed her more. That's if they still lived there. From Orion's note, she knew the chateau still existed. She pulled herself up from the kitchen floor, it was getting quite dark now. Switching on the small table light, she walked across to the kettle; she needed of a cup of tea. Closing her front door, Claire pulled the windows closed. She made her tea. Then, settling into the pretty chintz armchair that had belonged to her mother; she carefully opened the letter and began to read...

Dearest Claire

If you are reading this letter, then I will have passed away. I want you to know before you read this that you were my world. There was never a day in my life that I wasn't proud to call you my daughter. I have something to tell you, something that I couldn't face telling you whilst I was alive. I wanted nothing to spoil our wonderful relationship or the love you had for your father. You were his world; he adored you. I know this won't be easy for you to read, but I have to tell you. I am not sure where to start, but the beginning is probably the best place...

GLORIA

Chapter 12

Gloria stretched and yawned, feeling the cool morning air wafting in from the slightly ajar window of the tiny workers' cottage in the grounds of Chateau Le Grand Fontaine. The chateau was situated in the beautiful Auvergne mountains and it was the summer of 1983. Gloria had been extremely lucky to have secured a post as an au pair for the Le Fontaine family, who had specifically wanted a young English woman to teach their children. Gloria felt so lucky to have secured this post, despite both her parents thinking it wasn't a proper job.

Living at home with her parents, devoutly religious, had been oppressive. No freedom; her parents watching her every move, life hadn't been her own. She was so thankful for the day that she had sat in Hyde Park in her lunch hour. She had picked up a newspaper, left by a previous occupant, and spotted the advert for an au pair for two children in France. Gloria had re-read the advert more than once. When she got home that night, she sat down to write a letter, using her friend's address. To her delight, after a secret telephone conversation that had taken place at her friend's parents' house, Gloria had been offered the position on a month's trial basis. Telling her parents she was leaving for France had been horrendous. Her mother had practically packed her bag for her, almost throwing her out on to the street. Her father, never one to speak up to his wife, had watched from the sidelines.

Gloria no longer cared; she needed to escape. It was her way out. A ticket to a new life. As she boarded the bus to Paris at Victoria coach station, Gloria had heaved a sigh of relief. Finally, she was on her way; an adventure, freedom. Albeit being slightly nervous at what lay ahead. Arriving in Paris, she had been overwhelmed by the hustle and bustle. Thankfully, the family had sent their chauffeur to collect her. He tipped his cap at her as he loaded her tattered suitcase into the boot of the Bentley. Gloria suddenly felt like the poor town mouse. Never before had Gloria ridden in such style.

During the four-hour trip south she had dozed on and off, waking on occasion to take in the glorious scenery. The flat lands of northern France turned into rolling hills, then to mountains as she reached the Auvergne. Many girls of Gloria's age had never made it out of London, let alone abroad. As the car turned into the driveway of La Grande Fontaine,

Gloria had been stunned. Large, imposing gates graced the gravelled driveway which stretched ahead of them. In the distance, two beautiful turrets stood guard either side of the grand building. Suddenly, she felt overwhelmed. What had she done? Lying here now, some months down the line, she could remember that feeling so well.

The family had been wonderful, especially the suave and handsome Mathieu, younger brother of the Marquise. He would often appear when she was playing with the children in the garden. They loved their Uncle Mathieu. He would rough and tumble with them on the manicured lawn and Gloria loved to hear them giggling. Mathieu used to come up close to Gloria, occasionally placing a hand on her shoulder. He would grab her hand when playing with the children or tickle her to make the children laugh. Gloria lived for the moments that they would see each other. He was so much older, but a child at heart. When she was teaching the children English, he would walk past the room, pulling funny faces through the window. The children used to think this was hilarious.

Then, one evening, when Gloria had been out walking by the river, he had appeared from nowhere. Sitting by the river, they had talked until the light had faded. Mathieu had taken her back to her cottage. He knew his way around the estate, even in the darkness. In the moonlight he had pulled her to him, kissing her softly. Gloria remembered that feeling of his lips touching hers. Then, without a word, he had just disappeared off into the night.

Turning on her side now, she took in the outline of his handsome face lying beside her. Those dark eyes she had fallen for opened and Matthieu grinned a lazy smile back at her, caressing her bare back. Glancing at the clock, he asked her what the time was, his eyes too tired to take it in. '6.30,' Gloria replied.

Mathieu threw back the sheets to get out of bed, planting a lingering kiss on her lips as he reached for his clothes. Gloria inhaled the remnants of his expensive French cologne. She felt she would treasure that smell forever. 'I have to go, mon chéri, before my sister wakes, they must not find me here.' Again, he kissed her tenderly.

Mathieu was eighteen years older than Gloria, a bit of a playboy, and she adored him. Her head told her she should never have gotten involved. Her heart couldn't stop her, she was in too deep. Pulling the warm sheets around her, she buried her face in his pillow. It was if he was still there.

Mathieu Le Fontaine was the brother of her employer. It just would not be done to have him fraternising with the employees. He had explained all this to her when she had asked why he wouldn't be seen publicly with her. His family came from a long line of aristocrats. You only married into your kind, he explained. They would never allow him to have a relationship with an employee. It was frowned upon. Mathieu had made Gloria vow to keep their love affair secret. Gloria longed to be a normal girlfriend, to be seen together in public, to stroll through one of the beautiful markets. In her dreams they would link arms as they walked together. They would spend lazy afternoons on the riverbank in the grounds of the chateau, lying in each other's arms. It made Gloria feel sad to know that these dreams would never be fulfilled.

Sighing, she got herself out of bed. Walking across to the shower, she pulled her dressing gown off the hook, then went into the kitchen. Outside, she glimpsed Maurice, the chef, selecting fresh vegetable from the vegetable garden. As if sensing he was being watched, he turned towards her window and waved. Gloria waved back as she plucked an apple from the table. The workers' cottage, where she lived, was adorable. A little stable door led out into the tiny garden. There, in the distance, was the magnificent chateau standing regal and proud, with the morning sun sending rays of light over the beautiful gold and maroon tiled roof. The tiles looked like actual gold, she thought as they glinted in the morning sun. The mullioned windows cast a romantic facade to the chateau. The stunning rose garden in front of the chateau was a gardener's dream.

Looking at her watch, Gloria wondered how long Maurice had been there. Had he seen Mathieu leave? Hopefully he could be trusted, she thought as she stepped into the shower. The cool tiles were lovely on her feet. She began shampooing her blonde hair. It had become even blonder, this year, in the constant sunshine. Later that morning, as Gloria made her way across to meet the children, she saw Mathieu leaving in his little green sports car. She wondered where he was off to, who he would see. Would he think of her? The sadness overwhelmed her again. She just didn't understand his reluctance to go public; he blamed it on family; she was just staff to them. Gloria had been quite put out. This is 1982, she thought, not 1910. Her sadness, however, was short-lived.

There, running down the path to meet her, were Elodie and Thierry. 'Mademoiselle Gloria,' they called in unison.

'Mademoiselle Gloria, bonjour.'

They threw themselves at her. Laughing, she scooped them into her arms. 'Bonjour, petite enfants,' she smiled.

'What are we going to do today?'

'Oh, let's swim in the river Mademoiselle, Gloria, please. Please can we?' they sang, almost in tune, pulling at her arms as they did so. Gloria found it extremely hard to say no to the children.

Taking each by the hand, they walked back towards the chateau. 'I must speak with your mother first,' Gloria explained. 'Then, if she says OK, then maybe today we can also swim, as well as lessons. Would you like that?' she asked.

The children frowned at the thought of lessons. Then let out a cheer at the thought of swimming. Gloria pushed open the enormous oak door at the back of the chateau that led directly into the large, cool kitchen. Cook, a bright, bustling lady, was busy preparing not only the lunch, but the evening meal for the family, under the instructions of head chef Maurice. Maurice was one of those lovely men you could take home to Mum. You were guaranteed that any mum would fall head over heels in love with him immediately. He had trained in London, The Royal Savoy Hotel, under the master chef. Then, at twenty-five, he had taken off around the world. However, his travels had only got him as far as Chateau Le Grand Fontaine, where he had remained. That sort of summed him up a little. Not a lot of drive, but he excelled at what he did. Gloria couldn't blame him though for not wishing to move on from his glorious life at the chateau.

Maurice waved, beckoning Gloria over. 'Hey, Gloria, try this,' said Maurice, pushing a tiny silver teaspoon towards her mouth, laden with a chocolate-looking sauce. Laughing, Gloria couldn't resist, she let him slip the little silver teaspoon into her mouth.

'Oh my goodness, that is amazing,' laughed Gloria, licking her lips and rolling her eyes.

'I'll save you some for later.' Maurice smiled.

Maurice and Gloria had become firm friends in her six months at the chateau, they shared games of cards some evenings. Often with a little wine that Maurice had sometimes declared had no further use; it being the last drop in the bottle, of course. Maurice was shy; he watched Gloria longingly from a distance, Gloria being completely unaware of his feelings. She just enjoyed his company, comfortable company, for what it was.

Walking away towards the stairs with the children, Maurice watched her go, sighing. If only she knew. Maurice had never felt this way about anyone until he had met Gloria. He wasn't stupid, though, he knew she just saw him as a friend. For some time now he had seen the brief glances between her and Mathieu. He had seen him sneaking away from her cottage in the early hours of the morning. He just hoped no one else had. He turned his attentions back to his menu.

It didn't take Gloria long to find Madame. Her singing echoed down the long stone hallway. Liselle had such a pretty voice; it was like bird song filling the air. Madame had been an opera singer, but once she married Marquis Le Fontaine, she had had to leave it all behind her. His ancient family roots would not have allowed her to carry on. Love had won. Liselle had given up her celebrity lifestyle, joining him at his wonderful chateau. Despite what she had given up, Gloria knew Liselle had never looked back. She was a picture of complete happiness; contented with her life and she adored her children.

Gloria knocked gently on the door to the bedroom.

'Ah, Gloria, bonjour. Come in, ma Cheri. Ah, my little angels too, come to Mama.'

The children flung themselves at Liselle as Gloria looked on with a smile. She hoped, one day, she would have children, too. She wondered what it was like to have your world revolve around little people, to be the person they looked up to, the person whose example they followed. The unconditional love that only a mother can experience. Gloria laughed, watching Liselle play with the children.

'Can we swim, Mama? Can we? Please, can we?' they begged.

'Of course, my angels, if that is OK with Mademoiselle Gloria.' Liselle glanced over at Gloria as she spoke, smiling her sweet smile.

Gloria laughed. 'Of course, I can't think of anything better, it's a beautiful day for a swim in the river.' The children cheered.

The water was icy-cold, compared to the thirty-degree heat of the day. Apart from the initial shock, it was very refreshing. Despite shivering as the water enveloped her, Gloria felt alive. The children splashed and played, throwing water over each other; protesting, but laughing.

Elodie swam towards her. For her six years of age, she was a fantastic little swimmer. Thierry wasn't too bad either, but he was a little more reluctant. At eight years of age, he was the eldest of the two, but definitely the quieter one. That said, he always had a go, and he didn't mind being ducked under the water by his sister.

In the distance, Gloria heard the crunching of gravel. Looking up, she saw Mathieu arrive back with a couple of his friends. His friends climbed out of the sports car, waving their tennis rackets in the air as they made their way into the chateau. How Gloria would love to be introduced to them as his girlfriend; she would love to join the house parties. That feeling of sadness overwhelmed her again.

Suddenly, Thierry's yelling broke her thoughts. He was spluttering. Elodie, looking on, was laughing and calling him a baby.

'Elodie, you mustn't be so mean to your brother,' cried Gloria, lifting Thierry from the water. She held him tight, wrapping him in one of the soft towels.

Thierry buried his head into her shoulder, giving his sister one of those told-you-so looks.

'Come now, both of you,' Gloria instructed, 'it's time we headed back for lunch.'

Wrapping a towel around Elodie, she took both their hands. They started their walk up the long pathway lined with beautiful mimosa trees. The little feather-like pink flowers wafted in the warm summer breeze, sending a heady fragrance along their path. Up ahead she could see Mathieu sprawled out on the grass, his friends lying beside him. Mathieu had his white tennis shorts on now, showing his muscular, honey-coloured legs. He was stretched out lazily. Squinting in the midday sun, he waved to Gloria as she passed. Gloria waved back. One of his friends turned to him and said something. Whatever it was, it caused them to laugh out loud and Gloria felt herself blush slightly. She would ask Mathieu later what had been said.

Grasping the children's hands again, she led them up to the kitchen door. Pushing it open, she felt the welcome coolness of the stone-flagged kitchen; a stark contrast to the hot day outside. Gloria suddenly felt very hungry. There, laid on the little table, was lunch for herself and the children. Maurice never failed to have it ready.

Smiling, he came over, tickling Elodie then Thierry as he passed them. 'Mademoiselle Gloria, your lunch is served,' he announced, with a grand bow. This made the children laugh. Gloria thanked him before turning her attention back to the two hungry children. They all sat down together at the table, tucking into the lovely, healthy spread that had been prepared for them. Lush, freshly picked tomatoes, still warm from the sun. Crisp, cold cucumber. Boiled eggs that had been freshly laid that morning. This was all served with the most delicious bread. It was scrumptious.

The children talked amongst themselves, recounting the tales of their morning swim. The staff in the kitchen went about their business and Gloria sat gazing out of the small kitchen window. There again, in the distance, Gloria saw Matthieu and his friends. They were drinking and eating now. Something was obviously causing great laughter as they sat and ate. Mathieu looked so handsome; his shirt taut across his chest. It made her own chest hurt with the love she felt for him.

Maurice watched her gazing longingly at that worthless Mathieu. Just what did she see in him, he wondered. A toned physique. Family wealth. He couldn't compete.

For the rest of the afternoon, Gloria put thoughts of Mathieu to the back of her mind as she looked after the children. They played games in the garden; picking rose petals and placing them in a bucket of water to make perfume for Mama. Gloria herself had done this as a child in her grand-mothers' garden, loving the smells of the different-coloured roses. She could remember it so well. The children wanted to put them into bottles and Gloria had promised she would ask the housekeeper if she had anything that they could use.

As she read to them, they lay on the rug, getting quite sleepy. Suddenly, a car door slamming in front of the chateau woke them all up. 'Papa, papa!' cried the children, jumping to their feet and running along the grass.

Pierre looked over and waved; he was back from a business trip to Paris. The children knew he would have gifts for them. Gloria watched, smiling, as the children threw themselves into their father's arms. He had been away for a week, striking deals for his winery. He would have done very well, which would be reflected in the gifts for the children and for his wife. The front door of the chateau opened. A thrilled Liselle came running down the steps. Gloria looked on as the family stood there, arms around each other. She saw Pierre kiss Liselle tenderly on the lips, as the children giggled. How lovely it was to watch a family's love, she thought to herself. Gathering up the books and her rug, Gloria knew she would no longer be needed this evening.

Liselle looked over and waved. 'Thank you, Gloria, it sounds like the children have had a wonderful day today.

Please, tomorrow, take the day off. We are going to go out

as a family. Take some time for yourself.' Liselle smiled. 'You
have been a fantastic help this week.'

Gloria called back, 'Thank you, Liselle. Goodnight, children, see you soon.' The children waved as they blew her
kisses. Gloria blew them back. As she made her way back to
her cottage, Gloria wondered what she could cook for dinner
tonight. It would be nice to have a day off tomorrow, but she
wasn't sure what she would do. There was only one person
she would like to spend tomorrow with, and Gloria knew that
wasn't going to happen. Walking back along the path, the
evening sun was sending out its rays of deep-orange light,
which dappled on her little cottage roof. The jasmine was
in full bloom around the front door, and its heavenly scent
lifted her mood as she pushed it open.

Glancing down, Gloria noticed a basket, covered with the
checked cloth, at the side of the little porch. A handwritten
note sat on top... Some leftovers for you. Enjoy, Maurice.

Ah bless him, she thought. Picking up the basket, she
pushed open the door into her own little kitchen. Placing
the basket on the table, Gloria lifted the cover, smiling. Inside there was some cold salmon steak, a lovely green crisp
salad, cold new potatoes. Nestled at the bottom was that
delectable chocolate dessert she had sampled earlier. How
wonderful, she thought. She must remember to thank Maurice tomorrow.

Turning to the sink, she placed that morning's dishes in,
turning the copper tap to hot. Picking up the washing up

liquid, she squirted some of the honey-lemon-scented liquid into the bowl. Claire stood watching it froth up, running her fingers through the fluffy bubbles in a little world of her own. She kicked her shoes to one side, slipping off her cardigan at the same time. She could feel the cold tomette tiles on her feet. Instantly she felt cooled. Suddenly, sensing the feeling she was being watched, she slowly turned to the door. There, stood leaning against the doorpost, was Mathieu. He smiled; his eyes covered with dark sunglasses.

Picking up the tea towel, she wiped her hands slowly, walking towards him. He, in return, put out his arms to her, pulling her close. Gloria took in the aroma of his aftershave and perspiration, burying her head into the warm crook of his neck. Mathieu kicked the door shut with his foot, holding her tight. Lifting her chin, he quietly placed his lips on hers. She tasted him, his mouth warm, moulding against her's. Gloria knew then she loved this man with all her heart. Taking her hand, he led her towards the bedroom door. Dinner would have to wait, she thought, as the door clicked shut behind them.

Maurice looked out of the kitchen window as he put the desserts on the plates. That was him finished for tonight, he thought. How he wished he could walk across to Gloria's. How lovely it would be to share the supper he had prepared for her. It wasn't to be; he thought sadly, closing the kitchen door behind him. With a heavy heart, he made his way up the stone steps of the kitchen's chilly turret to his room on the third floor. Tired, weary and feeling lonely, he lay on the bed; no lights, just the golden glow of the evening sun bathing him.

With a sigh, thinking of Gloria, Maurice closed his eyes. He drifted off to sleep.

Chapter 13

Gloria inhaled the sweet summer scent of freshly mown grass. She felt heavy, weighed down. Every moment she spent with Mathieu was wonderful, but they could never chat about hopes and dreams or their future.

What future, she thought, there was no future. Not for them, anyway. Why would he not take that chance to reveal to his family his love for her? He said he loved her. His actual words were, 'I love you differently from the way I love my family?' What exactly did that mean, she wondered.

Turning away from the window, she wondered what she would do with herself today. She had the day off. It would have been wonderful to have shared some time with Mathieu. However, he had meetings, he had informed her, kissing her tenderly. Questioning what meetings, he had replied, 'I have to help my brother-in-law with the wine sales.'

He kissed her again. That was Mathieu's answer to everything, she thought, kiss me and I will forget! Feeling cross with herself, she walked over to the coffee percolator on the ancient stove and switched on the gas. Maybe she should write to her parents, it was something she had been putting off for some time. She could imagine them tutting when reading of her life in that foreign country where all they did was drink wine and eat snails and frogs' legs.'

Turning again to the window, she saw Maurice making his way across to the vegetable plot. Walking over to the stable door, she opened it and called out good morning. He stood up from the potato plants. Grinning, he waved to her.

'Have you got time for a coffee, Maurice?' Gloria called.

'That would be lovely,' he replied, putting down his vegetable basket. He stretched as he stood up. Two minutes later, he appeared in the cottage garden. Gloria gestured to the little table. 'I'll bring it out,' she called. 'How about a croissant? I have some if you would like one.'

Maurice grinned. 'Have you ever known me turn food down, especially when it is being served by such a pretty woman?' He laughed and Gloria swatted him playfully. Walking back into the kitchen, she quickly saved the coffee from over percolating.

Maurice always seemed to cheer her up, she thought, reaching for the two pretty floral mugs.

'Sugar, Maurice?' Gloria shouted over her shoulder.

'Is the pope Catholic?' he replied.

Gloria loved to hear Maurice laugh; it was deep, infectious. Filling the two mugs with steaming coffee, she placed them on the tray. She reached for the two matching tea plates, popping a croissant on each. The aroma was making her mouth water, too. Ready, she lifted the tray off the table, walking carefully back out into the glorious morning sunshine. Gloria squinted in the sunlight as she placed the tray on the table. Maurice was sat reclined in the chair, feet up on a large rock on the edge of the grass. Gloria couldn't help noticing how at home he looked. They chatted easily over their lazy breakfast.

'Do you think you will continue working here, Maurice, or do you have an urge to move on and find something else?' Gloria asked as she took another bite of her buttery croissant.

Maurice said, 'I don't see how I can better this just now.' He wiped a few crumbs from his mouth as he spoke. 'I like the family, all my colleagues, it's such a relaxed place to work.' Maurice, looking pensive for a moment, added, 'Maybe I should be a little more adventurous. After all, I did want to go off around the world.' He laughed. Then, finishing his croissant, he asked, 'What about you, Gloria, what are your thoughts on your future?'

Gloria sat quietly for a moment, then replied, 'I don't really know, Maurice. I am enjoying life here too, but long term I won't be needed, especially as the children will go away to be schooled in Paris from September. I am guessing they will only come home for weekends. Liselle hasn't really said much.

It is probably a conversation that I should have,' she mused.

Interrupting her thoughts, Maurice continued, 'So, Gloria, what are you going to do with your day off today?'

'I am not sure,' she said, shrugging. 'I have to write to my parents, so I thought I might do that after breakfast. What about you, what do you have on today?'

'Well, like you, I have been given the day off.' Then, thinking for a minute, he said, 'look Gloria, I don't want to push myself on you, but, well, I was thinking of going to the little market in Moulin. Would you fancy a ride out? We could get some lunch somewhere.' He was a little hesitant, wondering if he was being too forward. Why on earth would a pretty girl like Gloria want to spend the day with him? Sitting in his battered little Renault, visiting some poky little market?

'That would be lovely,' exclaimed Gloria. 'I would love to spend the afternoon with you. I adore that little market.'

Maurice, grinning from ear to ear, said, 'Then so we shall. Let's say we will be ready to leave about 11:30? Is that OK with you? It will take half an hour to get there. We can grab some lunch first; I know a lovely restaurant in the centre which I think you will enjoy.'

Maurice left the cottage to collect his abandoned potatoes from the vegetable garden. Nothing could take the grin off his face. He almost wanted to do a little skip and fist punch, but then regained his composure. It was just a trip to the market. Maurice, more than anyone, knew Gloria's heart lay elsewhere.

Their day off turned into a wonderful afternoon togetherer. They had arrived in Moulin and had gone straight to the beautiful Cafe de Bourgogne. It had a wonderful art deco interior, mirrored walls ran floor to ceiling. The waiters were decked out in black and white, complete with bow ties, and the ambiance was one of days gone by. Gloria just loved it.

Maurice had guided her through the menu, starting with snails! Gloria could just imagine her mother and father's face if they knew what she was eating; her mother would have been disgusted. Gloria had to admit, she was actually a little hesitant herself at the thought. However, how could she say she had spent time in France and not tried any of their delicacies? With Maurice's encouragement, she had stuck the little silver fork into the shell, pulling the snail out. There it sat, glistening on her fork with wafts of garlic!

'Oh, my goodness,' Gloria exclaimed. 'I can't believe I'm doing this.'

'Go on, you can do it.' Maurice laughed, watching her face. 'Honestly, it will be fine.'

Maurice took her hand with the spoon, guiding it into her mouth. Its texture felt rather like a slimy mushroom infused with garlic. The mixed sensations filled her mouth. She took a big gulp, shuddering as she did so. Then another, then another. On the fourth one she gulped, realising it was slightly stuck in her throat. Gloria felt her face redden as the snail slipped slowly down. Reaching for her glass of white wine, she took an almighty gulp, then let out an enormous sigh.

Maurice, looking on with amusement, laughed. 'Well,

there you go' he said. 'You have eaten your first snails.'

'Oh goodness, Maurice, I don't think I want to do that again.' Gloria grimaced, then laughed.

Maurice loved watching her laugh. Her beautiful blue eyes lit up and her long blonde hair seemed to flutter as her shoulders went up and down. His eyes fell on her breasts; how he longed to touch her, make love to her. This woman had stolen his heart. Her heart, however, was with someone else.

'Now!' he exclaimed, snapping himself out of it. 'Now we will try the beautiful Confit de Canard. Honestly, Gloria, the meat will melt in your mouth.'

Maurice was always enthusiastic where food was concerned. He loved food and he loved sharing his knowledge, he had such passion for it.

Maurice was right, thought Gloria, taking another mouthful of the delicious duck. The meat melted in her mouth; the sauce was to die for. It was so pleasurable. The little dauphinoise potatoes accompanied it beautifully, along with the slightly al dente green beans. It really was a superb meal.

'I'll never be able to walk this afternoon,' she lamented to Maurice, rubbing her hands across her stomach. Maurice laughed. He insisted on paying the bill.

Stepping outside into the afternoon heat, both of them commented, simultaneously, on how hot the day had become. Looking up the narrowed cobble street, they could see three lines of market stalls. Gloria loved the colours, the smells, such a wonderful ambiance. Walking over to the fruit stall, Gloria wanted to touch everything, to inhale its perfume. The vivid colours shone in the afternoon sunshine, the red apples were like traffic lights, the strawberries seemed to ooze their scent everywhere. This was one thing that she loved about France: all this fresh produce was amazing.

Maurice was busy chatting with the lady on the stall. She watched them, animated in their conversation. Gloria wandered on a little, leaving him to do his deal for produce for the chateau. She heard some laughter up ahead. Looking up, someone caught her attention. Gloria, with a start, realised it was Matthieu. She quickly slipped into the shop's doorway. Standing still, she was wondering if she should say hello or just hide. Gloria wasn't that sure that he would he want her to say hello? Mulling it over, she turned back to look again. This time there was a very elegant young lady exiting the doorway, with three men. They must be his friends, she thought. It was probably another long lunch on daddy's money. Gloria then realised she was actually feeling a little jealous. Mathieu was laughing with the two men. The young lady came to his side, smiling. Still laughing, he lovingly put an arm around her shoulder, affectionately kissing her on the cheek. Gloria froze, then, feeling an arm on her shoulder, she turned round to face Maurice.

Fighting back tears, she dipped her head, rummaging in her bag for a tissue to hide the fact. Not realising what Gloria had seen, Maurice was laughing and telling her about Marie-Claire on the stall, recalling a story she had been telling him. Gloria, nodding, glanced over again to the restaurant doors. Mathieu and his entourage were gone. It was just a friend, she told herself, it must be. He loved her. He said he did. Smiling at Maurice, trying not to let on what had upset her, she linked her arm through his.

'Come on, Maurice, let's go look at the cheese stall.'

Gloria was going to be rational, not think the worst of Mathieu. He was allowed friends. He had only kissed her on the cheek. She wouldn't let her silly thoughts spoil her afternoon. They wandered, amicably, along the rows of colourful stalls, it felt so French. Finally, they came to the cheese stall. That said, you could actually smell it from about one hundred feet away. Such an overwhelming mix of aromas: Bleu d'Auvergne, Saint-Nectaire, Tomme de Montagne. They were all there. The owner of the stall, Pierre, was a friend of Maurice's. He supplied cheese to the chateau, especially for dinner parties.

'Maurice, mon ami!' Pierre grabbed him by the shoulders, then planted a kiss on each cheek. 'You must try this Saint Nectaire. It is fresh from the cave this morning and has been maturing for almost three months.'

Swiftly, professionally, he sliced a small corner off the cheese, handing it to Gloria, then Maurice to try. The flavour was almost nutty, slightly mushroomy, with a creamy texture. It just melted in the mouth. Gloria could just imagine this washed down with a glass of Bourgogne red. *Ooh, get me,* she thought.

Maybe she was learning something about this wonderful country. As Maurice did another deal with Pierre, Gloria stood watching fondly. He had such a simple way with people, was so kind. He was very genuine in the way he listened to what was being said. No wonder he was so knowledgeable, he spent so much time listening to others.

Gloria was sure, one day, he would go far. She, more than anyone, would love to see him fulfil his dream of owning his own restaurant. *Good old dependable Maurice*, she thought. Why could she not fall for someone like him? The rest of the afternoon went by quickly. They sat amicably, in the little cafe, off the market square. The heat of the afternoon was filled with the aroma of coffee and cigarettes. Burly stallholders sat at the bar with their small glasses of beer, laughing; real belly laughs. Another young couple, behind them, were holding hands, not taking their eyes off each other. Their dog, a spaniel, at least she thought it was, lay at their feet, snoozing.

Over coffee, Maurice told her stories about the hotel he had worked in. Gloria had never laughed so much in a day and she thanked Maurice for a wonderful afternoon. Reluctantly they left the cafe, strolling, easy in each other's company, back to his green Renault spotted with delicate blotches of rust.

He opened the car door for her and she climbed in, realising suddenly how tired she actually felt. 'You look a little pale, Gloria, are you OK?' asked Maurice as he switched on the engine.

He opened the windows for her. 'I'm just a little tired.' She sighed. 'It has been a wonderful day, thank you.'

The little car sped along the rural lanes. The evening breeze was wonderful, cooling her face and body. Rising magnificently in the distance, Gloria could see the large volcano of the Puy de Dôme. The sun was setting, lighting up the entire mountain in its hues of orange and gold. The mountain appeared to become black as the evening sunset sent out its rays of liquid honey across the landscape. What a magical time of day, she thought, look at the beautiful colours.

Sighing, she closed her eyes, letting the breeze fan her face, her head resting on the worn leather of the seats. Soon they were turning into the driveway. The sun had set, the little lamps lit the way ahead. In the distance she could see the dark silhouette of Chateau Le Grand Fontaine. Little lights glinting from each room, like stars in the sky, casting its romantic spell over the grounds of the chateau. This chateau wrapped her in love and comfort, it made her feel so at home.

Maurice pulled the car up near her little cottage. She stretched her long legs out onto the grass verge, then, swivelling round, Gloria planted a friendly kiss on his cheek.

Smiling, she thanked him again for a wonderful time.

'We will have to do it again,' he said tentatively.

'That would be wonderful, I would really like that,' Gloria replied, yawning.

Maurice was surprised, even slightly taken aback, he hadn't expected such an enthusiastic reply. As she stood on the grass, the evening air made her feel even sleepier. Maurice waved, then drove away. Gloria fumbled for her key in her purse. Pushing open the little gate, she walked up the gravel path to the front door and, turning the key, entered her cottage. Her thoughts took her back to the afternoon, to seeing Mathieu with his friends. She must ask him about that, she thought. In a nice way, though, she didn't want him thinking she was jealous. Gloria imagined that would make a man like Matthieu rush in the other direction. How perfect it would have been, she thought, to have spent the day with him, to have fallen into bed together, talking about their adventure. Instead, here she was in the cottage, alone.

Switching on the light, Gloria wandered into the kitchen noticing there was a single red rose with a brief note which read: *For you, mon chéri, I am sorry I missed you!*

Gloria's heart didn't know what to do first, leap or sink. He had come to see her, leaving a rose. She had missed him! She lifted the rose to her nose, inhaling its perfume, cut short in its beauty. Reaching for a glass from the cupboard, she switched on the tap, filling the glass with water. Carefully, she placed the rose into it. Then, with a smile, popped it on the window ledge. Oh well, she thought, it wouldn't do him any harm to know she had a life outside of him.

Tiredly, she made her way up to her room. She was going to take advantage of an early night. Climbing into bed, she played back the day's events in her mind. What a lovely day it had been; she was very lucky to have a friend like Maurice. It took her seconds to fall asleep that night.

Three weeks had passed since her little afternoon out with Maurice. Gloria had filled her time with the children and their activities. It was getting close to September 1st, time for them to go away to school. Gloria had had the conversation with Liselle about what would happen when the children departed. Liselle had been very kind, saying that Gloria could stay on in the cottage working part time for her. You could be my personal assistant, she had suggested. Gloria had thought this a wonderful idea. She had taken great pleasure in writing to her parents to tell them she was going to be a personal assistant to the Marquise Le Fontaine. Ha, she thought, that would certainly be one for her mother to tell her cronies down at the church hall on Sunday.

Gloria had asked Mathieu, casually, about the time in Moulin. Mathieu, in his typical way, shrugged it off as an afternoon with friends. 'Why are you worried, ma chéri?' He smiled, kissing her tenderly on the nose. Mathieu then pointed out the fact that she had spent the afternoon with Maurice.

'Should I not be worried too?' He frowned.

Gloria had laughed. 'Maurice,' she chuckled. 'Maurice is just a friend.'

He had pulled her into his arms, leading her to the bedroom, kissing her, whispering in her ear all the things he knew she wanted to hear. She had never experienced such passion before. Mathieu was wonderfully attentive, so different from the quick fumble behind the school bike sheds or her first, disastrous time in the back of a car with her boyfriend. But that was all forgotten as she lay in his arms.

Chapter 14

After the children went away to school, Gloria started working for Liselle during the day. They had agreed Monday, Wednesday and Friday. Thursdays had now become a regular trip out with Maurice, to visit his various suppliers. Gloria was slowly getting to grips with the language and meeting all the suppliers had helped with this. She had to admit she was in her element. Afternoons were spent helping him select cheeses, charcuterie and fish. It was such an exceptional learning experience; Gloria loved this friendship.

Today, Wednesday, was a working day, and Gloria was up and about. She had been asked to come a little earlier to the chateau that morning. Liselle had told her that her planning skills were in demand. Gloria had been intrigued: what could it be? Wouldn't it wonderful if it were an event at the chateau? The chateau would really come to life then; it was such a stunning building, built to entertain.

Feeling very excited, she got herself ready. She hoped it would be something she could sink her teeth into. However, she also had to admit; she was feeling exhausted this morning. She didn't feel hungry at all. Making her way through the kitchen, Gloria reached for a banana from the bowl on the kitchen table. Such a pretty little bowl in the traditional blue Toile pattern. She wished it could talk, telling her where it came from. It looked old; she was sure it had been in the family for many years.

Taking the path up through the woods, she arrived at the back door of the chateau. There was a slight early morning chill in the air. It was now early September, so it took a little while for the mornings to warm up. In the distance, she could hear the hum of tractors through the vineyards: it would be a very busy time for the workers now as it was grape harvesting time. Everyone joined in with this. She was tempted to ask if she could spend a day helping out. In fact, yes, she definitely would.

Gloria let herself in through the back door. The kitchen was a hive of activity; staff making packed lunches for the workers on the vines. Maurice waved and smiled. He was busy, she could see; she carried on up the stairs to the family's private wing. It was cool in the chateau. It would soon be time to light the enormous fires. This always had to be done by mid-September, so by the time the cold weather really kicked in, the heat from the fires would already have penetrated the chateau walls.

Knocking on the door, she stood and waited. She could hear the click, click, click of heels across the floor.

'Ah, ma chéri, thank you for coming, come in.' Liselle pulled the door wide open as she gestured to the two armchairs in the large bay window. 'Ah, that is good, I see you have your notebook with you.'

Gloria held up her favourite floral fabric coloured note book, smiling.

Liselle laughed, gesturing to Gloria to take a chair.

'This has to be the best place in the chateau,' Gloria said.

The beautifully landscaped gardens of the chateau lay like a patchwork quilt. The river ran along the bottom of the grounds, making Gloria think back to the days with the children paddling and playing there. Then, for as far as the eye could see, vines, row upon row, upon row. She could make out the dotted heads of pickers bent with their baskets, the little tractors going back and forth, collecting the vast baskets of picked grapes.

'Liselle,' Gloria said, turning to look at her as she spoke. 'How would you feel about me helping out with the grape picking for a day? When I am not with you, of course!'

'I am sure Pierre will welcome your help. Yes, you must experience this. Everyone should do a day picking grapes.'

'Now, listen. We are going to host a party for all the workers at the end of the grape-picking season. I may even sing! The party is to be a thank you for all they have done this year and, of course, everyone gets a box of wine each.'

The two of them sat for the next couple of hours, their heads bent in deep conversation. They agreed on the food, stressing that Gloria would run this past Maurice of course.

Chef always had the final say.

Their attention was distracted by a rap at the door.

'Ah thank you, Edith that is wonderful,' said Liselle. 'We've earned our morning coffee and cake!'

The party would be taking place in three weeks' time. By then it would be the beginning of October, nearly time for the children to come home from their school in Paris for the autumn break.

Goodness, just where had this year gone? thought Gloria.

Gloria sat, sipping coffee, taking in the stunning view. The weather was still good for September. A storm was brewing and the pickers were having to work extra hard to get the crop in.

Finishing her coffee and closing her notebook, Gloria said, 'Well, I have lots to do.'

'Thank you, Gloria.'

Making her way out of the drawing room, Gloria took the back corridor that led back down to the kitchen. The kitchen, as always, smelled heavenly as she made her way through, waving again to Maurice as she went.

Stepping outside into the late morning sunshine, Gloria felt she needed a walk. She would drop the notebook back at the cottage, grab a towel, maybe she could brave a swim. There wouldn't be many more opportunities to do that now autumn was setting in.

Once back at the cottage, she collected her book and a towel. Picking up her cardigan off the back of the old kitchen chair, she tucked it in her bag. She followed the little path that wound down towards the river, to a little cove Mathieu had shown her. She knew it would be quiet there. Gloria could relax, swim, read her book. There would be no interruptions.

Reaching the spot, the water looked so serene, only birdsong filled the air. It was just past midday; the sun had reached a pleasant temperature. Placing her blanket on the floor, Gloria stretched out, feeling the warm rays on her body. Her skin had a lovely golden glow to it, it had been an amazing summer. There were little white marks where her straps on her tops had been, her long legs looked toned. Must be the tan, she thought.

Having read a few chapters of her book, Gloria felt a little uneasy all of a sudden. As if she was being watched. A branch snapped. She sat up. There, grinning, stood Mathieu. He was looking extremely handsome in his white shorts and polo top, his dark hair a little ruffled, smiling that cheeky grin as he walked towards her. Gloria took a step toward him. She could feel the hot stones under her bare feet, the river trickling over her toes.

'I didn't expect to see you here,' she cried, hugging him. 'Ah, I was in my room looking out. I saw you disappearing off down the path. I knew you were coming to our little place, our little cove. So here I am. I wanted to surprise you.' He grinned with mischief. 'Nobody will know we are here,' he said as he nibbled her neck. His kisses were becoming more passionate, his tongue pushing inside her mouth. She could taste him, smell his aftershave, feel his warm skin. He peeled back her t-shirt, then her skirt, as he slipped out of his clothing too. He carried her to the water, wading into the river, the water icy-cold on their bodies. It sent a chilling, tingling sensation across her as they gasped for breath. Then he dunked her under the water until it gushed around her, the chill enveloping her entire body. Yet she was hot from his passion.

Later, as they lay on the rug on the riverbank, he slowly ran his fingers up and down her back. 'You are beautiful,' he murmured. 'I have a little gift for you, Gloria,' said Mathieu, reaching into his pocket of his shorts cast aside on the rug. He pulled out a small box. For a moment Gloria's breathing seemed to stop: it couldn't be a ring, could it?

Smiling at her, he opened the little box. There, nestled in the deep-royal-blue velvet, lay the prettiest necklace she had ever seen. The tiny heart locket was engraved with a tiny rose and a lily. 'The rose is for my English rose,' he laughed,

'the lily for you to remember the French.'

Gloria was blown away, she didn't know how to react, 'You don't like it?' said Mathieu sadly.

'Oh no, Mathieu, no, it is beautiful. I am just very surprised, and it is so pretty.' Tears filled her eyes as she spoke.

Mathieu took the chain from the box, gesturing to her to

lower her head. Then, as she did, he placed the chain around her neck, tenderly kissing her hairline. Gloria shivered with the electricity that ran through her. She lifted her head back up to him and they kissed again.

'I have never had anything so pretty, thank you so much,' she said, fingering the delicate gold locket on her neck.

They lay on the bank of the river, each deep in their own thoughts. Their bodies were entwined in the warm sun. Time was soon no longer on their side.

Mathieu pulled Gloria to her feet. 'Come, my love, we must go.' He placed his arms around her and Gloria buried her head into his warm chest. Pulling away, he said, 'I forget, Pierre asked me to pass on a message to you if I saw you. He said he would welcome your offer of grape picking, how would Saturday suit you?' His tone was slightly bewildered. 'I am surprised you wish to do this. Is it not beneath you?' he said, looking puzzled.

Gloria laughed. 'Not at all. How can I come all this way and not partake in such a fantastic experience as picking grapes?'

He shrugged. To him it was strange, you would never catch him picking grapes!

It was almost six; the evenings were drawing in quickly now. 'Come on,' said Mathieu. 'We will walk back to the clearing together. From there you can take the back path to the cottage and I will make my way across the lawn.'

The brusqueness of this caught Gloria; she was his secret.

He never wanted to be seen with her. She didn't share this feeling with him, just nodded and smiled. She didn't want to be difficult, make a fuss.

At the clearing, he planted a soft kiss on her lips. Without a backward glance, he was off, at a pace, across the lawn. Making it appear like he was just out for an evening jog. Why did she let him treat her like this? She was quite angry with herself now. Pulling herself together, she decided she wouldn't let it spoil a perfect afternoon. She would bide her time; there would be an opportunity to discuss her feelings with him. They couldn't go on like this forever, as much as she suspected he thought they could.

She drew the curtains in the cottage, then put a match to the fire she had prepared earlier in the day. Opening the fridge, she took out the cottage pie that had been given to her earlier from the kitchen. Gloria popped it on the table while she put on the oven on, then reached for the bottle of red on the countertop. Pouring herself a glass, she took a sip, then slipped the meal into the oven. A couple of sips later, and Gloria didn't like the wine. Maybe it was a bad bottle?

Popping her glass on the side, she turned on the tap for a glass of icy-cold water. That was better, she thought. Looking in the mirror, the pretty little necklace sparkled back at her. She held the cold gold in her warm palms, staring absent-mindedly for what seemed like ages. Suddenly she remembered the pie in the oven. Retrieving it before it burned, she settled down to eat. It was OK, but she noticed again she really didn't have any appetite. Maybe an early night would do her good so she could continue reading her book. Tucked up in bed, she managed all of a page before sleep engulfed her.

Waking the next morning, her head felt heavy and she was still tired. Looking at her watch, she realised she had slept for ten hours. A good shower would do the trick, she thought, as she trudged to the bathroom. Oh my goodness. Gloria quickly reached for the toilet seat, lifting it as she promptly vomited into the stark white porcelain bowl. Then again. Sitting there afterwards, Gloria felt wiped out. It must have been the pie she ate last night, that and too much sun, she thought.

Wearily, she returned to bed. Thank goodness it was her day off. Sighing, she crawled back under the duvet. Sleep, yet again, engulfed her. Gloria really didn't feel right for the next few days. She had had struggled through her meeting with Maurice for the menu. Maurice had commented on how peaky she looked, but she just brushed it off, saying it must have been too much sun. She hadn't seen Mathieu for the rest of that week; she lay low, resting up.

Chapter 15

Gloria's alarm woke her. Reaching over, she hit the off switch. 5am. You needed to be up at the crack of dawn for grape-picking. Climbing out of bed, she was relieved that she seemed to feel much better this morning. She was really looking forward to today.

Just a virus, she thought. She showered and dressed in cropped trousers, a vest top and a checked shirt, then popped her feet into plimsoles.

Gloria grabbed her bottle of water off the side, too early for breakfast. Walking out over the grounds, she looked across at the chateau. It was a stunning morning; the sun was breaking over its rooftop.

The workers were stood around in groups, quiet and subdued. Tired from their previous days work and the apprehension of another busy day ahead. Henri, the vineyard manager, split everyone into groups and handed out the large wicker baskets. As the morning wore on, people started chatting. Gloria was finding it quite hard on the back. At one point, she actually felt a little dizzy.

Morning came and went. As the church bells chimed twelve in the village, work stopped for lunch. They all sat around the long trestle table, shaded by the leaves of the popular trees. Cheese and charcuterie were served, accompanied by delicious, freshly baked baguettes. The wine had flowed freely. She had been a little surprised at that, considering they all had to continue working that afternoon.

Gloria had stuck to water. She didn't want to take any chances, after being under the weather. The grape picking continued after lunch. The heat beat down on them. Once or twice, she took a seat for five minutes in the shade.

Despite that she was thoroughly enjoying the experience. Sharing conversation with her new Australian friends had been wonderful. They had agreed to exchange numbers. Gloria offered to help them with places to stay once they got to the UK. As the light went down, everyone returned their baskets. The camaraderie had been lovely; The workers had obviously all built up a bond. Not surprising with all the time they had spent together. No doubt she would see them all next Saturday at the party. Gloria wiped her stained hands across her brow. She was exhausted. What a great day's work, though.

Thanking Robert and Elaine for their company, she wished them luck with the rest of their adventure. After promises to keep in touch, Gloria slowly made her way back out through the vineyard, heading to the lawns of the chateau. She was feeling overwhelmingly tired. Touching her forehead, it felt clammy. It had been a hot day. What she needed was a good cup of tea, then feet up for the evening.

As she took a few more steps, her head swam. Little stars seemed to flutter in her eyes, she tried to wipe them away but they wouldn't go. Seeing the tree trunk in front of her, she stumbled to reach it. Claire knew she needed to lean on it. Her palms touched the gnarled bark it rubbed her already swollen hands. As she put her hand to her head, she could hear someone calling her name in the distance. Slowly, she felt herself slipping. Then everything went black.

When Gloria came to, she was lying on her bed in her cottage. The bedside lamp was on.

'Gloria, it's Dr Pérotin.'

Trying to sit up, Gloria's head swam again. The doctor put his hand on her shoulder.

'Sit still, mademoiselle,' he said firmly, patting her hand to reassure her.

The doctor explained that she had passed out on the lawns of the chateau. It had been Maurice who had been calling her. Maurice, luckily, had been taking a break before evening service. He had seen her walking back from the grape picking. Calling out to her, he saw her slump to the ground. Shouting to the housekeeper to help, they had got her back to the cottage.

Fortunately, the doctor had been at the chateau visiting the gamekeeper after he had broken his leg the previous week. I am going to need to run some tests for you,' the doctor explained. 'I am going to take your blood. You will also need to supply a urine sample.'

At that point he helped her out of bed, then handed her a test tube. Gloria went to the bathroom. She still felt wobbly but filled the tube. Back in her bedroom, she handed it over to the doctor. Sitting on the bed, the doctor wrapped her arm in the tight blood pressure arm band. Then, quickly and expertly, he slipped a needle into her arm to draw the blood. Gloria felt like this was all happening to someone else. She just wanted to sleep, to be left alone.

The doctor said he would tell the La Fontaines that she was a little under the weather and asked her to make an appointment for four days' time, at his surgery. He could discuss the results with her then.

Gloria rested for a couple of days, Maurice bringing her food from the kitchens; homemade lemonade and freshly baked cake.

Liselle had come over once to see her and had insisted that she took the instructed time off to make sure she was fully recovered for the event at the chateau this coming Saturday. There were flowers from staff, books left for her to read. One person, though, had been conspicuous in his absence. Not a peep from Mathieu. Gloria felt hurt. Surely he could have made one visit to see how she was?

That evening, the embers in the fire were fading, but the heat remained. Switching off the kitchen light, Gloria went through to her bedroom where she slipped out of her clothes and put on her nightclothes. As she stood, brushing her teeth, Gloria thought she must take one of the vitamins she'd been forgetting to take of late. Gloria opened the bathroom cabinet door in search of the bottle. As she pushed a packet of paracetamol to one side, a box of Tampax fell out, landing in the sink. Reaching to pick it up, she froze. *Oh my goodness. Oh no!* When was my last period? Shutting the cabinet door, she stood, rooted to the spot, hand pressed on the cold glass door.

Eventually, pulling herself together, she went to find her diary. Picking it up, she turned the pages, flicking back through the dates. She was desperately trying to remember what she had been doing; it was all a blur. Suddenly it came to her. Yes, it had been the last week the children had been here before they left for Paris. She remembered not going swimming with them for that reason. Sinking into the armchair, it hit her. Gloria buried her head in her hands.

The next morning, sitting in the doctor's waiting room, Gloria felt chilled to the bone. What on earth was going to happen? Maurice had kindly driven her there, saying he had some stock to sort.

'Mademoiselle 'arper,' called the receptionist.

Why could the French not pronounce H? she thought irritably as she stood up.

The doctor gestured to her to take a seat whilst he flicked through her notes. Then, looking directly at her, confirmed she was pregnant. Her eyes brimmed with tears. Doctor Pérotin spoke kindly as he talked through her options. He explained that abortion really wasn't an option, not in France, under Catholic law. She would have to return to the UK if she didn't wish to keep the baby. Gloria knew returning to the UK, to her parents, pregnant, was out of the question.

He patted her hand, asking gently, 'Can the father help?'

Gloria, fighting back tears, said, 'I don't honestly know.'

The doctor nodded. He had his suspicions about who the father was. Being a frequent visitor to the chateau, he was well aware of the gossip in the staff quarters. Gloria left the room. As she stepped out of the dingy doctor's office, the cool air washed over her, making her shiver again.

She had an hour before she needed to meet Maurice, so she walked, trying to get her head together, tears streaming down her cheeks. Eventually, as she made her way back to the marketplace, she could see Maurice waiting. What would she say? She really needed a friend just now. Could she put this on Maurice, though? Lovely, kind Maurice who she trusted unreservedly. No. It wasn't fair.

Maurice looked up and smiled as she approached. He drew out a chair for her to sit on. It was obvious to him that all was not well. He could see that she had been crying. His heart ached for her. Deep down, he had an inkling of what she was going to tell him. Gloria really hadn't planned on telling him, not yet, but she couldn't stop the tears spilling out. Even the waiter, delivering their drinks, looked a little embarrassed. Setting down the drinks down, he quickly disappeared.

Through sobs that wracked her body, Gloria found the inner courage to tell Maurice. He said nothing, just held her against him as she cried and cried and cried. Eventually, drawing breath, Gloria reached for the hanky from her jacket pocket and dabbed at her blotched face.

Maurice took a deep breath, then, boldly said, 'It's Mathieu's baby, isn't it?'

Gloria nodded reluctantly. 'Yes, yes it is.'

'Come on,' said Maurice. 'We need to get you home.'

They had driven home in silence. Maurice offered to come in with her, but Gloria needed some time alone. She needed to take this all in, needed time to think. As Maurice drove off, Claire ran her hand over her stomach. 'It's you and me now,' she whispered in the evening air.

Chapter 16

Waking up the next morning, Gloria felt a little better. She was pretty sure once Mathieu knew everything, he would stand by her. Of course he would! He would want to marry her. She was having his child. Mathieu loved her; he told her so frequently. She looked at the clock. She really ought to get up. Somehow she had to put the pregnancy to the back of her mind. This evening had to be a success for Liselle; Gloria knew how much this party meant to her. As far as she was concerned, it was going be the best party the chateau had ever witnessed.

Up and dressed, Gloria made her way across to see how things were going. Maurice was deep in conversation with his staff. Gloria felt relieved; she could do without having to discuss her problem again today. There was far too much to do.

The day went by in a whirl. No time to think, or catch your breath. Gloria oversaw every detail in the beautiful ballroom. The flower arrangements; roses in delicate shades of cream and peach, eucalyptus leaves enhancing their subtle tones. Silver cutlery, polished to within an inch of its life, gleamed on the tables. Crystal glasses twinkling in the lights of the chandeliers that graced the ballroom. Gloria couldn't help but feel proud of what had been achieved. Taking one last glance around, she just had time to get back to the cottage and make herself look presentable. A quick backward glance at the room, made her smile. She knew that Liselle would love it. Gloria had certainly excelled herself here, even if she thought so herself.

Walking back to the chateau as the light started to fade, lights shone from every window. The candles lining the driveway flickered and Gloria could see a snaking line of motors making their way up the long driveway. Before long, the party was underway. The music played; people were already dancing. Gloria caught sight of Liselle across the ballroom; she looked absolutely stunning in a gown made of gold chiffon. It was encrusted with tiny diamante that sparkled with her every move, shimmering in the light from the magnificent chandeliers. She looked just like a princess.

Gloria, glancing down at her gown, had to admit that she had shaped up well tonight, too. She was wearing a stunning red gown that she had bought in one of the exclusive shops in Moulin. Gloria had spotted it on one of the afternoon trips with Maurice. It had been displayed in the window. Maurice had encouraged her: 'Try it on, you deserve to treat yourself,' he said.

Gloria had hesitantly gone into the shop. Stepping out from the changing room, she had seen him stare in awe at her. The red silk clung to her lithe body, swirling as she moved. It had cost her nearly a month's salary. To Gloria it was worth it to know that Mathieu wouldn't be able to resist her when he saw her in it. Gloria had imagined that she too was a Marquise. Wouldn't that be good; there would certainly not be any class issues then, she thought wistfully. Mathieu would be thrilled to marry her.

Everyone was happy, chatting away, laughing. The clink of cutlery and glassware sounded almost musical. In the background the band played discreetly. To Gloria, it all felt very Viennese. Not that she had ever been to Vienna. After dinner the dancing began. Gloria looked around for Mathieu; he was still nowhere to be seen. The anticipation of telling him their news was now bubbling up inside her. He would take her in his arms, announce to the world that they would get married. He would kiss her tenderly, tell her he loved her.

The music suddenly became louder, bringing Gloria back from her daydream. Some of the grape-pickers had taken to the floor with their traditional dances and onlookers applauded as they swung across the ballroom. Gloria looked at the grand clock next to the fireplace; it was nearly time for the star attraction. Liselle looked beautiful as she stepped on to the stage. The French songs she sang brought tears to Gloria's eyes. She was feeling very emotional just now; it took very little to make her cry!

Gloria ran her hand over her stomach, feeling the silk of her gown, not quite believing that a new life was beginning inside of her. Smiling, she turned her thoughts back to the evening. Liselle had been bubbling to tell her something. Gloria hadn't a clue what. Every time she tried to get to talk to her, Liselle had been whisked away. She looked like she was in her element. The whole evening had been a huge success. Lots of people were saying the food had been utterly delicious. There was Maurice to thank for that. He was certainly getting lots of compliments; he certainly deserved them. He was destined, one day, to do amazing things in the culinary world, but, for now, Gloria was extremely grateful to have him as a friend.

Suddenly the lights were switched on in the ballroom; glaringly white, a stark difference to the muted glow of the chandeliers or the flickering candles on the tables. The whole ballroom looked stunning. Gloria stood, feeling quite proud of what she had created. Putting her hand up to shield her eyes for a moment, she glimpsed Mathieu with a handful of his friends, male and female, standing around him. She couldn't help noticing that the stunning woman who had been with him in Moulin was also here. She certainly was a beauty; her crimson gown sparkled magnificently in the bright lights of the ballroom. The tiara on her head looked like it had come off the pages of a fairy tale. It was a very different world, sighed Gloria. She wondered what was happening. This certainly wasn't part of the well-planned itinerary.

Looking back over to Mathieu, Gloria's stomach did a flip. Tonight would be the night. Gloria knew he would come to her after the party. He would appear at her little cottage and she could tell him about the baby. He would stand by her and the Fontaine family would welcome her into their life.

Liselle and Pierre were now on the stage, thanking all their workers and their families for the wonderful job they had done with the grape-picking this year. They announced that they expected it to be an excellent vintage. Everyone, of course, would get a box of six bottles of wine, as a special thank you. This announcement brought a loud round of applause from everyone. Liselle then took the microphone from Pierre. Her sweet voice filled the room. 'My dear friends and colleagues, it is with great pleasure that I stand here before you tonight to share with you some wonderful news that our family has received this week.'

Turning, she gestured to Mathieu to join her on the stage. Liselle continued, 'It is with the greatest pleasure that I announce to you all that Mathieu has proposed to the wonderful Viscountess Lydia Serrenday.' A huge around of applause shook the ballroom. 'And' continued Liselle, holding Mathieu's hand, 'Of course she has said yes!' Another enormous cheer went up around the room, everyone clapping. The band struck up. Mathieu kissed his sister affectionately on each cheek. Pierre shook his hand before they both took it in turns to congratulate Lydia, who was smiling.

Mathieu then took Lydia by the hand, placing a tender

kiss on her lips. Everyone cheered, followed by another loud round of applause, which echoed around the ballroom. Gloria was frozen to the spot, but the room was moving in slow motion. She couldn't breathe, the pain in her chest hurt so much. Her heart was beating as if it was going to burst through her chest. Clutching her hand to her mouth, she suddenly felt an immense wave of nausea come over her. All the colour had drained from her face. She had to get out of the room.

Back in her garden, Gloria sat, tears streaming down her face. How could he? How could he have not even told her first, how could he be so heartless? He knew how much she loved him. The handkerchief in her hand was soaked. She turned as she felt a hand on her shoulder. No words were needed as Maurice pulled her close. She sobbed until there just wasn't anything left inside of her. Maurice held her.

As dawn broke, Gloria, exhausted, turned to Maurice, trying to smile. 'I'm s-s-s sorry.' She breathed deeply, trying to get her breath. 'I c-c-can't believe just how callous he has been. How could he stand there and do that to me? How could he not tell me first?'

Maurice shook his head. He too was in disbelief; how could anyone treat a woman they supposedly loved with such disregard? As he sat there, holding Gloria, he yearned to tell her he loved her. This was not the right time or place. Would there ever be a time and place for them? His heart ached to see Gloria in so much pain, but also with the secret he was so desperate to keep He loved her so much.

Chapter 17

Maurice and Gloria sat in the garden until the sun was fully risen. Gloria had eventually laid her head on Maurice's shoulder and closed her eyes. Now, as the dawn chorus broke, he nudged her gently. For a moment, Gloria couldn't work out why she was sitting outside with Maurice. Then the events of yesterday evening flooded back. Sitting up straight, she looked at Maurice. 'I'm so sorry. Have you sat there all this time with me?' Maurice nodded.

'Why don't you have a shower, I can put the kettle on?' suggested Maurice.

Rubbing her eyes, Gloria nodded, then walked to the cottage door. Turning at the door she looked back at the chateau, her dreams shattered. Standing in the steaming hot shower, she ran her hand across her belly. She still couldn't take in that there was a new life growing inside of her.

Turning off the shower she stepped onto the mat, reaching

out for the warm fluffy towel she wrapped it around herself. Gloria felt cocooned from the outside world. Stifling a yawn, she knew she must rest. She needed to save her energy.

Maurice called up to her. 'Coffee is on the table. Rest now. I will be back later this afternoon to see how you are.'

'Thank you.' She needed to lick her wounds in private. Collecting the coffee from the table, she made her way back to the little bedroom. That was painful too – it held memories of Mathieu. Somehow, climbing into bed, she felt comforted. She pulled the duvet up around her. Minutes later, she was asleep.

Gloria woke at about three that afternoon. Climbing out of bed, she wrapped her towelling dressing gown around herself, pulling the belt tight, then went downstairs.

Maurice had brought a meal for her. 'Ah, love, you look a little better,' Maurice said, gesturing for her to take a seat in the armchair. He put the kettle on.

'I don't think I can eat, Maurice.' Gloria sighed.

'Look, love, you have to keep your strength up. You're not just looking after yourself, you have another little one to think of now.' Maurice cleared his throat.

'Gloria, I have had a hard think about things. Life is going to be very difficult for you. You can't stay on here easily unless, of course, you want him to know about the child.'

Gloria's eyes brimmed with tears again. 'Maurice, I know. What can I do? My parents will not welcome me back with open arms. My mother is a devout Catholic; she will be horrified. She won't want anyone to know, she'll hide me away.' Gloria could already see her mother and father's faces!

'I know love, listen. Please hear me out,' Maurice pleaded. He needed to say this. 'Look, why don't you and I get married in a registry office here?' Maurice saw the look of amazement in her eyes. Not letting that stop him, he continued. He was going to get this idea out in the open. So he kept going. He didn't want to give Gloria the opportunity to say anything, so he shushed her and continued, 'We can get married here and you can tell your parents it was three months ago, tell them you have been plucking up the courage to tell them; they never need to know.'

Maurice waited for her reaction to his idea, his palms feeling slightly sweaty.

'Oh, Maurice, you would do that for me,' Gloria said in disbelief.

Maurice nodded. 'Of course,' he replied with a smile. 'Gloria, you need to know I have been *in love* with you for some months now,' Maurice said, quietly, not looking at her. 'I have hated seeing what Mathieu has done to you, it has broken my heart.' Maurice looked her in the eyes. Taking her hands in his, he said, 'I know you may not, for now, love me like you do him, but I hope maybe one day you will.'

Gloria gripped his hand tight. It took a little while for it all to all sink in. What a wonderful man; taking her and her unborn child on.

'I need time to think. But from the bottom of my heart,

thank you.'

He understood.

He would give her time to think it all over. They could meet again tomorrow, he suggested, as he cleared her empty plate away. Gloria hadn't realised just how hungry she had been. It had been well over twenty-four hours since she had last eaten. She sat with her eyes closed in the armchair. Maurice had lit the fire for her, and the room was quite toasty now, which was making her even sleepier.

'Look love, get yourself to bed. I can lie here on the couch tonight if you like, however if you want to be alone, that's also good. I understand'.

Gloria smiled a watery smile. 'Maurice, you have done enough, get yourself a good night's sleep, let me do the same and let's talk tomorrow.' Gloria looked into his eyes as she spoke. She was so lucky to have a friend like Maurice. However she needed time to think.

He smiled, then kissed her gently on the forehead, wishing her a good night's sleep. Gloria wearily made her way back to bed. It was a good job it was the weekend. The family had given her the following week off. They were going away on a late autumn trip to visit Pierre's parents in Paris. They would then drop the children back at school, returning once again to Le Grand Fontaine. Gloria lay in the darkness of her bedroom. Sleep would not come. There were so many thoughts chasing around in her mind. She was still reeling from the kindness of Maurice's proposal. What a man! Gloria also knew her choices were limited. Eventually, as the little clock turned to midnight, she drifted off. Tomorrow would be another day.

Maurice lay in his turret bed, staring out of the window. The stars seemed far brighter than usual tonight. He knew in his heart he had made the right decision. One day, Gloria would also love him as he loved her. It was a chance he was prepared to take.

Maurice woke the next morning. With the family being away, there was only the staff in the chateau and they could look after themselves. Maurice was pleased there was no Mathieu. It would give Gloria the space she needed. Looking at the clock, he thought he could prepare some lunch for Gloria. They had agreed he would go over about 1pm, so he would take it with him then. He so hoped her answer would be yes. Maurice knew he was selling himself short, asking a woman who didn't love him to marry him. He also knew, that given time, perhaps she would come to love him as he loved her. Packing up the little picnic basket, he felt very nervous as he walked across the grounds to Gloria's little cottage. The front door was open.

Gloria was up and about, feeling much fresher. The worst of the morning sickness seemed to have passed, but she was still weak from what she had been through. She knew she would need to rest and take better care of herself to protect her unborn child.

Maurice's kind-hearted offer still amazed her. If she said

yes, was she destroying his life? If she didn't, what life would she have, a mother of a bastard child? She took her coffee out into the garden.

Gloria was overwhelmed with sadness, knowing she would now have to leave here. How could she stay, how could she see Mathieu with his fiancé? Then, eventually, he would have his own family. He would never know that her child was his. She knew what her answer was, and she had to go, she couldn't stay.

Looking up from her cup of coffee, Maurice was just walking through the garden gate. Gloria watched him, her friend. It made her think about his hopes, his dreams, maybe he would want to open his own business one day? Maurice had wanted to travel the world. What right had she, taking that away from him? But maybe they could work together, maybe she could help him fulfil his dream of owning his own business. These thoughts certainly gave her a little injection of positivity.

Maurice smiled at Gloria as she sat drinking her coffee at the garden table. He loved this woman so much. It pained him to think of the child not being his. Maybe, one day, they could go on and have a child of their own. It was certainly a possibility. This brought a smile to his face. He had been pacing about all morning, preparing himself. He was convinced Gloria would say no. Why would she want to spend her life with someone like him?

Gloria smiled at him. 'Come, come sit down, Maurice,' she said, kindly, pointing to the garden chair. Reaching for the spare cup, she poured him a cup of coffee. Handing it to him, she smiled.

Maurice smiled back at her. Maybe he wasn't being too hopeful after all. 'Gloria,' he said quietly, trying not to look her in the eye, 'Gloria,' he went on. Gloria looked at him hesitantly.

'Yesterday I suggested marrying you. I have thought more about it since then.' He took her hand as he spoke. 'I think we should leave here altogether, go back to the UK, get married there as soon as we can.

'Whilst the family are away, we could pack up and leave, be back in the UK by Friday. We could apply to get married straight away, before we head to your parents. We then tell them we got married three months ago, that you fell pregnant straight away.' He tried to judge her response from her face but nothing was obvious. 'They don't need to know about what has happened here.' He paused, for a moment, looking at Gloria. Tears were sliding down her cheeks, falling into the teacup she still held in her hand. Maurice knew it. She wouldn't agree to his idea. She still loved that imbecile. He pushed back his chair to stand up.

Gloria put out her hand, touching his arm gently. 'Maurice, please, please sit.'

Maurice sank back down in his chair, turning to look at Gloria. She was smiling at him.

'You would do that for me,' said Gloria, her voice almost a whisper. 'I can't believe you would take me back to the UK, marry me, bring up my child.' She shook her head in amazement. 'I can't let you do that; you have your whole life ahead of you,' Gloria said, wiping her eyes before continuing. 'You have dreams, ambitions, you want to travel. We would only hold you back, all this with someone else's child.' Gloria shook her head, still in disbelief. 'Maurice, how do you know you wouldn't hate me for it?'

Taking her hand, Maurice looked tenderly at her. 'Gloria, I have loved you for some time now. I never told you, as I knew your heart was elsewhere. We have spent some lovely times together, I think you are fond of me too.'

Gloria nodded. She certainly was. However, it was hard to believe what she was hearing. They talked for what felt like hours and, finally, he convinced her.

Maurice and Gloria would leave on Wednesday, returning to the UK. They would arrange a quick marriage before returning north and facing her parents. Maurice said that his only stipulation was that Mathieu's name was never mentioned again. Maurice also promised that he would bring up her child as if it were his own.

Gloria knew she had no other option. What would life be like if she turned down this offer? And she was extremely fond of him. They could make this work.

As Maurice was about to leave, he took Gloria's hands in his. 'We will keep this to ourselves, no one must know.' Gloria nodded in agreement.

'I will see you on Wednesday night at 10pm.' Maurice

smiled as he looked into her eyes 'We can make this work, Gloria. Everything will be OK. You'll see.'

Chapter 18

Maurice was true to his word. At 10pm exactly he drew up in his battered little Renault. Gloria was ready. All her possessions were packed into two suitcases and a box. The night air was cold and only an owl hooting broke the silence. The full moon lit up the front garden. Maurice left the car running as he quickly went to the front door to meet Gloria. She opened the door, handing him her two suitcases. He took them away, then returned for the box. Gloria shivered again, pulling her coat around her. 'The car is warm, Gloria, you will be fine once we get going,' he said, taking the box from her.

'I just need a moment,' she said.

'No problem, I will see you at the car,' replied Maurice.

Gloria switched off the lights. She stood looking around her small cottage, the brightness from the moon lighting up the small kitchen. Taking a deep breath, she pushed away the memories. That was what they would be now, just memories. It was no good standing around; nothing was going to change. Pulling the front door shut, she took her last walk up the garden path. There was no looking back. Maurice was all she needed now.

The busy port and town of Dover was a stark contrast to the undulating hills that they had left behind in the Auvergne. Lorries piled off the ferry. Their fumes made Gloria want to choke as she put her hand to her mouth. Maurice looked tired and drawn. It had been a long, hard drive north through the night. They had only stopped to grab some food and coffee to keep them going. Everything they owned was packed into three large suitcases and a couple of boxes. They were all crammed into the boot and backseat of the tiny Renault.

The ship's chain clanked as cars filed down the exit ramps. It was a cold, wet, miserable morning. Even the seagulls weren't their usual persistent selves. Gloria was chilled despite Maurice turning up the car's heating. They were making their way to a tiny hotel just on the outskirts of town where they would stay for three nights. They had booked a slot at the registry office for tomorrow. There would be no pomp and circumstance. They would just grab two witnesses off the street.

The hotel was dingy; they needed to save what money they had. Gloria sat down and wrote to her parents to tell them she was back home in the UK and was married to Maurice. She would post it after the wedding. She could just imagine the shock on her mum's face. Sadly, she also knew the hurt that she would have caused them by not telling them about Maurice. Putting the pen down, Gloria thought back to Mathieu. The tears had dried now; the anger welling up inside her replaced them. How could he have been so cruel to her? How long had he known about the engagement? If you loved someone, you didn't treat them like that. Gloria felt used, abused even.

On the morning of the wedding, Gloria wore one of her best dresses. A pale-blue cotton dress with a full skirt. She knew it brought out the blue of her eyes. Maurice thought his heart was going to come through his chest as he stood looking at her in the registrar's office. Finally, Gloria would be his. Gloria looked at Maurice and smiled. Many women would have fallen over themselves to have a husband like him. That morning, at 11am, Gloria promised herself to him. They had thanked the two witnesses, who had been happy to help. Maurice took Gloria's hand as they left the office. 'Well, Mrs Fitzgerald. Let's get some lunch. We can even treat ourselves to a bottle of wine,' he laughed. Gloria squeezed his hand and smiled. They were now husband and wife.

Maurice and Gloria had rented a tiny flat on the outskirts of London. This would be better for Maurice's chances of getting work back in a hotel, he had said. The first night in their new home, Maurice had carried her over the doorstep.

'Maurice, you will put your back out!' exclaimed Gloria, laughing as her feet waggled in the air. He had placed her gently down on the sofa in their new living room, bending to remove her shoes for her.

Leaning forward, he kissed her lightly on the lips. For a moment Gloria hesitated, but then gave in to his touch. Maurice had been kind, understanding. Gloria knew it mustn't have been easy for him, either. Afterwards, as they lay in each other's arms, she knew that every day they spent together would be another day that they could build on. Together they would be the best parents possible.

One evening, as they sat talking, the baby suddenly kicked. Gloria was startled for a moment. 'I think the baby just kicked!' she said.

'Really? What did it feel like?' he asked. Getting up from his chair, he came to sit with her. Gloria took his hand and laid it on her swollen stomach. They sat for a few minutes, then suddenly again there was a kick.

Gloria turned to Maurice. 'Did you feel that?' she asked.

'I did,' he said, grinning from ear to ear.

It warmed Gloria's heart to see him so happy.

Maurice's parents were just as kind and empathetic as Maurice. They had welcomed Gloria into their home, just an hour north of London. Maurice's mum, Ethel, had got the cakes made. The tea was brewing, ready. Harold, his father, was such a kind man. He had taken great delight in showing her around his vegetable garden. They were absolutely made up with the news that they would be grandparents. So much so, Gloria felt quite guilty at the deceit but knew, heart in heart, it was the absolute right thing to do. Maurice certainly didn't appear to have a problem with it.

Today she had to get through seeing her parents. It had been put off far too long. Gloria hoped they would be excited about the pregnancy news. They had made brief contact by letter, which is always difficult. Things don't always come across as they are meant. Her mother had written back to her, curtly, taken aback that Gloria was informing them she had married. That said, her mother also wrote, she would look forward to welcoming them both to their home soon. Which, in Gloria's mother's language, meant you had better get up here damned fast. They set off that sunny morning in the little battered Renault, making the drive up to Butteroak, where her parents lived in the thatched cottage which had been Gloria's grandmother's.

Her mother was quite stiff and abrupt with her initially, her father much warmer. They had invited them both into the little sitting room, offering to take their coats.

Gloria knew before she removed her coat she had to get the baby news out of the way. Coughing nervously, she un-buttoned her coat. 'Mum, Dad.' She swallowed again quickly. 'Maurice and I have some other news for you.' Gloria cringed as her mother's eyes bored into her.

'Well go on then, Gloria,' her mother had chipped in.

'Maurice and I are expecting a baby.' There it was, out.

Gloria continued on quickly. 'I'm due in September.' Gloria stood still, waiting for her mother's response.

Her mother seemed to tense slightly for a moment. She could almost sense her father cringing, waiting for his wife's response too. 'That is wonderful news, congratulations to you both.' Her mother was almost smiling. 'Arthur, get the sherry out, will you? We need to have a little toast.'

Gloria knew that once the news had set in, she would take great delight in telling her Sunday Club cronies all about it. Thank goodness, thought Gloria, thank goodness they had said they had been married earlier than they had. She was eternally thankful to Maurice. Her mother would never have to know that he wasn't the father. Gloria checked herself quickly. She had to believe Maurice was the father.

They had driven back down to Hertfordshire that evening. It was a long journey and Gloria had slept for most of it. Maurice had been delighted with her mother's interest in his culinary skills. He felt they would get on extremely well. Maurice could see though that Gloria and her mother rubbed along. She was obviously very close to her father. He was so looking forward to becoming a father; he was going to do everything in his power to provide for his new family. Gloria opened her eyes briefly, smiling a tired smile at Maurice. She reached out and placed her hand on his knee, squeezing it. Every day she was learning to love this man more. She knew just how lucky she was to have met him. Having a kind, caring, happy relationship was more than most people could ever ask for. Gloria knew, with him, she had this. Maurice woke her when they reached the car park of their flat.

Gloria stretched and smiled. 'Thank you for taking me to my parents today, I really appreciated it. Then, laughing, she said, 'It wasn't anywhere near as bad as I thought it was going to be.'

Maurice laughed too. 'I think your mum is lovely, really. I think we will get on like a house on fire.'

'I think it was news of the baby that did it,' smiled Gloria.

Then, looking at him, she said, 'Our baby.'

Maurice worked hard. He arrived home late most nights. On the evenings he was home, he would spend hours in the evening talking about names. He hoped it would be a boy, but so long as it was healthy, he really didn't mind. Maurice had secured a job at a large local hotel as head chef. Gloria was becoming used to spending her evenings alone in their two-bedroom flat. Maurice had also bought her a TV; it was quite a novelty. She didn't really watch it much, preferring to spend her time reading or knitting. There was a pile of baby cardigans and jumpers building up in every colour of the rainbow. Gloria was feeling increasingly tired and tonight was no different. Hearing the click of the front door, she placed her knitting down on the table.

'I'm home, love,' called Maurice.

Gloria pulled herself up from the cosy armchair, walking slowly to the kitchen. 'I'll put the kettle on,' she called.

Maurice's face peered around the kitchen door as he swiped out a bunch of daffodils from behind his back.

Gloria took them from him, smiling, 'Oh, how lovely,' she said, reaching for a vase from the kitchen shelf.

Maurice came rushing to her side to help as she yelped.

'Are you OK, love?' he asked, the concern in his voice obvious.

Gloria turned to face him. 'I think so, but that was a sharp pain,' she said, rubbing her back.

'Here, you sit down. I'll make the tea,' he offered, leading her into the lounge.

Another pain tore through her. She gripped his arm. 'I think I might be going into labour,' she cried.

Maurice, calm as ever, got her to the chair. 'Now, where is the bag you got ready?' he asked.

Gloria pointed to the dining table. 'Under there. Ouch,' she cried again.

Maurice wasn't going to take any chances; he grabbed the bag from under the table. Going into the hallway, he put his shoes on. 'I think we need to get you to the hospital,' he said, gesturing for her to slip her feet into the shoes that were next to the armchair. Gloria did as he asked, letting him help her out of the chair and down to the car. On the journey to hospital, the pains were coming quicker. Maurice was timing the contractions and they were now five minutes apart. She knew it could take hours with the first one and the pain was awful; she didn't feel she could cope.

'Nearly there now, love, just hang on.' He was finding it incredibly hard to see her in so much pain.

The staff were wonderful at the hospital, fetching a wheel-chair to the car, they took Gloria to the labour ward. Maurice went to park the car, then, grabbing her bag off the back seat, he ran back round to the maternity unit. The nurse showed him to the labour suite. Gloria had changed into a hospital gown and was crying out in pain. The midwife was wonder-ful, her voice soothing and caring. 'Come on, Mrs Fitzgerald, let's get you on the bed.'

Gloria felt like she was in another world. All that mattered was the baby. She could cope with this pain so long as the baby was OK. For hours, the pains came and went. Maurice mopped her brow with a cold flannel and Gloria inhaled the gas and air. Then, finally, at 7am, Claire Louise Fitzgerald came into the world, weighing in at a healthy 7lbs 10oz. A mop of dark hair, cute little dimples. It had been an excru-ciating eleven hours. Gloria had done it. She was exhausted.

Maurice was elated. Never had he looked at someone and felt so much love from that very first minute. Well, no one except Gloria, of course. Maurice tenderly kissed Gloria on the forehead. 'Well done, my love, just look at her!' he ex-claimed. 'Such a beauty.' He grinned. 'Just like her mother.'

Gloria smiled fondly back at him, holding his hand, staring at her beautiful daughter. She could not fail to see how sim-ilar to Liselle her new daughter looked. A tear rolled down her cheek. Maurice was too busy holding Claire to notice. Gloria knew he would just think it was a happy tear, a tear for her new daughter.

Every time Gloria looked into Claire's eyes, she saw Mathieu. She knew she had to stop this, forget about him.

Gloria swore that day that she would protect herself and Claire from ever knowing the truth. Mathieu Le Fontaine would no longer exist.

Chapter 19

Maurice and Gloria had eventually moved to Cheshire, where, finally, on their tenth wedding anniversary, Maurice had opened his own restaurant. It had been a huge financial risk for them; they had put everything into it. It was Maurice's pride and joy, well after Gloria and Claire, of course.

Gloria was in her element, organising everything, and Maurice was extremely proud of her. Both their sets of parents had eventually passed away, leaving Gloria and Maurice financially secure. Her parents had left her the gorgeous little cottage in the picturesque village of Butteroak. Gloria knew, the day they moved in, it would be the perfect place to bring up their beautiful daughter. Over the years they had tried for another baby, but nothing had happened. It obviously wasn't meant to be. They were, however, both content with the life they had created. Gloria was very involved in village life. She often laughed at how like her own mother she had become.

Looking out of the kitchen window on this particular morning, Gloria was watching the birds feed off the bird table in the garden. It was a beautiful spring morning in Butteroak. Claire was at school. Maurice had just left for the lunch preparation. Gloria thought she had better start the ironing. She pulled the large board out of the cupboard in the hallway, then switched the iron on. Just as she was spreading out Maurice's shirt, there was a knock at the door. Switching off the steam iron, Gloria wondered who it could be. She wasn't expecting anyone or any parcels. Well, none that she could think of. Probably a door-to-door salesperson, Gloria thought to herself.

Wiping her hands on her apron, she removed it before going to the door. Pulling open the front door, she froze. There, stood in front of her, was Mathieu, Mathieu La Fontaine. Gloria felt the colour drain from her face as she leant on the side of the front door for balance. Trembling, she wanted to slam it shut, pretend this wasn't what she was seeing. There was no doubt whatsoever that it was Mathieu. Gloria remembered him like it was yesterday.

'Gloria, it is me, Mathieu,' he whispered in his lilting French accent. He could see the reaction on her face; she looked like she had seen a ghost. To him, though, she looked the same Gloria that she had all those years ago. The beautiful woman he had always remembered, the one he had dreamed about finding, night after night, for the last ten years. Mathieu had never loved a woman like he had loved Gloria. He needed to see her, to speak to her. His daughter had drowned last year, his life was in pieces, he needed his Gloria to make him feel better. He hated this empty, lonely feeling. His wife was deep in depression. He, too, just wanted to curl up and die. It had taken every ounce of his strength to search for Gloria. His agent had been working on it now for two years. Now, here at last, Gloria stood in front of him.

Gloria was shaking. She didn't know what to do, except that she needed to get him in off the street. She gestured to him to come through the door, pointing to the lounge at the front of the house. The room they only used for special occasions, like birthdays or Christmas, or the small gathering they had held after her parents' deaths. Mathieu stepped over the doorway, brushing past Gloria. His closeness was almost too much to bear. Seeing the fear in her eyes, he almost regretted coming to see her. *What had he done?* he asked himself. The pair stood, a respectful distance apart in the lounge, just looking at each other. 'What are you doing here, Mathieu?' stammered Gloria. 'Why have you come now, why?' she pleaded with him.

Mathieu stood looking at her. Yes, why had he come? Why had he done this to her? The years had been kinder to her than him, he could see that. In return, Gloria noticed the dullness of his eyes.

'I needed a friend, Gloria. I needed to see you,' said Mathieu, turning away to look out of the lounge window.

'Mathieu, I married Maurice. Do you remember? The chef?' Gloria told him, still in disbelief that he was actually standing in front of her. Mathieu nodded. He knew all that. Some information he had squeezed from Madame Rencurrent in the kitchen. She had told him that Gloria and Mathieu had gone back to the UK. Mathieu had hired a private investigator to look for them. He also knew that Gloria now had a daughter, which he assumed was Maurice's child. He told all this to Gloria. Gloria felt sick to the pit of her stomach: what should she do now? Tell him or lie.

It was a beautiful little thatched cottage, a far cry from his chateau. How homely Gloria had made it. The pretty chintz curtains that hung at the window, the two lovely red velvet armchairs with their arm protectors that looked like they had been hand embroidered. He would bet anything that Gloria had made them, Mathieu thought to himself.

Gloria was panicking now. Should she tell him about Claire? Did he have a right to know? What was right for Claire? Maurice? The decision was taken out of her hands. Mathieu glanced over at the tiled fireplace surrounding the open fire. There, on the mantlepiece, was a photo of a young girl. Before Gloria could stop him, he had reached to pick up the frame. Gloria's hand was on his arm. He turned to look at her, then back at the picture. Then a tear slid down his cheek. The child was the spitting image of his sister, of his mother also when she was a child. Mathieu didn't need to say anymore; he knew, just knew, that this child was his. His and Gloria's. Gloria now had tears spilling down her face too.

'Mathieu, no. Please, no,' sobbed Gloria. 'Please put the photo down.'

He shook his head. 'Gloria, please, please tell me this is not my child.' But he knew, looking at Gloria, it was.

Gloria didn't need to say anything. It was written all over her face.

He placed the frame back on the mantelpiece. Slowly, he stepped towards her. Feeling him, smelling him, all so familiar yet only a memory, Gloria stood, rooted to the spot, feeling his arms around her, burying her head in his shoulder. She let out a sob. Mathieu pulled her closer, rocking her gently in his embrace, tears also spilling from his eyes. He wanted to know everything.

Gloria came to her senses and stepped back. She didn't want Mathieu holding her. What if Maurice appeared? What on earth would he say? Maurice had never liked Mathieu; despising all that he stood for and had done. Gloria loved Maurice very much and there was no way she would let this man pull it all apart.

Mathieu felt embarrassed, thinking back to the night of his engagement to Lydia. He had behaved appallingly. What a coward. How had he not had the guts to tell her himself? He was sick to his stomach at the way he had treated her. He was only here now, out of selfishness, to make himself feel better; he could see how life had turned out for her. He could see that she loved Maurice.

Gloria's voice brought him back to the present. 'What is it you want of me, Mathieu?'

He gazed back at her, taking her hand in his. 'Gloria, I have no right to make any demands on you. I will never forgive myself for what I put you through.' Selfishly, he had let family honour come before love.

Now, after all these years, he realised that nothing should have stood in their way. He shook his head. What a wasted opportunity. Looking at Gloria, he realised he still loved her with all his heart, but he could not destroy the life that she had created, nor the life of her child. Their child. 'I am so sorry, Gloria. I am sorry I have turned up like this. I have already caused you enough pain.'

Gloria spoke. 'Go, Mathieu, please go. Please, don't come here again. You cannot upset our family, nor our child.

Please, Mathieu, just go.'

Mathieu sighed and nodded. 'I know, Gloria. I promise you I will never do this again. You do not deserve this. I am sorry, sorry I came, sorry I put you through this. I needed to see you one more time, just one more time,' he breathed out, then turned around.

Gloria, reaching for the photo of Claire on the mantlepiece, wiped away a tear. Handing the picture to Mathieu, she then pointed to the front door. He turned, opened the door, then left.

Gloria watched him walk down the street, shoulders hunched. Mathieu had found her. And now she was letting him walk away. It was the right choice, the choice she had to make. She knew that she and Maurice would carry this secret to the grave with them. She had to forget about him. Gloria swore that day that she would protect herself and Claire from ever knowing the truth. Mathieu Le Fontaine would no longer exist. She took off the little gold chain she wore, with the rose and lily engraved on it, then, taking the pouch that her wedding ring had come in, she carefully placed the locket in her purple box. She would keep the box and its contents, but it must go up in the attic. Then, sitting down, she wrote a letter to Claire, trying to explain what had happened. Gloria popped the letter inside the purple box. Maybe one day Claire would find it. Claire could then make her own choice. As she placed the box away in the attic, Gloria knew, for her, the lid would stay on that box for ever.

CLAIRE

Chapter 20

Putting the letter back in the box, Claire could feel tears spilling down her cheeks. Her poor mum, to have had her heart broken so brutally. She did not deserve that. Claire felt anger and hatred for this man she had never met. My father! No, Mum must have been mistaken. My father is Maurice. Not Mathieu, that can't be right. She read and re-read those last few lines again and again. Now her head hurt, her eyes ached. Standing up, she went for a glass of water, mind whirling. Claire couldn't take all this in. Her hands clenched the side of the sink as the ice-cold water spilled into the glass.

Her head throbbed. How could she go through life not knowing who her actual father was? What parent had the right to deprive another parent of their child? She felt desperation, then anger, then more anger at the way Mathieu had treated her mum. How good, kind Maurice had stepped in, been the father she had known. But the other part of her wanted to know more, more about her actual father, his life and the chateau. Oh, my goodness, she thought, a chateau, it was just too much to take in.

Late that afternoon she had drifted off to sleep on the sofa. It had been too hot to sit outside. Claire wasn't used to this heat. Today, in particular, she felt fragile. She had thought about Googling to see what she could find out, but it would only cause more pain. There would be time enough for all that. She wished she had someone to share all this with. Someone to hold her and tell her it would be alright. She felt lost and alone. She was in a new country, a new home. Not only that, but, on a whim, she had taken it on for six months. That was a long time to feel this unhappy. Exhaustion overtook her, and she drifted off to sleep.

When she woke, she couldn't take in where she was for a moment. Then the letter had come flooding back, like a bad dream. She wished it was only a bad dream. Why had she lifted the lid on the box? The question went round and round in her mind. Her mother obviously knew that Claire would find it one day. 'Why didn't you talk to me, Mum?' Claire whispered to the empty room.

Pulling herself up off the sofa, she knew she had to get focused. There was much to do in the cottage. It would give her something to take her mind off things. She needed that. She couldn't lie down all day feeling sorry for herself. Searching for the nails she had purchased yesterday, Claire decided where her two pictures were to go. Lifting up the one of her dad, Maurice, Claire held it, at arms' length, just staring at it. This is my dad, she thought, how could I ever replace him? Carefully she knocked the nail into the wall, then hung the photograph.

Holding the other one of her mum in her hand, she stood still. Her mum had been everything to her. They were close. They laughed and cried together. How come her mother hadn't been able to share the biggest secret of all with her? Claire knew now she would never know the answer to that question. It made her both sad and angry at the same time. From reading the letter it had given her the sense that her mother wanted her to find her father. How did she know it wouldn't be too late? Mathieu could be dead now, for all Claire knew. He would be in his eighties. Claire hung the photo of her mother next to her father. Standing back, she looked at them both.

'I will do my best, Mum,' she said out loud. Claire knew now there was no going back; all she could do was start the search. If life wasn't complicated enough before, it certainly was now.

Deciding she needed some fresh air, she slipped on her flip-flops that lay by the front door. Walking outside, she turned onto the little country lane. It was 7pm, the heat from the day lingering. The storm last night didn't appear to have cleared the air completely. As she walked, she thought back to the storm. How scared she had been. She laughed as she thought of herself cowering under the sheets. Such a childish thing to do. Walking up towards the pond, one of her new neighbours waved. Claire waved back. The old lady gestured to her to wait a moment. Returning a few minutes later, she handed Claire a jar of jam. As the lady pointed towards the tree, next to the farmhouse, Claire realised she was trying to tell her it was cherry jam.

Smiling, Claire hoped the lady knew that she understood. 'Merci,' Claire said in her best French.

The lady gave an even bigger smile, revealing two missing teeth.

Claire held out her hand. 'Claire,' she said.

The lady held out her own hand to Claire. It was warm to touch, wrinkled from years of sunshine. They shook hands.

'Agatha,' the lady said before she shuffled off back towards the farmhouse. How lovely, Claire thought, such a sweet thing to do.

By the pond a cat prowled. Claire didn't think he would get much of a catch in the village pond, but you never knew. There was an old bench to one end, walking over, she sat down. The view from the bench looked back down the village towards her own home. Claire sighed. Yesterday she had been so elated. Finding the cottage, meeting Adam for coffee. She smiled at the thought of Adam. Part of her wished he could be here now, holding her hand and telling her everything would be OK. Claire couldn't believe she was already thinking of him like this. She had never met anyone that had made such an impression on her. She had only told herself days ago that she wasn't ready for a new relationship, yet here she was, fantasising about being with Adam. A man she hardly knew.

The sun was warm on her face. The silence was broken by a loud rumble, something was coming down the lane. Claire looked behind her to see where the noise was coming from. A large tractor loomed, its wheels twice the height of Claire. She shielded her eyes from sun to look. The old man in the cab waved as he passed. Claire waved back. Everyone seemed so friendly.

Realising that the mosquitos were starting to eat her, she got up from the bench. It probably wasn't the best idea to sit around water at this time of night. As she walked back towards the cottage, the cicadas struck up their evening chorus. For some reason this always reminded her of holidays in Greece. They chirped away. On the wall to her right sat a little kitten licking his paws. Not a care in the world, Claire thought, as she reached out to stroke it. The kitten was having none of that and shot off the wall. Probably feral, she thought. Her cottage looked so pretty in the evening light. Yes, it could do with a bit of sprucing up. A bit like herself, she thought. She tried to smile at the thought. Tiredness was draining her; she was mentally exhausted. Hopefully she would sleep tonight.

Inside, Claire popped the kettle on. A cup of tea was what she needed. Why did the English always have a cup of tea in a crisis? There wasn't too much in the fridge, she could deal with that tomorrow. Maybe she would see about getting a TV as well. Nights could be very lonely, she thought, especially once the winter arrived. She would need some company. The cottage was silent, so was the village. Claire wondered what everyone did in an evening. Maybe one night I could walk to the lake, she thought, as she spread Boursin cheese on her bread. A pizza might be nice. Picking up her book, she tried to read but the words on the page seemed to blur into one. She was too tired for reading.

Placing the book back down on the sofa, Claire thought about getting the letter out again to read. It wouldn't do her any good going over and over it. Nothing would change. Those words would still hit her like a ton of bricks. It was read, now the secret was out. Nothing would ever change that. There was only one thing for it; she would have to go to bed. Locking the front door, she pulled over the little lace curtains and placed her mug and plate in the sink. They could wait until tomorrow.

With one last check around the room, she made her way wearily up the stairs. The bedroom windows were open but, tonight, to avoid any problems, she would pull the shutters over. They wouldn't bang and wake her up tonight. At least they still let the cooling air into the room. Undressed and in her nightshirt, she snuggled down into bed. The room was dark with a shaft of moonlight coming through the join in the shutters. It cast a light glow across her bed. In the distance an owl hooted, it was quite soothing. Her eyelids were as heavy as her heart. Sleep won.

Chapter 21

Claire was happy in her cottage; she had been there a couple of weeks now. Settling into village life, she had spent a lot of time out and about exploring. Her article on La Creuse region was coming along nicely. At least the writing gave her an income. Claire hadn't dared to look any further into Chateau Le Grand Fontaine or Mathieu. She would know when the time was right. It wasn't yet. Today she had given herself the day off. Claire was just thinking about getting some weeding done when her mobile rang. It was a French number. *I wonder who this is*, thought Claire. Hitting the green button she said, 'Hello, Claire speaking,'

'Claire, it's Adam.'

At first she was a little surprised, then she thought how warm his voice sounded.

'I hope you don't mind me ringing,' he said hesitantly. 'I have a client near Besoin I am due to visit this coming

Monday.' There was a hint of nervousness in his voice. 'I am currently in Paris, but plan to make my way south in the morning. How about we meet for a lunch tomorrow, is that too presumptuous of me?'

Claire was secretly delighted. 'Adam that would be wonderful, yes, I would like that.' Claire was a little taken aback by how pleased she felt at the thought of seeing Adam again. The butterflies in her stomach took her by surprise. Agreeing to meet at the little restaurant at about 12.30, they exchanged a few more pleasantries. As Claire put the phone down, she was beaming from ear to ear. For the first time since she had read her mother's letter, Claire was feeling elated. She was really looking forward to seeing Adam again.

Saturday morning was the perfect morning; the sun shone and the birds were in full song. Claire woke and stretched. Glancing at her clock, she was surprised to see it was already 9am. She was certainly sleeping well now. Washed and in her dressing gown, she went down to the kitchen. She needed a coffee. Then, when refreshed, she would decide on what to wear. It had been ages since she had been on a date. If indeed this was a date. Claire wasn't sure what direction this was going in just now. Again she wondered if she was ready for this, too soon she mused? Those little butterflies were back, fluttering around her stomach.

Coffee done; it was in the shower. Now for the big decision. Her phone beeped. There on the screen it said Adam Johnstone. Claire, for a few seconds, felt deflated. He was calling it off, she thought.

Opening the message, it read: Journey going really well be with you by 12.30, Adam.

She was quite looking forward to this lunch. Especially to talking with someone in her own language. Half an hour later, Claire was ready. She shifted through the papers on the sideboard and found her keys. Clutching them, she made her way out of the door, pulling it shut behind her, turning the lock as she did so. Locking your doors round here wasn't really a necessity, but old habits die hard. She had spoken to an English couple up the road. Whenever they left the house, they literally just pulled the door to, no lock. She hadn't, as yet, felt confident enough in doing that.

Setting off down the lane in her little car, Claire took in the beautiful countryside she now called home. She never tired of its beauty and today it looked lovely. The lanes wove in and out through the fields. For as far as you can see, it was green. A rural landscape with tiny dots of Limousin cows scattered across the hillsides. Pulling the car into La Terraine, Claire headed for the little car park behind the library. There was only one space at the far end. It was, after all, market day today. Claire knew the town would be bustling.

Strolling up through the little passageway that took you to where the fountain was, Claire looked across the street. The lovely little cafe was spilling with people. She made her way under the ancient port into the market square. The majestic church loomed in front of her. It always took her breath away. Boxes of geraniums adorned the market square. Their vivid petals wafted in the welcome breeze. Claire glanced at the little market bar in the corner. Every table was full, people were sitting, drinking, laughing, deep in conversation. A little puppy playfully barked as she passed. She smiled at his owners.

Taking the stone steps up, she walked along one of the medieval alleys to the square. Claire knew the route to this restaurant well now. For a moment, a wave of fear came over her. What was she doing? This all seemed to be happening quickly. It was hardly any time since they had bumped into each other. Hardly any time since she had left her marriage. Taking the three steps up to the large medieval oak door of the restaurant, she told herself, 'I can do this!'

The proprietor smiled as he opened the door for her. 'Ah, Claire, it is lovely to see you. How are you?' he asked in his broken English, kissing her on each cheek.

'I am good thanks, Sebastien. I am meeting Adam Johnstone for lunch, I think he has booked a table,' Claire asked, hesitantly.

'Ah yes,' smiled Sebastien 'He is outside on the terrace, second table on the right.' He pointed towards the back of the restaurant.

'Thank you.' Claire smiled and walked through into the

pretty courtyard. There were only another couple of tables.

Claire had no problem locating Adam: he was the only man sat alone on the right. Adam looked at her and waved. Standing up from the table as Claire approached, he held out his hand to her. She took it. Hesitantly, he stooped to kiss her on both cheeks. Claire inhaled his aftershave. She approved. He was slightly taller than she remembered, a little greyer too, not that that mattered. His eyes smiled. She had to admit he looked rather handsome stood there.

'Claire, you look lovely,' he said, gesturing for her to take a seat opposite him 'Life is obviously treating you well.'

Claire laughed as he pulled out the chair for her to sit down on. She instantly felt at ease with him. He was just as kind as she remembered him. Sebastien arrived with the menus, asking if he could get them a drink. 'I'm driving, but I will have a glass of wine with my meal' she said. 'Could I have some Perrier as well please?'

Adam had a small beer; they placed their order. 'Tell me about you, Claire. Where has life taken you?' He was kind in the way he asked. It didn't feel obtrusive.

Claire told him how she had split up from her partner, the story of spotting him kissing their next-door neighbour. How that had resulted in her being in tears the day she had met him. She filled him in on the writing she had been doing, the move to France, how she had felt so at home here. Then the painful bit.

Adam could see her eyes cloud over, her posture change

as she explained about her mother and Maurice. He realised with a shock that Claire was talking about his boss's Uncle Mathieu. Chateau Le Grand Fontaine was no surprise to him. Suddenly it was all falling into place. He couldn't quite believe he was sitting here with Claire, most likely, the daughter that Mathieu was searching for. Adam had to keep this to himself; he had to be sure before he said anything. How on earth had this happened?

'So, Adam,' asked Claire, 'what are your plans this weekend? Where are you staying tonight?'

Adam explained that he was booked in at this restaurant. Claire had forgotten there were rooms here. She laughed and said he didn't have far to travel to fall into bed then.

Adam thought she was so pretty when she laughed; her entire face lit up. Talk continued as they had made their way through a delicious starter of moules served with parsley and garlic, probably the biggest moules Claire had ever seen. She hadn't been able to resist dipping the fresh bread into the juices on the plate. Next, they had moved on to confit de canard, which had been sublime, the meat falling away, and the sauce was to die for. Neither had room for dessert, but they decided they would share some cheese. Louis the server had wheeled over a trolley with about fifty cheeses on it. It was a difficult choice, but they decided they would go along with his recommendations. They were certainly not disappointed.

Before they realised it, two hours had passed and they were almost the last two left in the restaurant; it had been a long and easy conversation. Moving on to coffee, Claire plucked up the courage to make a suggestion. 'Look, Adam, I don't want to put upon you, but I have really enjoyed lunch.' Hesitating a little she then went on, 'I wondered how you would feel about a brief ride?' He would probably have lots to do work wise. He had also had a long drive today. Why on earth, she thought, would he want to spend time with her?

'Claire, that would be a genuine pleasure. I would love to explore the area,' Adam replied, smiling. Claire grinned like a Cheshire cat, then checked herself; don't show him you're too keen, but there was no mistaking the little flip her heart had just made. Another move by the new Claire, she thought.

Adam stood up from the table and gestured to Claire to take his hand. Smiling, she pushed back her chair, placing the crisp white napkin back on the table. Taking his hand, she allowed him to help her up. 'Now, lunch is on me. No arguments.'

'Are you sure? I am more than happy to pay my own way.'

'I won't hear of it,' Adam replied as he walked over to the desk where Sebastien stood. In perfect French, Adam asked for the bill to be added to his room. Claire watched him chat briefly with Sebastien. He had a lovely stature about him; tall but not too tall. His dark hair was peppered with grey, crisp jeans worn with an even crisper white short-sleeved shirt that only helped to emphasise his deep tan. Glancing down, she took in the brown leather loafers and no socks. She loved it when a man wore no socks! He turned to her and smiled. She smiled back. Sebastien came over to open the restaurant door. Kissing her on each cheek, he wished her an enjoyable afternoon. He shook Adam's hand and said he would see him later, that he hoped he enjoyed exploring the beautiful Creuse countryside this afternoon. They stepped out into the heat of the afternoon sun.

Adam gestured to his Jaguar parked up in front of the hotel. 'I'll drive,' he offered and, for once, Claire was happy to accept. It had been a long time since a man had driven her anywhere. Climbing into the warm car, Adam started the engine, flicking the air conditioning switch on. The cool air blasted out. He shut the doors, standing outside with Claire.

They waited for the car to cool down.

'This is such a lovely street,' commented Adam.

'Isn't it just?' said Claire. 'See the building there?' Claire pointed to the large building next door to the restaurant. 'That is the ancient mairie building; it is used now for concerts and theatre and meetings, but it is a lovely building inside.'

Then, squinting in the sun, she pointed across to a house at the top of the street. 'Isn't that beautiful?' she said. 'Just look at that amazing rambling rose draping itself across that impressive gate.'

Adam looked over and agreed.

'I've always thought it would make a lovely B&B. Just look at the courtyard; it would be perfect for serving breakfast. You would have a wonderful restaurant on your doorstep for evening meals too.' Claire was full of enthusiasm as she spoke.

'Is that something you fancy doing, Claire?' Adam asked, looking over at the house.

'I'm not sure, maybe one day I will. I certainly enjoying writing about them, but it would be different to running my own place. Who knows! Being here has certainly made me think of it a little more.'

Adam reached over, opening the passenger door for Claire, smiling she slipped into the cool leather seat. The air conditioning was blowing icy-cold air, it was really refreshing after the afternoon heat. Adam climbed in the other side. Claire felt so comfortable in his presence. It was almost like she had known him for many years, yet this was what, their third or maybe fourth meeting, none of which had been for very long. She glanced over at him, taking in his face and eyes. Once again, she thought how handsome he was. Feeling herself flush, she reprimanded herself. She must stop this. They were just friends, enjoying an afternoon out together.

Chapter 22

The rest of the day they meandered around the lanes of La Creuse countryside. Eventually they arrived in Crozant, a medieval village on the Santiago di Compostela route, where thousands of pilgrims trod the path each year. They enjoyed climbing the ruins, looking down at the river as it wound its way towards Eguzon. Claire explained that Eguzon, a bustling watersports lake, was incredibly busy in the months of July and August. They had walked along by the gorge crossing the bridge to the other side. There they sat, high up, on the terrace of the hotel. They watched the kayakers on the lake. It was a busy place. Claire explained to Adam that in the winter it would all be shut up. He laughed and said that was like most of France in the winter months. Walking back up to the village, they bought an ice cream from the little grocery store. The lady serving must have been ninety if not older; a tiny little woman, her skin creased like a walnut.

She sat with a traditional apron wrapped around her waist. When she smiled, some teeth were missing. This all seemed to add to her charm. They had both wished her a good day; she had smiled back with her toothless grin.

Adam was very easy to chat to. He filled her in on his family, the upbringing he had. He had no brothers or sisters. His parents had conceived him late in life, both had now passed on.

Claire hesitated for a moment. 'What about you, Adam? Do you have any children?'

Adam shook his head. 'No, it never happened. I was married though; my wife Angela and I were together for fifteen years. He swallowed. Claire realised it was obviously a difficult subject. Adam went on. 'She passed away from cancer of the liver three years ago. For once, his eyes didn't sparkle. He looked deflated.

Claire, without thinking, placed her hand on his, squeezing it gently. 'I'm so sorry, Adam.' Adam smiled. Squeezing her hand back, he said, 'Come on, it must be coffee time.'

Claire didn't push any further. The last part of the afternoon was coffee in the little bar come restaurant in Crozant. It was run by the lovely Francine. Claire had enjoyed many a coffee on her terrace whilst visiting the village. It had been her go-to-place for a morning coffee and croissant when she had first moved here, alone. Not really knowing anyone, Francine had been lovely to her.

As the afternoon turned to evening, they made their way

back to the car to star their journey back to La Terraine. Arriving back outside the restaurant, Claire felt sad that the afternoon was ending. 'What are your plans for the rest of the weekend?' Adam asked.

Claire laughed. 'I have more boxes to get up in the loft. I have a garden to tidy up, especially the front of the cottage.' It must sound very mundane, she thought to herself.

'Claire, if you would like me to, I would be thrilled to come and help.' He hoped he wasn't pushing too soon.

'Ah, bless you, Adam, I can't get you to do my jobs. I am sure that is the last way you want to spend your weekend. Especially if you have work on Monday,' said Claire.

'No, seriously, I would be delighted to have the company.'

Claire laughed. 'OK, but remember, you offered.' Adam looked delighted. 'I just have a couple of emails I need to send first thing. If you would have me, I would love to come and help. I could be with you around 10:30 if that's not too early?' Adam looked so enthusiastic; Claire couldn't help feeling the same. Although still a little hesitant about letting a man into her new cottage. Goodness me, she thought, he is only offering to come and help, not move in. 'Adam, that would be really kind of you but I have a condition,' teased Claire.

'OK, what is the condition?' he said, looking at her with quizzical eyes.

'I will do lunch for you, it would be the least I could do,' said Claire.

Adam said he accepted the condition. He would be delighted to join her for lunch. Claire got out her mobile phone, texting him the address. 'If you get lost just call, and, Adam, thank you so much for a lovely afternoon.'

Adam smiled at her and took her hand. 'It has been my pleasure, Claire. Honestly, I have had a lovely time. Thank you.'

Bending down, Adam planted a kiss on Claire's cheek and saw Claire to her car. Waving, they both went their separate ways.

Sunday morning was another glorious day. Claire was up and about with great enthusiasm, wanting to get down to the baker's early to get some of their lovely bread. They were lucky that the little bakers were open on a Sunday morning in the village. In fact, it was just as busy as any other day of the week. Bread bought, back at the cottage, she rummaged through the fridge looking for what she could make for lunch. She decided on a platter of charcuterie, salad and trimmings. Claire had a glut of blueberries in the fridge. That's easy then, she thought, a blueberry tart. Claire cheated using supermarket pastry she had picked up earlier in the week. It was already cut into a circle, so perfect for popping into a dish; just add the filling. Forty minutes in the oven and it was ready. Glancing at the clock, it was already 10am; he would be here in half an hour. She hoped he would find it OK.

Her phone beeped. She picked it up from the kitchen worktop. Just leaving, read the message. Claire felt a warm feeling creep over her. It was the thought of another day with Adam. She had felt so sorry for him hearing about his wife. At least Sean hadn't died. She couldn't even imagine how it had been for him. Looking at herself in the mirror she thought she had better tidy herself up a little. Looking around the cottage she smiled. It always seemed to make her do that. Such a perfect little place. She hoped Adam would like it. As she was combing her hair, Claire heard a car outside. Glancing out of the window she could see it was Adam. A quick skip down the stairs and she was at the front door. Outside, Claire waved, beckoning him to park his car next to her's. There would be just enough room. It would keep his car off the road. The road, however, was rarely used, especially on a Sunday! Adam climbed out. He had a bottle of wine and an enormous bunch of carnations and roses. He handed them both to Claire, bending to kiss her cheek again. 'Oh, Adam, look at these, so beautiful.'

'Look at this cottage,' exclaimed Adam in return. 'Just as beautiful as its owner.'

Claire blushed, whacking him playfully. 'Thank you,' she smiled. 'Come on in.'

They walked into the house. Adam was really struck by the prettiness of the open-plan room. Tastefully decorated; a lovely, homely feeling. He told Claire so and she smiled and thanked him.

'Would you like a coffee?' she asked, opening the little glass cabinet to take out two mugs. She placed them on the marble sink drainer. Claire turned, and he nodded. She couldn't help smiling at him again. It made her feel sixteen. It had been a while since she had felt these sorts of feelings for anyone. Claire could just imagine what her mum would say about Adam.

'What are you grinning at?' Adam asked, nudging her in a friendly manner. A drop of coffee splashed onto the table.

Laughing, Claire turned to him. 'I was just thinking what my mum would say,' replied Claire.

He smiled back. 'What was your mum like, Claire?'

Claire handed him his cup of coffee, gesturing to go out into the garden. 'Come on, we will take this in the garden,' She led him out through the door. Adam loved the little garden, so feminine, just like Claire, he thought as he watched her place the coffee cups on the table. Adam pulled out a chair for her to sit down on. They sat and drank their coffee, talking a little about Gloria. Adam could see it was still painful for her. It hadn't been that long, really, he thought. He knew bits from what Mathieu had told him. Still, he was keen to move the conversation away from her mum for fear of saying something he shouldn't. After their coffee was finished, Adam said, 'Right, come on, what jobs have you got for me to do? We can't sit around all day chatting.'

They spent a brilliant afternoon moving boxes, then some furniture around. Before they knew it, it was already 3pm and they hadn't eaten.

'Goodness, I've been making you work so hard, just look at the time. We haven't even had lunch yet.' Claire felt quite apologetic.

'Slave labour,' replied Adam, shaking his head as he pulled a sad face. His eyes twinkled as he playfully put an arm around her shoulder. 'Just what does a man have to do to eat around here?'

She pushed him away, playfully. Then, gesturing to the bathroom, she said, 'Wash up. I'll get the beer.' Adam headed to the bathroom and Claire went to wash her hands in the kitchen sink. Picking up the pretty rose-patterned tea towel from the hook, she dried her hands.

Opening the fridge, Claire took out the two plates she had prepared earlier that morning. Placing them on the tray, she took a wine and a beer glass down from the shelf, placing them both on the tray alongside the plates. The aroma from the fresh bread made her suddenly feel starving. As they ate lunch, they chatted easily to each other in the afternoon sunshine. Claire was surprised at how much they seemed to have in common. Lunch finished; Claire suggested they took a walk. They set off, walking comfortably, side by side. They stopped at the little pond at the top of the village to admire the ducks waddling around. 'It makes it feel very English having a village pond,' she laughed. 'Although it's not as pretty as an English one,' she added. They sat for a moment, on the bench, looking at the view.

Claire pointed to her cottage. 'I can see this view every morning.'

He smiled. 'You really have struck lucky here. It is a lovely cottage. I am quite envious, actually.' Standing up, he put out his hand to pull her up, 'Come on, let's walk on.'

The lane rarely had any traffic on it; it made for a very pleasant walk. Adam was funny, telling her stories about wine tastings that he had done all around France. He told her his favourite area was down near Cahors. 'Have you been there?' he asked. Claire replied that she hadn't.

'Next time I am heading down that way, I will let you know. Maybe you would like to join me?' he suggested. Claire said that sounded a lovely idea.

As they walked, quietly, side by side. Claire's thoughts drifted to Chateau Le Grand Fontaine. She wasn't sure she was ready to discuss this right now with Adam. Maybe when she had some answers herself, she could confide in him. Adam had tentatively broached the subject with her on the walk. She had side-tracked him, thankful that he had taken the hint.

Continuing, they came to the end of the lane, where the road opened to expose a wide expanse of water. It was a beautiful lake, in the late evening sunshine looking like a sheet of glass. The water sparkled like a thousand diamonds glittering away; it was something you wanted to take a photo of, but you knew you just wouldn't capture its beauty. Not like you would with the naked eye.

'Wow,' said Adam. 'This is a beautiful spot, Claire. You are so lucky to have this right on your doorstep, what a find.'

They looked over at the children playing on the man-made sand beach, splashing in and out of the water, the puppy doing the same. It looked like it was having just as much, if not more, fun than the kids. The children were squealing and laughing as the puppy, getting more excited by the minute, joined in with them barking in delight. Claire and Adam stood and watched, laughing away. There was a young couple lying on the grass under a tree. They hadn't come up for air the whole time they had been standing there.

'Young love,' laughed Adam. 'The beach bar is over there,' said Claire, gesturing ahead of them. 'Great, I am ready for a beer, it's my treat before you say anything.' His eyes twinkled at her. Claire knew, looking at those eyes, they were enticing her into something she didn't know if she was ready for yet!

Sitting opposite each other at the table, Adam asked,

'Where do you think your writing will take you to now, then, Claire?'

'Well, I have always thought I would like to write a travel guide on France. I have one or two things I need to sort out first though.'

Adam noticed her eyes cloud a little. He could tell that, whatever it was, it was painful for her. Maybe, as time went on, she would open up a little, but that, of course, would put him in a tough position, one he couldn't really talk to her about just now either.

'Have you always worked in wine,' asked Claire, turning the conversation back to him.

Adam talked happily about his career. He had started work in a little wine shop in Coppice Common, a small town that Claire knew of about thirty miles from Butteroak. They had lived so close but had never known each other. Working there, Adam explained, he had developed his interest in wine. That interest had led him to take up a wine sommelier course in a renowned wine school in Bordeaux. He had studied there for three years. It was a dream come true that he had landed his current job, working on a wine estate in the Auvergne. Adam then turned the conversation back to Claire again. He didn't want to talk too much more about his job. Drinks finished; they made their way slowly back up the lane.

The evening sun was setting; the lane was bathed in a beautiful glow smothering the countryside. They heard the cicadas chirping away in the fields, cows were lazily chewing grass. The village was silent as they arrived back. There were very few streetlamps and the lanes were getting dark. Claire shivered a little. It was now late September; the days were still full of heat, but the evenings cooler.

Standing at the front door by the car, Adam turned to Claire. 'Thank you so, so much for a wonderful day. I have felt so relaxed. I can't remember the last time I enjoyed myself so much.'

'You too, Adam, thank you.'

Her eyes were soft, her features aglow with the sunset

and Adam couldn't help himself as he gently leaned across, kissing her on the cheek, lingering for a moment, a moment longer than he should. 'Claire, I would really like to do this again sometime if you would,' Adam said hesitantly.

'That would be lovely,' she replied shyly. 'If you're passing, call me.'

'I can do better than that, Claire,' Adam said.

'I will be back this way in a week's time, would it be possible to meet up again?'

'I would really like that.'

'OK, I'll be in touch then,' he said as he touched her cheek. 'Thanks again, Claire.' Adam climbed into his car and waved as he drove off down the lane. Claire stood at her little cottage door, watching him drive away. The sun had almost set; it sent a beautiful hue of apricot over the entire house and garden. The honeysuckle at the front door, past its best now, still smelled lovely, Claire sighed. It was a happy sigh. What a wonderful day it had been. It didn't take her long to tidy up and get ready for bed. Then, switching off her bedside light, she pulled the duvet around her, feeling the warmth, the comforting smell of freshly laundered bedding. Part of her wished she had Adam's arms around her tonight. With this thought, she drifted off to sleep. Claire had no idea of the position that Adam now found himself in.

Arriving back at the small hotel, he was feeling very relaxed after a day in Claire's company. What a warm, friendly, caring person she was. Claire was everything he wanted in a woman. Climbing the stairs to his room, Adam threw his car keys onto the small dressing table. Sitting down with a sigh, he pulled the paperwork together that he had left strewn across his bed that morning. Claire had asked a few questions that had been close to the bone and Adam knew that if he was to continue seeing Claire, he would need to tell her. Sighing, he opened the file. How he was going to do that was another matter.

It had been completely by chance that he had landed the job, working for Theo and Elodie Levant, straight out of wine school. He was the same age roughly as them; they had a very privileged upbringing and had been born into one of the best wine merchant families in France. Adam had learned so much from them over the last twenty years. They had introduced him to Elodie's Uncle Mathieu quite early on, and Mathieu had taken him under his wing, teaching him everything he needed to know to make a successful career in wine. Mathieu Le Fontaine trusted Adam like his own son. It had been shortly after that first meeting with Claire, in the Dusty Miller pub, that Mathieu had opened up to Adam, telling him the story about Gloria.

Mathieu had been amazed that Adam had lived not far from where he had last seen Gloria. Such a coincidence. Mathieu had eventually asked for Adam's help to track down Gloria. Adam had felt that he couldn't do anything else other than agree. He had made some tentative enquiries which had led him to the nursing home. Here he had been informed that Gloria had died. Adam had returned to Mathieu to let him know this. Of course, the old man had been devastated by the news.

Adam, at that point, thought that would be the end, but then Mathieu, out of the blue, told Adam that he had fathered a child with Gloria, a girl. Mathieu had begged Adam to continue with his search, to see what information he could find out about his daughter. He told him not to contact her, but if he could find out her whereabouts, that would be a start. Mathieu had said to Adam that he was now in his last years of life. The cancer was progressing. He desperately wanted to put right the wrongs of his youth. His home, a magnificent chateau, would belong to his daughter one day. That was if she wanted to know him.

Shortly after this meeting with Mathieu had been when Claire had contacted him to meet for a coffee. That was when the penny had finally dropped. By sheer coincidence, Adam was talking to Mathieu's daughter. Hearing about her mother had confirmed it all. Adam felt like a complete coward, but he just didn't know how to bring the subject up with Claire. They had only just had a first date, if you could call it that. Claire had been very keen to see him, just as he would like to see her. How did you tell someone you were working for their father, that she was the person the father was looking for?

It was a very troubled Adam who tossed and turned all night in bed, but he knew, somehow; he needed to tell Claire the story. If it went on much longer, it would be a disaster.

Chapter 23

Claire woke the next morning, smiling as she thought of yesterday with Adam. Claire had loved his simple company. He had a great sense of humour. It felt like she had known him such a long time. Claire secretly hoped it would go further, but she would not push anything for now. It was certainly a change of heart from not wanting to get involved with anybody. Life was short, thought Claire, and she had concluded that you needed to grab happiness when you could. She also knew she had to make a start on finding out more about Chateau Le Grand Fontaine and her biological father.

Claire lay there wondering if her father would still be alive. By her reckoning, he would now be almost eighty-three. Once again, Claire felt quite hurt that neither of her parents had ever discussed it with her. There was nothing linking her age to her parents' marriage. Judging by the birth certificate, it was only a few months after she would apparently have been conceived. Maurice was amazing to have taken on someone else's child. He had given her the love and devotion any father would. Her parents had always been there for her. Claire, with what she now knew, loved him all the more for it. Did she really want to get to know someone else, especially at this late stage; time certainly wouldn't be on their side. However, it was no good lying here pondering, she needed to get up and make a start somewhere.

Up, dressed, and downstairs in her little kitchen, Claire went about making some breakfast. Her phone vibrated on the table. Reaching across for it, she saw Adam's name on the screen. She smiled, opening the message. Thank you again for a lovely day yesterday! Looking forward to Saturday. Adam had signed it with a kiss.

Claire stared out of the window, grinning to herself, then had to give herself a shake. Taking a bowl of cereal, she picked up her coffee. Sitting down at the kitchen table, she lifted the lid on her laptop. Claire took a deep breath. OK, here we go, she thought. Tapping on the keys, she put in Chateau Le Grand Fontaine, Moulins. Up popped a website and images of the chateau. Blimey, thought Claire, that is some chateau. The photos showed an amazing roof. The bright gold and burgundy roof tiles were stunning. It looked so majestic, especially with the clear blue skies and the beautiful gardens. She then read a description of the chateau. It had been in the La Fontaine family for over 300 years; passed down from father to son, it read. Currently Mathieu La Fontaine was the

resident Marquis, but he was the last of his line and the chateau would be inherited by Thierry Le Fontaine, his nephew.
Claire wasn't sure she wanted to read anymore, but the article got the better of her and she continued. The Marquise
had a daughter called Angelica. Claire let out a deep breath.
Shocked, she read on. She actually had a half-sister, then?

Reading more, she discovered that the daughter had died
in a swimming accident in the river aged nine. How awful,
thought Claire. She felt an overwhelming sadness for someone that she had never met. The article then continued, stat-
ing that the Marquis' wife had never recovered from the loss
and had taken her own life five years later, after a history of
depression. Claire couldn't imagine how any mother coped
with the loss of a child, how tragic for the family. If that wasn't
bad enough, the sister and husband had died in a car accident
about ten years ago. What a tragic life, thought Claire. The
Marquis had never remarried and was rarely seen in public.

Reading on, Claire discovered his niece and nephew, and
their partners now ran the family vineyard business. There
was no mention of their names. That, thought Claire, would
make them her cousins. It was certainly a stunning chateau.
Claire closed the laptop lid. She was taken by surprise by the
tears sliding down her cheeks. Not sure why; shock maybe,
or because it was a sad story. Somehow it didn't feel connected to her life, yet it was very much part of her life, a part
Claire had never known. Claire was frightened, yet curious.

A 'family' she had never known.

All this made Claire think of her mother again. It was unbearable that her mother had carried this her whole life, never talking about it to anyone, well not that she knew of, anyway! Claire wondered how far she was prepared to take this. It was already consuming her emotional energy. She knew she had to work out where to go from here. As far as she was concerned, there were two options: ignore and forget or let the curiosity get the better of her and continue with the research. Taking a deep breath, she reopened her laptop. Selecting Google Maps, she put in the chateau's address. Maybe a trip out there would be good, just to look. She didn't have to take it any further.

Glancing at the clock on the kitchen wall, she saw it was already midday. She had wasted too much time already. Claire knew that was the danger of looking too much into something like this. She sighed. Maybe first she should find out more. Then again, there was always Adam, but she didn't know if she felt ready yet to unload this burden on to him. However, knowing his knowledge of the wine industry, it would certainly be an advantage. Maybe he could help further. She would see him for dinner on Saturday. Maybe then would be the right time.

For now, she had to get on with some work; she still had her article to file for next week's publication. Claire had enjoyed writing about La Creuse. It was a relatively unknown region of France; the Brits, slowly realising it, were flooding in. The fantastic property prices, along with great flight connections from the UK, made it an ideal holiday home destination. That said, Claire had discovered, more and more were actually moving here. Finishing the article, Claire decided she would get out in the garden for the afternoon. Some fresh air would do her good. It would fill her time before she made any rash decisions on visiting Le Grand Fontaine.

Before Claire knew it, Saturday was upon her. She was getting quite excited at the thought of seeing Adam again. Looking out her freshly laundered cerise linen dress, she hung on it on the wardrobe door. She then pulled out her linen-blend white cardigan with the pretty flower buttons down the front. This would look perfect with her little white wedge-heeled sandals. It would complement her summer tan beautifully. Scrabbling in the bottom of the wardrobe, she finally found her little cerise pink handbag. Brilliant, she thought, she was now date ready. Standing in front of the Venetian glass mirror, she carefully pulled the straighteners through her long hair. It had really grown this summer. It must be all the wonderful sunshine, she thought.

A little smudge of pink lipstick. She was ready. Adam had agreed to collect her at 7pm. They were going to take a ride out to the lovely auberge by the river in Laselle. Claire loved this restaurant. Even the ride out was all part of the experience. Hearing the scrunching sound of gravel, Claire glanced out of the window. There was Adam, climbing from his car. She couldn't help noticing again how handsome he was. He was dressed in dark jeans and a crisp white linen shirt. He had his pale-blue cashmere sweater slung around his shoulders. Locking the car door, she saw him lift his sunglasses up on to his head. Adam turned towards the door. He must have sensed that Claire was watching him. She had no option but to wave. He smiled, waving back. With a quick hop down the stairs, she greeted him.

'Claire, you look amazing,' smiled Adam.

'You don't look too bad yourself,' she laughed. He bent slightly. Placing a soft kiss on her cheek, she smiled shyly. There was a loud beep and a wolf whistle. Claire looked up, it was Henri the gardener passing by in his little Renault van.

Claire laughed and waved, telling Adam who he was.

'Ah, so you have another admirer.' He feigned a hurt look.

'No, no,' laughed Claire as she filled him in about Henri. 'He is married,' she told him. Then, with a cheeky smile, she added, 'I think his wife is a very lucky lady.'

Adam laughed, but Claire couldn't help noticing that he was looking a little uncomfortable. 'Is everything OK?'

Claire hoped he wasn't having second thoughts about their night out.

'I have a little problem I need to discuss with you before we leave.'

Claire looked at him, waiting for him to continue. 'I have a problem. I was due to stay at this little B&B twenty minutes from here. They rang to say that they have a major problem with their septic tank. They have had to cancel their bookings for this weekend. Could you recommend anywhere else?' asked Adam. 'Or' he went on, 'I can drive back to Besoin tonight and stay there.'

Claire thought for a moment. 'Look, Adam, it's not the comfiest, but you are welcome to my small spare room. It only has a single bed. It may not be quite long enough, but I don't have a problem with you using it,' explained Claire. She was not quite believing what she was saying. The old Claire would never have been so brave. They were both adults, she told herself.

It was Adam's turn now to feel uncomfortable. 'Claire, I wasn't asking so that I could stay here. I didn't want to be that presumptuous,' Adam replied, frowning a little as he spoke.

'Look, Adam, it's no problem. We are both adults. It would be nice to have your company,' Claire said. 'I was going to ask you if you wanted to have lunch here tomorrow, anyway.'

Adam was pleasantly surprised. 'Thank you so much. That would be lovely.' He gave her a small hug, pecking her on the cheek again. She swatted him playfully. 'Flattery will get you everywhere,' she giggled.

Adam loved how her eyes smiled when she laughed. 'Come on, ma'am, your chariot awaits. Let's go to dinner.' The ride out to the auberge was a very pleasant one indeed. The chat was easy; they talked about wine, France, cheeses and life in the country. The lanes leading to the little town were beautifully bathed in the last colours of the day and a buzzard or two swooped overhead. The heat was going down, and the smell of fresh grass filled the air through the open car windows. As they came down the hill into the small town, they wound round the corners, the little stream babbling alongside them. Eventually, as the town opened up in front of them, so did the river. A couple of anglers were lining the riverbank, some children paddled in the river close to the bridge. Their parents watched on as they splashed and played. Claire wasn't sure she would brave the river at this time of year, but the children didn't seem to mind.

The little auberge was lit up with its lanterns, fairy lights adorning the garden.

'Wow!' said Adam. 'What a beautiful place, excellent choice.'

Claire, smiling, told him she loved this village. The restaurant had the best fish and chips in France and it was the perfect setting as far as she was concerned. Parking alongside the river, they climbed out. Adam tentatively took her hand as they strolled alongside the river to the auberge. Claire thought how right it felt. She glanced up at him just as he glanced at her, their eyes smiling into each other. They both laughed, feeling a little like teenagers again.

They were welcomed warmly by the owner of the auberge who Claire had got to know. He showed them to a table, looking out over the river. Adam ordered a Kwack beer, Claire a Kir Royale. They settled down at the table and Adam felt content. This was the first woman, in many years, he had felt comfortable with. She was natural, no pretences. Adam realised, even though it was only a short time, that he was falling in love with her.

How on earth could he tell her he was working for the

father she had never known? It really didn't bear thinking about, but he had to do it sometime, just not now. He had to see how it all went. He could always tell Mathieu that he didn't want to work on the assignment anymore, but Mathieu had been a great friend over the years. How could he lie, telling him there was nothing about his daughter when here he was enjoying her time and company?

'Of course, you could always catch that pig flying over there,' said Claire, slightly annoyed.

Bemused, Adam looked her in the eye. 'What? Oh yes, pigs,' said Adam, looking very puzzled.

'Adam, you were miles away,' said Claire. 'Am I boring you?' Claire scowled at him, pretending to be annoyed.

'Claire, I am so sorry, my mind just drifted. I was looking at you and thinking how beautiful you are.' Adam laughed.

'Nice try, Adam, not sure that redeems you, though,' grinned Claire.

The young girl from the bar then appeared with two plates of fish and chips. 'Saved by the food,' said a relieved Adam, laughing. From that point on, Adam gave her his utmost attention for the rest of the evening, pushing any thoughts of Mathieu from his mind.

Claire was really enjoying herself; he had a witty, even sightly quirky sense of humour. They had laughed all evening.

It was now getting chilly. Paying the bill, they made their way back to the car. Adam's hand had found hers again.

It felt so right, so comfortable. Claire gave a silent sigh of contentment. They drove home a little quieter than their journey out. In no time, they had pulled up at the front of Claire's little cottage. Adam jumped out and came around to open the door for her. They went into the cottage, Adam bringing his small overnight bag with him.

'Would you like a glass of port or brandy, Adam? Or a whisky?' offered Claire.

'That would be lovely, thank you, I'll have a brandy.'

'Pop your bag upstairs, it's the first room on the right. I'll get the drinks out.'

Adam made his way up the wooden staircase. As he disappeared from sight, Claire quickly straightened her hair in the mirror, checking her appearance as she did. Glasses out and brandy poured, Adam appeared in the lounge. Claire gestured to the sofa. They sat nursing their brandies in silence. Claire was very conscious of his body; she could feel his warmth penetrating her left-hand side. It all felt comfortable in one respect, but a little uneasy in another. They both knew really what would happen next, as if both sensing the feeling, they turned to face each other. Adam leaned forward, putting his brandy glass down on the coffee table. Turning to Claire, he took her glass from her hand. Cupping her face in his hands, he gently placed his warm lips on her's. The kiss was gentle at first, their lips laced together. She could feel his hands on her face, she tingled with the excitement, apprehension. They pulled apart slightly.

Adam whispered, 'Claire, you are beautiful.'

Claire smiled as their lips once again met, this time with more passion and pressure. His tongue explored inside her mouth, as Claire gasped with pleasure. It seemed like a lifetime until they eventually pulled apart. Claire, taking the opportunity, rose from the sofa, putting out her hand to Adam. He accepted it. He pulled her closer. Claire, pulling away, gestured towards the stairs.

'Are you sure, Claire?' asked Adam. 'I don't want to push you.' He caressed her face as he spoke. 'I want to be with you,' he sighed, tightening his grip on her hand.

Without a word, she tugged at his hand as if to say come on. They made their way up the stairs, Claire leading him toward her bedroom. At the door they stopped and Adam tenderly kissed her again, this time not releasing her as they stumbled into the bedroom, falling onto the bed. They laughed as they fumbled with their clothing. Claire wanted to feel his bare skin. She had never wanted someone so much; it was quite overwhelming. He gently peeled back her blouse, tenderly caressing her breasts through the thin fabric of her bra. She sighed, arching herself towards him. He pulled her closer.

Adam was a tender lover, like none Claire had ever experienced. That night, as he slept, Claire lay contentedly in his arms. She could see the full moon glowing outside, the distant owl hooting between his gentle snores. Adam looked so peaceful. Curling into his body, she let the tiredness take over, drifting off to sleep.

Chapter 24

Claire stretched, yawning and blinking in the morning light. For a moment she wondered what day it was and last night came flooding back to her. Claire turned to see an empty place in the bed and wondered where Adam was. Pulling herself up, she was just about to climb out as Adam turned up at the door.

Grinning at her he said, 'Ah-ah, lady, back to bed.'

Adam had discreetly crept out to the bakers to buy some fresh croissants. From the garden he had picked one of Claire's beautiful autumn roses, placing it in a small champagne flute on a tray with coffee.

'I hope you don't mind,' he said tentatively. 'I had a little rummage around the kitchen.'

Claire smiled. 'Of course not. Oh, Adam, that is so thoughtful of you.' Claire couldn't believe the trouble that he had gone too. The tray looked so pretty. Plumping up her pillows, she made herself comfortable in the bed. He placed the tray on her lap. Smiling, he climbed on to the bed beside her, pouring out two coffees, which he placed on the bedside tables. Claire grinned at him as he tore a piece off the croissant. Holding it to her lips, he kissed the tip of her nose. She took the croissant into her mouth. What a wonderful way to wake up, she thought. Turning to Adam, Claire gently kissed him on the cheek. They ate breakfast together side by side, enjoying the moment. When finished, he took the tray from her lap, placing it on the little dressing table. Climbing back on to the bed, he kissed her toes, then her knees. Slowly, he made his way up her body. Then pulling her to him, she rolled on to him. The perfect way to start a day. She sighed.

They spent the Sunday in complete bliss doing minor jobs around the home, then taking an early evening walk up to the little pizza restaurant by the lake. Autumn was coming, the evenings chilly. They walked back comfortably side by side up the little windy lane. It was almost dark. Adam placed an arm around her shoulder to keep her warm. She smiled as she snuggled up to him. Back at the cottage, Adam made them a cup of tea. Watching him, Claire smiled at how quickly Adam had familiarised himself with her home. If you had asked her four months ago about having another man in her life, she would have run a mile. Claire, stretched, then yawned. Turning to Adam. 'Will you stay again tonight, Adam?'

Adam nodded. 'I would love to, if you're sure that I am not

intruding.'

They sat together on the small couch, quietly, both in their thoughts. Claire was still amazed how comfortable it felt with Adam after such a short time. It would be a shame he had to leave tomorrow. She had to admit she had enjoyed having a man around the home again, more than she had thought she would. 'Where are you off to this week?' Claire asked, lifting her head from Adam's shoulder to look at him.

Adam explained he had to go to near Bordeaux until Wednesday. After that, Toulouse for a wine fair on Thursday and Friday. Then his plan had been to head home.

'Do you work from home?' Claire asked.

'Yes, I do, but I am usually only in the UK one week a month, then I go to my office in the Auvergne, which will be the week after next,' Adam explained. Claire thought about it for a moment. 'Do you have to go back to the UK?' she asked. 'No, in theory, not really. Why?' Adam asked.

Smiling, Claire said, 'Would you like to work from here that week before you go to the Auvergne?' She was secretly delighted at the thought of it.

Adam, however, was a little taken aback. Claire read this completely wrong. 'Oh, I am sorry, Adam. I know, too much too soon.' She turned away, feeling a little hurt, then felt his hands on her shoulders.

'I would love to. Honestly, it would be a pleasure to spend more time with you, but only if you're sure. I really don't want to impose on you.' He saw the relief on her face. 'Come here, give me a cuddle,' Adam laughed, pulling her back on to the sofa. Tenderly he took her face in his hands, kissing her warm, flushed cheeks. Claire buried her head into his shoulder, inhaling his scent. A warm, tingly feeling filled her body. Her feelings for him were slightly overwhelming. Was she getting in too deep, too soon?

The next morning Adam departed from Claire's with the promise he would be back by lunchtime on Saturday. He had left a bag of clothes and Claire said she would put them through the wash for him. This week, she was determined she was going to find out more about Chateau Le Grand Fontaine. She might even take a drive over to see the chateau. She was feeling braver than she had felt in a long time. Adam had certainly boosted her confidence.

She could look at the chateau from a distance, of course. Claire knew she didn't have to rush into anything at this stage. Claire opened her MacBook. Clicking on Maps, she looked again where Chateau Le Grand Fontaine was. By her reckoning, she could get there in about one hour and forty minutes. It had to be worth a drive, just to have a look at; thought Claire. She knew that there was another chateau connected to it but hadn't found out any more than that.

Thinking about it again, Claire wished she had sought Adam's advice. She didn't, however, want to burden him with her problems. So far, she had kept the information she had found to herself. She felt that if she shared it; she was admitting it was true. Maybe if things developed a little further between them, then the time might feel right. After a little more reading, she decided tomorrow would be the day. Claire planned to leave early. She would take a drive out just to see where the chateau was. Her phone pinged. On the screen it said Adam. Opening the message, it just said: Miss you xx. Claire laughed, sending a quick reply: U2 xx. Claire realised she must have looked idiotic sat staring at the phone, smiling!

Shortly after Adam had left that morning he had taken a call. It was Mathieu La Fontaine, asking how his search for his daughter was going. Adam could not bring himself to say he had found her. He knew how much this all meant to Mathieu. And yet how could he jeopardise his relationship with Claire? How on earth was he going to tell her he worked for her cousins? The thought filled him with pain. Claire was the first woman he had felt comfortable with in a long time. He didn't want to lose that, but how could they start a relationship with lies? She had let him into her life, cautiously at first, but they were opening up to each other now. Adam was falling in love with her and he knew she was fond of him too. She wouldn't have asked him to come and stay for a week if she wasn't. He knew they would have to take it steady. In relationship terms things were already going quicker than he had thought. He was ready to let a woman like Claire into his life. Ready to love again, but this issue with Mathieu was causing him concern. He would have to get it out in the open; he just needed to find the right moment.

Tuesday was a glorious autumn morning; the sun shone, the dew glistened on the grass and a light mist hung on the fields opposite her house. Morning bird song was in full flow as she sat sipping her coffee. Packing her small picnic into a little wicker basket, Claire hummed to herself as she poured boiling water into a coffee flask. Opening the fridge, Claire took out a small bottle of water. In fact, thought Claire, I'll take two. Selecting an apple from the fruit bowl on the oak kitchen table, Claire carefully placed that alongside the sandwich in her basket. There, I am ready. That might not be entirely true: her stomach had been churning all morning. She told herself repeatedly, you're only going to have a look, you will not be seeing anyone, just a look, just to see how it all feels!

The drive over was lovely. Claire left behind La Terraine, taking the N145 towards Montlucon. Despite being a busy road, for rural France, it was nothing like the M25 in London. What made it even better was the amazing countryside that was laid out before her. Tiny villages dotted the horizon.

An occasional chateau loomed up magnificently from the hillsides.

Once past Montlucon, she decided she was going to switch to country lanes to take in some of the villages. After all, thought Claire, I have all day! The lanes wound around the patchwork of fields and valleys. Every corner held a new sight. Some of the sleepy villages were so pretty. The autumn colours had the hillsides in a blaze of oranges and reds, the sunbathing them in its rays.

Every moment seemed to take her breath away. Passing through another village, Claire noticed a cafe. Looking at the sat nav, she was only twenty minutes now from Le Grand Fontaine, so she had time for a morning coffee and a croissant. It was, after all, only 10am. Claire was pleased she had left early. It had been a beautiful drive with the sun coming up, the glorious morning colours filling the horizon. Pulling her little blue fiat into the car park, Claire turned off the engine.

Locking the car with a click, Claire made her way across the street, stopping to look at the florist shop. Such a pretty display thought Claire. It took her back to the morning that she had seen Sean with Jacqueline. It still hurt, but not quite so acutely. She brushed the thought from her mind. The cafe was busy, mostly men propping up the bar. Another couple of men sat in one booth, both with daily newspapers. There were three ladies sat around the table, another lady sat alone.

Claire wouldn't feel out of place here, she thought as she

went to the bar to order her coffee and a croissant. The wait-ress smiled. 'Where will you be sitting' she asked Claire.

Claire pointed out onto the street. The young girl, still smiling, said she would bring it out.

'Is there a toilet I can use please?' Claire asked the young girl in her best French. The waitress pointed to the back of the room. Claire smiled, thanking her. Her coffee and crois-sant arrived. Thanking the young girl, she handed her a five euro note. The waitress reached into her money belt to get some change, but Claire motioned to her to keep it. Smiling, the girl thanked her. It was a lovely cup of coffee. The crois-sant, flaking all over the place, was delicious: Claire thought she could almost admit to wanting to eat another.

Across the street, she saw a large jeep pull into the car park. A beautiful young woman stepped out, long hair flow-ing down her back. Reaching into the back of the car she opened the door, out stepped a young boy and a girl, who Claire thought were about twelve or fourteen. The girl had the same pretty hair as her mother. The boy and girl were teasing each other, and the mum reprimanded them. Urg-ing them on, she led them across the road to the cafe where Claire was seated. Speaking to them in French, they were instructed to sit nicely at the table and the mum went inside to order. The boy said something to the girl and she pushed him a little too hard. The boy, falling off his seat, bumped his head on the table next to him. Claire jumped up from her table, reaching out a hand to him to pick him up from the floor. The little girl looked on, laughing. Then her face turned to concern as she realised there was a trickle of blood running from his eyebrow.

Claire reached for her serviette to dab his face. His mum returned, issuing a flow of words at the children, who both took to their chairs, sitting solemnly as their mum turned to Claire. Speaking in French, Claire really wasn't one hundred per cent sure what the lady was saying. After a minute, the lady realised. 'Ah, you are English. I am so sorry, thank you so much for picking my boy up.'

Her eyes twinkled at Claire. 'This pair are always fighting.' Then, holding out her hand to Claire, she said 'Elodie'.

Claire took her hand. 'Claire, pleased to meet you.'

Elodie was probably about five or six years older than Claire, she thought. Elodie looked at the children. 'This is Pierre, he is nine, and this is Lucille, she is eleven,' offered Elodie.

'Ah, a little younger than I thought,' said Claire.

'Are you from around here, Claire?' Elodie enquired. Claire explained that she lived near La Terraine, that she was on a day trip out to have a look around the area. The two ladies chatted away for about half an hour, about the area and work. Elodie explained that her husband owned a chateau near to the village; he was a wine producer. 'You would be very welcome to come and have a look sometime.'

Claire thanked her, but not today. She really wanted to get on now and see Le Grand Fontaine. She was almost about to say to Elodie, then checked herself. Better not for now, thought Claire, not being sure how this was all going to feel.

It was as if Claire couldn't bear anyone to know her secret.

Elodie reached into her handbag and pulled out a business card with the name Theo Levante on it. 'Here,' said Elodie. 'This is our card for the chateau. If you're back this way again and would like to have a look, please just call or email,

I would love to show you around.'

The children were getting bored and restless, so Elodie bid Claire farewell as she ushered the two children back to the car. As Elodie drove out of the car park, she waved at Claire, who waved back.

What a lovely family, she thought. Drinking the last sip of her now-lukewarm coffee, Claire got up to leave, saying 'Au revoir' to the people next to her table.

Here we go, she thought, as she turned the keys in the engine. The rest of the drive was just as stunning, nothing around for miles, just vast open countryside. Claire marvelled as a huge buzzard swung overhead, such a huge wingspan. Claire had seen many of these in her short time in France. Their beauty always amazed her. The sat nav broke her thoughts. 'In 500m on the right you reach your destination,' it said with authority.

Slowing down, Claire pressed the button to open her window a little. She wanted to savour this moment. Slowly, the car crawled along the lane. Up ahead she could see the large wrought-iron gates. Claire could make out vines and grapes on them. The grass was overgrown around the gateposts and one gate hung slightly squiffy on its hinge, but it was still majestic. Looking for somewhere to stop the car before the gates, she spotted a little clearing. It was just perfect.

Climbing out of the car, she looked around, taking in the sight before her, savouring the moment. Walking up to the big iron gates, Claire gave a small push. The gates weren't fastened; they were loose, so pushing one open, she stepped through onto the gravel. There, lay ahead of her, a magnificent driveway lined with beautiful poplar trees. The drive had seen much better days, the gravel strewn with tufts of grass and weeds.

There, in the distance, the chateau stood. Mighty and proud, the autumn sun glinted off the gold and burgundy roof tiles. Claire was in awe. I wonder what mum must have thought the day she arrived here to work. She would have been amazed; she would never have seen anything like this in her life. It made Claire realise how brave her mum had been to step out on this adventure, alone, to a country she didn't know. Going to a family whose language she would have not understood. There would have been no way of knowing how they would have treated her. From what she had read on the internet, she didn't believe the chateau was lived in. It certainly didn't look it. She wondered if her father lived nearby, if indeed he was still alive. The article she had read had been an old one.

Claire still couldn't comprehend that thought, her father. It felt strange. Deciding there would be no harm in taking a walk, Claire locked up her car. Going back through the gates, she began the long walk up the driveway towards the chateau. Feeling pleased she had thought to bring a jumper with her, Claire wrapped it around her shoulders. There was definitely a chill in the air or was that just trepidation about what she was actually doing, Claire wasn't sure.

Just before the chateau, she noticed an overgrown path going off to the left. Deciding to go that way, Claire took the little path along to see what was there. Walking out into the clearing, in front of her, Claire could see a sweet, tiny cottage, intact but in disrepair. Not dissimilar to the one she lived in now. There were tiles clinging to the ancient drainpipe. Windows had smashed panes of glass. The little garden gate was hanging off. The rambling roses and honeysuckle were vastly overgrown. It then dawned on Claire this must have been the cottage her mother had lived in. Turning to look across, Claire took in the back of the chateau. So grand, so beautiful, what a view to have had from your front garden. Claire could imagine her mother here, pottering in the garden, sitting drinking tea after a day at work. Was this where she met Mathieu, was this their meeting place, Claire wondered? It was certainly very close to the chateau, but then still quite discreet, thought Claire.

Feeling overwhelmed with sadness, she sat down on an old tree trunk. It was strange to have these thoughts about her mother. Claire had only ever known her love Maurice. They had seemed so perfect together. She couldn't imagine her with anyone else. Her emotions were erratic. One moment she felt anger, then sadness, then humiliation for her mum. Claire suddenly wondered if she was back where she was conceived. It was highly likely.

Looking across at the chateau, the gardens had seen much better days. Claire could also make out the walled garden, probably the vegetable patch. Suddenly Claire shivered. This was all too much. She needed some food and a drink. Turning back, she then hesitated at the path. Maybe she could just explore on a little more. Taking the path to the right rather than back the way she had come, Claire continued. It wound through the trees, eventually coming to a small clearing. There she could see a beach and the river. Oh, how pretty, she thought. Claire guessed her mother had been here, too. Her mother had loved water of any kind: river, sea or pond!

Ahead in a clearing she could see an old man, sat quietly contemplating the water, the view stretched out before him; he clearly hadn't heard Claire. In turn, she didn't want to intrude. Quietly turning around, she walked back. For a moment, curiosity getting the better of her, Claire turned back to look at the clearing. The man had gone. The opportunity was missed. It had struck Claire how sad he looked, even from a distance.

Following the path back up, past the little cottage, she veered to the right, back into the driveway. Opening the car door, she welcomed the warmth. Starting up the engine, she tried to get some extra heat into the interior. She wouldn't eat her picnic here. Claire felt she needed somewhere neutral to go to. For a moment, she wished Adam were here. It would be good to have someone to share this moment with. Someone to put an arm around her shoulder, to comfort her.

Parking the car in the picnic car park, Claire felt in a turmoil of emotions. Turning off the engine, she felt a tear slide down her cheek. Reaching up, she wiped it away. Then, with no control, Claire just sobbed. It took her by surprise. Why was she crying, nothing had happened? It could only be the fact that she had finally seen the chateau. It was certainly far more real now. There was an overwhelming sense of sadness, thinking of her mother, all that Gloria must have been through.

Sipping her coffee, she then bit into her sandwich. The food certainly made her feel a little better. Claire sat, pondering. She knew there was no going back now. She owed it to her mother to find the truth, to understand what had happened. Claire also wished she had never taken the lid off her mother's purple velvet box.

Chapter 25

It had taken Claire a couple of days to pull herself together. Adam had called to ask how she was, and she had played down her visit. Claire thought he seemed genuinely interested in her day out. He had listened intently, not commenting.

Inside, however, he was in turmoil. How bizarre the whole situation felt. Fate was certainly dealing a hand in all of this, but it didn't feel like a helpful one. Claire had told him about the beautiful chateau, describing the stunning burgundy and gold tiled roof. How the afternoon sun had lit it up. Adam knew this only too well: he had stood many times marvelling at the stunning architecture of the chateau. Adam kept the questions to a minimum, realising Claire had gone further than he thought she would. He had no option other than to tell her.

Claire, to Adam's relief, turned the conversation away from the chateau. 'I am really looking forward to seeing you at the weekend.'

'Me too,' Adam replied. Finally, saying goodbye, Claire put the phone down. Talking to Adam always made her smile. Thinking back to the conversation about the chateau she realised it would be good to have someone to share it all with. Maybe it was time to trust in someone again.

Saturday morning arrived and Claire busied herself tidying up the house, cleaning the bathroom and preparing a lasagne for dinner. It would be nice to eat in front of the fire tonight, she thought as she searched for some matches. They needed a fire in an evening now to keep the place warm. It might only be a small cottage, but it could soon get cold. Looking at her watch, she just had time to jump in the shower before Adam arrived. As she was towel drying her hair in the bathroom, she heard him shout from the front door.

'Come in,' Claire called as she hastily wrapped a towel around her hair. 'In the bathroom, just about to dry my hair. I'll be five minutes. Stick the kettle on,' Claire called.

Adam was just pouring the tea as Claire came down the stairs. She had on a pair of jeans and a white jumper. Her hair hung loose to her shoulders. Adam stepped towards her, Claire took his hand, and Adam pulled her in for an embrace. Silently they stood, entwined. Claire felt the warmth of his body, his familiar aftershave. She felt comforted, secure. Pulling away from his arms she laughed, 'My tea will be cold.' It was still warm outside despite being late afternoon, so picking up the teacups, they strolled out into the garden.

Chatting over tea, Claire filled in him on her day out to Moulin to find the chateau. Adam felt himself tense. He still had to cross this bridge with Claire. It worried him. How he was going to do that was another matter. Maybe it will just happen, Adam thought. Surely there will be an opportunity to drop it into the conversation. It was a bit of a bombshell, though, hardly just something to mention in a passing comment. Adam turned his attention back to Claire. She was still chatting away.

'Then, when I was in the cafe, I met this lovely lady called Elodie Lavant.'

Adam nearly choked on his tea, spluttering as he did so.

Claire laughed 'Why do you look so shocked?' she laughed as she handed him a napkin to mop up the spilt tea.

Adam put down his teacup. 'Err, Claire, well, I might as well tell you that was one of my bosses that you ran into,' Adam said. He was still in disbelief, watching Claire's face for a reaction.

'Really!' Claire exclaimed, eyes wide. 'Oh my goodness, what a small world it is, how weird is that.' Claire looked relaxed; this news didn't strike her as being odd. But then Claire didn't know who Elodie really was. He didn't want to spoil the moment. She was laughing, her eyes alight. Adam knew, if he told her more, he would risk everything, so, for now, he thought, just one step at a time.

'Elodie was lovely,' enthused Claire. 'She even invited me

to look at the chateau, Adam, how kind was that?'

Adam knew he had to play this carefully, there would be no harm in Claire meeting Elodie and Theo but somehow, for now, he would have to stop her knowing that their uncle was Mathieu La Fontaine. 'Maybe we could go together to the chateau sometime then,' Claire suggested tentatively. 'Would you be OK with that or is it mixing business and pleasure?' Claire asked, looking at him with her lovely brown eyes. eyes that he couldn't resist.

Touching her face, he replied, 'Yes, that would be a lovely idea. It is a beautiful chateau, Claire, the wine is fantastic.'

Claire was thrilled at the thought. 'I really felt she was someone I could be friends with,' Claire went on enthusiastically. Adam couldn't bring himself to tell her they were actually cousins! This was all such a mess, he thought.

They had a week ahead together. Claire put all thoughts of Chateau Le Fontaine on hold. Adam tried to do the same, too. He wanted it to be special. They fell into an easy daily routine. They set up their laptops at either ends of the table. Claire watched him tapping away on his computer, listening to the deals going on for wine selling, as she typed up another article; this time on the Correze, a department below La Creuse. She had to submit it by Friday. She knew, come January, that there would be more travel writing work for her. It was the time that people's thoughts turned to their summer holidays. There were still many places in France she wanted to write about. She had done some research and had some ideas to put to her boss next time they spoke. If Susan was happy, there would be enough work to see her through to the end of her six months. That and hopefully starting her guide on French accommodation, one day!

Their evenings were spent cooking, trying new wines, talking. It was comfortable, familiar. Claire couldn't quite believe how quickly they had become a couple. In the evenings, in front of the fire. Claire would sit with her feet up on Adam's lap. He would rub her toes as they talked, looking at her face in the firelight's glow. Sometimes they read, side by side. Sometimes there was just silence, a comfortable silence. They were content in each other's company. It had been hardly any time at all since they had met. Claire didn't care. They were happy. That was all that mattered.

It was now the end of November and December was approaching. It was fire-lighting time in the cottage. The cosy glow added to the ambiance, the romance of it all. Evenings with Sean had never been like this. Claire suddenly realised it was the first time in months she had thought about Sean. It all seemed a very long time ago. Claire thought back to that day she had met Adam in the little pub, how lucky she had been to bump into him later in France.

Here they were now, acting like an old married couple.

'What are you thinking?' asked Adam as he leaned over and tickled her, making her squirm. She tried to break free from his embrace. Adam tightened his grip on her, pinning her down. First, he kissed her slowly, tantalisingly. Then with ardour and passion. Finally, they lay entwined together on the sofa. As they adjusted their clothes, Claire ran a hand through her hair.

Adam lay watching her. 'I can't believe how good this all feels, Claire,' said Adam sighing, a contented sigh.

Claire looked back at him and said softly, 'Me too.' Her big smile said it all. The passion was still very much at the forefront of their relationship. She felt herself blush, thinking about it. Later, when they turned off the lights. Claire thought how safe she felt, having the warmth of a man next to her. She felt protected. As they lay together, Claire listened to his soft breathing. It was the happiest she had been in a long time.

It would be Monday tomorrow. Claire felt sad knowing that Adam had to leave. He was off to Moulin to work at the chateau for the week. He had promised that he would broach the subject with Elodie about them meeting up. Adam also knew he was going to have to have a conversation with Elodie, somehow preventing her from letting Claire know that her Uncle Mathieu was Claire's father. Adam really wasn't sure how he would work that out. Maybe, thought Adam, just maybe, it would just be better to take the risk, tell Claire.

Adam knew the longer this went on, the more she would feel like he had deceived her. He was in a very difficult position. Claire wasn't ready to face her father yet; he could tell this from how slowly she was taking it all. He was also acutely aware that she hadn't completely opened up to him on the subject. From what he knew about her, she would have to feel sure before she did. And Adam didn't want to rush her. He certainly didn't want to lose her over all of this, not now when things were going so well between them.

As his car pulled away, Claire stood at the front of the cottage, waving. Returning to the house, Claire suddenly felt empty. She knew he would be back next weekend. That seemed a long time away. As she cleared away their breakfast dishes, she thought back to Elodie. Hopefully she could go with him to the chateau the weekend after next. It made her think again about Chateau Le Grand Fontaine. In her mind, there were two choices, she could go into it all further or she could just let sleeping dogs lie.

Claire had seen the chateau, the garden cottage, where her mother had lived, the beautiful river. Wasn't that enough for her? Then again, she thought back to the old man she had seen by the river; she wondered what he had been doing there. Had she really seen him? After all, when she had turned back to look, he had gone. Claire sighed, she wished her mother had told her more, then she would not be guessing, she would know what her mum would have wanted her to do. It made her wonder why her mum and Maurice had not had their own children? Maybe it had just never happened, she thought.

As she stood there pondering, she didn't know which way to go. She felt perplexed. The one good thing would be that she would have Adam by her side to help her. It was probably time she confided in him. Claire wondered how he would deal with her emotional baggage. Everything she had seen of him so far suggested he would be a support to her, but you never knew. It was a lot to take on in a new relationship.

Claire stared out of the window, thinking of him. As she tidied up, she saw her mum's purple velvet box sitting on the side. Picking it up, Claire took another look inside. No matter how hard she was trying to push this all to one side, the curiosity of it all was niggling away at her. She needed a coffee first, she thought, placing the box on the kitchen table.

Claire glanced out of the window again, the rain was pouring down. There was a fair wind today too. Claire wondered, with it being her first winter, if this was typical weather for the end of November. Her first winter in the cottage. The words made her smile. The log fire burned, its warm glow making the room feel cosy as Claire pulled up the little green velvet armchair closer to its warm rays. Her coffee sat steaming on the old wooden trunk she used as a coffee table. Slowly, Claire opened the lid on the box. Each time she looked, she discovered more of this secret life her mum had led. Despite the painfulness of it all, it was certainly intriguing. Mathieu, her father – she still couldn't get to grips with that – looked incredibly handsome. She could see why her mother had fallen for him all those years ago. The other side of Claire, though, thought he was a bit of a cad for all that had happened. Claire sat wondering if she would ever know the true story.

Sighing, she rummaged deeper into the box, pulling out photos. Claire looked again at the pictures of the two children. Studying the photo, she couldn't help but feel she had met the girl before; she seemed familiar. Down at the bottom, she found a few more photos. There was her mother sat at a little wrought-iron table. Very similar to the one she had in her own garden here. Gloria looked happy, relaxed, young and in love. Claire realised then that the cottage she had visited on the estate was definitely the one her mum lived in. The photo proved it was. Looking again at one of the other photos, which showed the children playing in the water, Claire realised that was the river where the old man had stood. She really should have spoken to him that day. He may have been able to help.

Digging deeper, Claire found a small velvet pouch. Curiously, she opened it. Inside was a fragile gold chain with a dainty locket hanging from it. Engraved on the front was a rose and a fleur de lys. An English rose and the French national flower. How romantic, Claire thought as she twirled it in her fingers. The gold was obviously an old gold. Claire gave it a little polish. In the middle of the rose appeared to be a diamond, well, she was no expert, but it certainly looked like a diamond.

On the inside were inscribed two letters: G M. It had to be from Mathieu, thought Claire, that would be their initials. Claire laid the chain gently back in its box. She was tempted to wear it, but it didn't feel quite right. There were some more photos of the chateau gardens, a picture of a very stunning couple which she thought must have been her mum's employers. The lady looked incredibly elegant; she was laughing with her husband and they were standing by some bottles of wine. Underneath this Claire found an old newspaper cutting dated September 30th, 1970. It was a photo of a man. It could be Mathieu, she thought, trying to look closer at the photo. He was standing with a stunning but fragile-looking woman. The article read:

The Count & Countess Serrenday of Paris are delighted to announce the engagement of their only Daughter Lydia Serrenday to the honourable Marquis Mathieu Le Fontaine.

The article said about the chateau, the wine history, talked about the family fortunes of the Serrendays. They were from a shipping background which had started with tea from India. The article detailed that the Count was extremely well regarded, not just in Parisian circles, but throughout the world; it appeared they had a vast fortune. How painful that must have been for her mother, Claire mused. Thinking about it further, Claire suddenly realised that her mother must have been pregnant with her when this had happened. Claire was stunned with the realisation. She had been born

24th April 1983, so her mother must have been about eight

weeks' pregnant when this had been announced. Instinctively, Claire touched her stomach. She wasn't sure why, it must have just been the overwhelming sickness feeling. The pain was unbearable for her, thinking of her mother knowing she was pregnant with Mathieu's baby. It was too much for Claire. She quickly put the lid back on the box, pushing it with force across the table.

Claire felt intense anger for a man she had never met. Her heart was overwhelmed with grief for her mother. Anger that boiled inside her. Sitting there, Claire remembered from the letter that he had come back to find Gloria. Could she show some forgiveness for that? Claire wasn't sure. How painful that must have been for her mother. What if, thought Claire, what if they had got back together? What if Mathieu had the chance to be her dad? Claire couldn't help wondering what life would have been like? Would they have moved to France? Would she have grown up in the chateau, would she have known her cousins? So many ifs, so many buts. It was all a little overwhelming.

With a heavy heart, Claire put the box away. She knew then that, until she had answers, she wouldn't be able to put this behind her. Claire needed to know what happened. Maurice would always be her dad but, deep down, she knew she needed to meet her father. Claire needed to hear his side of the story. Then, and only then could she decided if she could forgive the pain he had inflicted on her mum.

Chapter 26

Adam arrived back the following Friday evening looking tired and drawn after a heavy week's work at the chateau. He had been preparing for the wine festival in Paris. This was a big feature in the winemaker's diary. The chateau would have a large display. There had been lots to complete; it was only six weeks away.

Claire had made a chicken and leek casserole with mashed potatoes; Adam had declared he was in heaven. Sighing, he smiled. 'Claire, it really feels like coming home when I come back to you and this beautiful cottage.'

Picking up the empty plates from the table, Claire kissed the top of his head, but before she took them away, he pulled her on to his knee. Laughing, Claire tried to juggle the plates, kissing him at the same time. Wiggling herself free, Claire asked, 'Did you speak to Elodie?'

Adam watched her put the plates down by the kitchen

sink. 'I'm sorry, Claire, I didn't. I was flat out in the office all week; I hardly saw anyone.'

Claire, looking a little disappointed said, 'That's a shame, I was quite looking forward to seeing her chateau.' Then she turned her attention back to loading the dishwasher. Adam stretched as he got up from the table, carrying over the wine glasses and condiments. Claire shut the dishwasher door with a clunk as Adam pulled her into his arms, kissing her longingly on her lips.

'These last few weeks, Claire, have been perfect,' he murmured into her ear, whilst nuzzling it. Claire shivered, almost in anticipation, as he continued to kiss her neck slowly. 'Come on, leave the rest, I will help you in the morning.' Adam smiled, taking her hand, pulling her towards the stairs. Claire allowed him to lead her up the stairs. 'I think a long soak in the bath is in order,' he said, kissing her again.

The next morning, Adam was still fast asleep. Claire was feeling wide awake, energised. Their lovemaking had, as always, been amazing. They had finally fallen asleep, exhausted and content. She looked at him lying there peacefully. Claire felt so lucky to have found someone as perfect as Adam. Combing her hair in front of the bathroom mirror, she realised it was the happiest she had felt in years. It certainly showed; she was glowing. She decided to let Adam sleep. It would give her the opportunity to get tidied up downstairs, enjoy some coffee. Hopefully, if she crept around, he wouldn't be disturbed. He looked like he needed the rest.

Down in the kitchen, she busied herself tidying up. She had lit the fire, pulled back the curtains. There had been a few specks of snow overnight. How pretty it looked. The winter sun was shining on the frost, making the garden look like it was bathed in glitter. Claire noticed a little robin sat on the garden bench. How sweet, she thought to herself. The fire soon warmed up the room. She got the coffee on, then, reaching for the oven she popped in some frozen croissants. Adam's bag, along with a couple of folders, were lying by the door where he had left them last night. Bending down to pick them up, Claire thought she would move them. Then there would be no chance of her spilling something on to them. As Claire scooped them up, one folder slipped out of the pocket of the briefcase, sending its contents over the floor. Oops, thought Claire. Bending down, she quickly scooped up the papers. She hoped she had got them back in the right order. Suddenly one of them caught her eye: it was from Mathieu Le Fontaine.

Claire couldn't move, she was frozen to the spot. Shaking, Claire turned the paper over, it felt like she was operating in slow motion. Her heart was beating rapidly. A sense of fear was creeping through her body. It was indeed a letter from Mathieu to Adam, a letter from her father to her lover! Claire felt sick. She looked closer. The letter was a copy of an email to Adam giving him the information on her mother's name and last known address. He was asking for Adam's help to find Gloria and Claire, who he knew to be his daughter.

Claire was shaking. She steadied herself on the table. Oh, my goodness, she thought, No! Adam is working for Mathieu. Claire sat down with a thud on the kitchen chair. Aware of Adam now moving around upstairs, Claire felt panic take her over. This is all false, all this, all of Adam, all that we have shared. He has just been wanting to get to me for Mathieu. The anger was rising fast, along with the bile in her throat.

Aware of his presence, Claire turned to see Adam stood at the bottom of the stairs. He was in shock as he realised what Claire was looking at. How could he have been so stupid as to bring the paperwork into the house? 'Claire, please, I can explain. Please don't jump to conclusions. Please let me explain,' Adam pleaded with her.

'Get out, get out, Adam!' Claire screamed. Her face was flushed with anger as she screamed again, 'Get out of my house!'

Adam was horrified. 'Claire, please calm down, please, it's not what you think. Let me tell you, please?' Adam was begging her now. He went to walk towards her but stopped.

Claire was shaking, this time with venom. She said loudly, 'GET. OUT. NOW.' Her face was red, her eyes raw with the anger she was feeling.

Adam knew this was not the time to plead his case. He had to leave. Reaching for his car keys, he took his bag off the chair. Walking to the door, he tried again. 'Please?' he pleaded with her. 'Please, when you are ready, please call me, please give me the chance to explain.' With that, his face white, he walked out of the cottage.

Claire crumpled into the armchair. The room felt like it was spinning; she felt sick to the stomach; the anger raged through her body. Then slowly, one by one, the tears came. They flooded down her cheeks. Claire fumbled for the box of tissues. Not sure which hurt the most. Was it that once again a man she was in love with had betrayed her? Or was it because Adam actually knew her father and had kept it from her. The piece of paper with his contact information lay on the table.

Claire stared at it through the blur of her tears. She couldn't believe the man she had trusted, had fallen in love with, had done this to her. How could he be working for her father? Were the past three months all a sham to get her into bed, then present her to her father. How could he? Claire felt sick to the stomach. Her head ached; she was bereft. Walking into the bathroom, Claire fumbled for the paracetamol packet, popping two pills into her mouth and gulping them down with a glass of lukewarm water from the bathroom tap. Staring back at her reflection in the mirror, what a mess she looked. She sighed, then dabbed her face with a cold flannel.

Claire just wanted to lie down, close out the world.

Walking into her bedroom, she pulled back her duvet. Fresh tears welled in her eyes; only hours before she had lain here in Adam's arms, feeling secure and loved. The bedroom was too painful, so she took herself to the spare room, falling on to the small single bed. Burying her face into the pillows, she sobbed before finally falling asleep, exhausted.

Claire woke with a start. Glancing at her watch, she was amazed to see it was 2.30pm in the afternoon. She had slept for hours. The realisation of the morning came flooding back to her, the overwhelming sadness made her body ache. Claire knew she needed to pull herself together. At that moment, the decision was made. There was only one thing to do; she had to get in contact with her father, there was no option.

Suddenly, hunger seemed to take over. She knew she needed to eat, so, pulling on a cardigan, she made her way downstairs. There were only embers left in the fire, quite ironic really now that she only had embers of another failed relationship. Taking the firelighters from the box, she inhaled their paraffin smell as she threw them into the grate. Claire struck the match, staring for a moment at the glow from the stick, then put match to lighter. A flame burst through, the logs began to crackle.

Adam hadn't known what to do when he left Claire's. He had driven a little way, then stopped for a coffee. He would have to head to Moulin. He had nowhere else he could really go. In his car, as he approached Moulin, his phone rang. Glancing at the display on the car dashboard, he saw it read Mathieu Le Fontaine. Adam quickly hit the decline button. He wasn't ready for Mathieu's questions today. He needed more time to think. Goodness knows how he was going to handle it. He knew one thing was for sure; it was playing heavily on his mind. He could confide in Elodie. That might be the option.

He pondered this thought for a moment. Elodie had coincidentally met Claire just last week. It was a huge risk. But Adam was certain Elodie would understand. The thoughts were going round and round in his head. What a mess, Adam sighed. There was only one thing for it. He would have to talk to Elodie. She would know what to do. He knew he would have to tell her the whole story; he was sure she would understand. Adam knew Mathieu had limited time; he had been diagnosed with cancer of the blood two years ago, it had now spread throughout his body. Mathieu managed dai-ly with help, but time was running out for him. Although it was slow, the doctors had intimated another year at the most. Adam knew how much Mathieu wanted to make peace with his daughter. He had desperately wanted to help him do so. Adam had never planned to meet Claire like this, never planned to fall in love with her. He knew more than anything he should have been straight with her from the start, but it was too late now.

Pulling up in front of the small chateau that belonged to Elodie and Theo, Adam could see the children playing croquet in the chateau garden. He spotted Elodie in the rose garden. Adam sat, silently watching her for a few minutes. He was trying to work out in his mind how he would broach this with her after all; it was actually her cousin that he was talking about. As if sensing she was being watched, Elodie looked up from pruning the roses and waved to Mathieu. He waved back, then, taking the keys from the ignition, climbed out of the car. Elodie was walking over to greet him, a basket of dead rose heads in one hand and secateurs in the other. On reaching him, they exchanged kisses and Elodie asked him how he was. 'You looked tired, Adam,' Elodie said, stepping back.

Adam nodded. 'Elodie, is there somewhere we can talk please?'

'Of course,' replied Elodie. 'The children are fine, they can amuse themselves,' she said, glancing over at them. 'Come into the drawing room. I'll get some tea sent up,' Elodie said kindly, touching his arm. They made their way in silence into the chateau. Elodie told Adam to go on up whilst she dropped the basket off in the kitchen, saying she would get the tea organised. Adam made his way through the grand entrance hall, with its huge portraits adorning the mighty walls. The floor was made of beautiful marble, the most luxurious chandeliers hung from the high ceilings. It had a certain chill to it on an early December day. There were beautiful touches around the chateau, he knew Elodie had made these. She had a real eye for detail.

Climbing the huge oak staircase, Adam turned to the left, pushing open the door to the drawing room. This was Elodie's personal space, a room she loved to spend time in, especially during the winter months with its huge stone fireplace. The stunningly large aspect windows looked out over the gardens of the chateau. Down below, he could see the children playing. The sounds of arguments floated in through the window, making Adam smile for the first time that day. Beautiful rose-pink velvet curtains dressed the window. He sat down in one of the soft chintz armchairs in front of the roaring winter fire.

It wasn't long before Elodie appeared. Her smile always lit up the room. Adam had thought many times what a lucky man Theo was to have such a beautiful wife, such an easy-going one, too. Born into a wealthy family, but so down to earth. She was also incredibly fond of her Uncle Mathieu. Loving to spend at least one or two afternoons a week in his company, listening to his stories of the 'olden' days of aristocracy in rural France.

Placing herself opposite, Elodie looked at him. 'OK, you had better start from the beginning. Something is obviously troubling you. I hope you're not planning to leave us,' Elodie said, looking rather concerned for a moment.

Adam, shaking his head said, 'No.' Starting at the beginning, he told her how her uncle had wanted to find his daughter. Elodie nodded as they went along. She was aware she had a cousin that she had never met, and that Uncle Mathieu kept a photo of her in his study. Mathieu explained how he had coincidently bumped into a very upset Claire in a local pub but hadn't realised that she was Gloria's daughter. He explained how they had then run into each other again in France. Claire had told him about her mother dying, then she had mentioned Chateau le Grand Fontaine. Adam explained he had then put two and two together, realising he was falling in love with Mathieu's daughter. He said he knew how stupid he had been to not tell her from the beginning.

Elodie could see from the way Adam spoke about Claire that he really had fallen in love with her, Elodie was intrigued to know more.

Looking at Elodie, Adam said, 'You won't know this, but you have actually met her.' Elodie looked very surprised, asking, 'How?' Adam explained about the day Elodie had bumped into Claire in the cafe near Moulin. The day she had been there with the children. Elodie was amazed to hear this.

'Oh my goodness,' she exclaimed, placing her hand to her throat. She was wide-eyed. 'Yes, I remember her so well. She was lovely company, so good with the children.' Elodie shook her head in amazement. Continuing, he told her about this morning; the moment that he realised Claire had found out. 'Adam, how could you be so stupid?' Elodie exclaimed when she heard that Claire had found the folder with Mathieu's contact details in.

Adam then said that he had tried calling about six times, but no answer.

'Claire just won't speak to me.'

'Do you blame her?' said Elodie, a little sharper than she had planned.

'No,' said Mathieu dolefully, placing his head in his hands.

Elodie could tell he was devastated. At that moment, there was a knock at the door. One of the kitchen maids appeared with a pot of tea for them, along with a slice of freshly made walnut gateau, a speciality of the region. He took the tea, declining the cake. He really couldn't eat just now.

Elodie, sitting back, looked at Mathieu. 'I will go to see her. Maybe she will talk to me. I can explain that you really aren't quite the baboon that you appear to be.' She smiled. He looked a little offended, but she was only trying to make light of the situation. It was an attempt to cheer him up. Adam wasn't sure about the suggestion, but on thinking more, he realised he probably didn't really have any other option, so it was agreed Elodie would go to see Claire.

Claire was pouring herself a glass of wine. It was just 5pm, a little early, but she needed it after the day she'd had. As she popped the bottle back in the fridge, she heard a car outside. Oh, please don't let that be Adam, she thought. I can't cope with all this now. She had at least six missed calls from him on her mobile. Under no circumstance would she be speaking to him today, or any day! Claire knew she needed time to think, to get her head around it all.

Glancing out of the window, Claire saw a red Range Rover Evoque parked up. She frowned; she didn't know anybody that drove one of these. Maybe they were just parking outside her house and going somewhere else? Claire watched as the car door opened and a young woman climbed out. She was dressed in jeans, a bright ochre roll neck that clung to her very slim body and draped with a cream and ochre wrap. How elegant, Claire thought, looking down at her faded denim jeans and loose check shirt. She was suddenly feeling incredibly scruffy.

Then, as the woman walked towards the house, Claire realised that it was the lady she had met at the cafe. The lady that she had later found out to be Adam's boss! Oh goodness, thought Claire, catching her reflection in the mirror. What on earth is she doing here? Quickly running her hands through her unbrushed hair, she reached for the door handle.

'Claire, hello,' said Elodie in her delicate French accent.

'Hello,' Claire replied.

'Nice to see you again,' said Elodie.

'Can I come in,' asked Elodie 'It's a little cold out here, I would really like the chance to talk to you.'

As she spoke, she glanced into the cosy little living room.

'Yes, yes, of course,' said Claire, coming to her senses. 'Sorry, yes, please come in.'

Claire opened the door wide, allowing Elodie to step past her into the living room.

Elodie could see why Adam was so in love with Claire. And her house was incredibly homely, something she sometimes yearned for herself after a lifetime of living in draughty chateaux.

Claire gestured to a seat and Elodie sat down, smiling. 'Thank you.'

'Would you like a drink,' asked Claire, looking towards the tiny kitchen.

Elodie said she would love a cup of tea. Making herself comfortable in the little fireside chair she said, 'You have a beautiful place here, so warm and inviting.' Elodie smiled at Claire as she spoke.

'Thank you,' Claire replied, handing her a cup of tea.

'Claire, we need to talk,' said Elodie, placing her cup on the little oak table at the side of the chair. 'We have to talk about Adam and Mathieu.' She smiled at Claire, trying to make her feel comfortable. This would be a difficult conversation.

Claire nodded, feeling herself blush a little.

'Adam came to see me today. He told me how you found out about his connection with Mathieu.' Elodie was watching Claire. She could see the pain etched in her face at the mention of Adam. Elodie explained that Adam had been in a very difficult situation; he hadn't known about the connection the first time or even the second time that they had met. It wasn't until Claire had explained about her mother Gloria dying that it had all fallen into place. Elodie reached out, touching Claire's hand. 'He was in a very difficult situation,' she said. He was compromised between loyalty to my Uncle Mathieu and falling in love with you'.

Claire looked at Elodie. 'Uncle!' Claire gasped, feeling the colour drain from her face. 'Yes, my uncle, Claire, he is the brother of my mother. Your mother used to look after me as a child. I have very fond memories of her.'

This was too much for Claire. A tear rolled down her cheek as Elodie continued to stroke her hand. 'That means you are my cousin,' stuttered Claire.

'Yes, I am your cousin, Claire,' said Elodie softly as she squeezed Claire's hand tighter.

'Oh my goodness,' sobbed Claire. She didn't know how much more of all this she could take. Elodie reached for the box of tissues on the coffee table, handing them to Claire. Claire took one. She didn't know how to feel. She knew, however, that she was delighted at the prospect of this lovely lady being her cousin. Claire squeezed Elodie's hand back. They had hit it off from that very first meeting. Now Claire knew why she had been so comfortable with her. The photos as well. No wonder Elodie had looked familiar.

The two women sat in silence for a few moments before Elodie continued. 'Adam has been fraught with guilt. He really didn't know how to tell you he worked for my uncle. Uncle Mathieu is not well, Claire, he has cancer of the blood. There is no more the doctors can do for him. He wanted to make peace with your mother before he died, but of course that cannot happen. I am so sorry for the loss of your moth-er,' she said kindly. 'Adam, finding you has added another dimension to the problem. Adam has not yet told my uncle any of this, only that your mother had died. It has broken his heart. The only hope he has now is to make amends with you,' said Elodie softly. 'Claire, he is not a bad man; he is kind, caring, caught in the past. A past that lives with him every day.' Elodie leaned across and placed her arms around Claire, who folded into them, sobbing. Elodie just sat, arms around Claire, letting her feel the comfort of family.

Chapter 27

They had talked long into the evening. Now 9pm, on this cold winter night, it was pitch black outside. 'Oh goodness, Elodie, I haven't offered you anything to eat. Could you manage something? I could rustle up an omelette for us,' suggested Claire.

'That would be wonderful,' agreed Elodie.

'We still have lots to talk about. I might find a local hotel so we can continue. You must have so many questions to ask,' said Elodie, reaching for her mobile phone.

Claire had a thought. 'Look, Elodie, why don't you stay here, stay in my spare room? It is not luxurious, but it will be comfortable, you don't have to go to a hotel room.'

Elodie was delighted. Claire pointed her toward the small spare room so that she could freshen up. Then, remembering she had lain on the bed earlier today, she told Elodie she would just need to straighten it up. Elodie told her not to worry. Claire told her where to find towels. 'They are in the cupboard on the landing and I can find you a nightshirt of mine to borrow if you like?'

Elodie laughed. 'That would be lovely. A girls' night in your beautiful cottage.' She grinned. 'I have a couple of bottles of our Grand Cru in the boot, we can open one of those, then I will leave the other with you,' laughed Elodie. 'That is if we don't drink it all.' They both laughed at this thought.

Claire was feeling a little brighter after their chat. Busying herself in the kitchen, she began making omelettes. Elodie went upstairs to freshen up. Walking into the tiny bedroom she thought how beautiful it all was. The room was bathed in duck-egg blue walls and the bedding was crisp white, a delicate lace finished it. A far cry from the large cold bedrooms at the chateau. Elodie was going to enjoy a night in here, she thought. Switching on the little pleated lamp at the side of the bed, she sat down. Well, she thought, that hadn't gone too badly. It could have been a lot worse.

Sighing though, she knew she really needed to broach the subject of Adam, that was what was important here. Adam had worked with them for many years now, he was more like a member of the family. Elodie was upset to see him so torn today, she knew he didn't have a malicious bone in his body; she knew, too, that he really was in love with Claire. Downstairs, Claire was ready to serve up the omelette, 'It's ready,' she called up the stairs.

'OK, I'll be straight down!' Elodie shouted back.

Claire set out two sets of knives and forks on the pretty gingham tablecloth, along with two crisp white napkins out of the drawer in the unit under the TV. Reaching for two wine glasses from the cupboard, she then turned and picked up the bottle of red that Elodie and left on the table. Turning the bottle in her hands, she squinted to read the label. 1994 Grand Cru Chateau Chenosay, it read. Turning the corkscrew in the top, she pulled out the cork with a pop. Inhaling the red wine aroma, she then placed it on the table. Orion would be proud of her.

Elodie was on her way down the little staircase, stopping when she reached the bottom step to pick up a photo of Gloria and Maurice, smiling fondly. 'Your mother was wonderful, Claire. Thierry and I loved her. We knew Maurice too. He used to make us amazing treats to eat in the garden. You were very lucky to have been brought up by two wonderful people,' Elodie said, placing the photo back. Claire noticed she looked wistful for a moment or two.

Elodie knew her upbringing had been entirely different to Claire's. Her father had worked away for long periods of time. Her mother, who had loved them dearly, had been highly strung. She would spend long hours in her room singing.

Claire interrupted her thoughts. 'Yes, I was very lucky. They were wonderful parents.' Elodie noticed Claire's eyes filling with tears.

Claire took a deep breath to compose herself, gesturing to Elodie to take a seat at the table.

'This all looks wonderful, Claire.'

I was very lucky. Dad taught me to cook from a very early age. He had his own restaurant in our local town for many years,' Claire explained to Elodie. The two sat amicably over their omelettes and red wine, chatting about Gloria and Maurice. Elodie told her how sad they had been on returning from Paris to find that Gloria and Maurice had left, had eloped together. 'Your mother was our friend, our companion. We had such fun with her, especially swimming in the river,' she laughed.

Finishing dinner, they put the plates away in the dishwasher. Picking up the wine and their glasses, they positioned themselves once again by the fire.

'What a wonderful evening,' Elodie sighed. 'You really have such a lovely place here, Claire, I can see why Adam loves it.'

Elodie watched Claire's reaction to Adam's name.

Claire sighed. 'I really thought I had found someone very special in Adam. I was falling in love with him, then this all happened.' She sighed as she continued sadly 'and when I found out he knew my father my world fell apart'.

Elodie patted her hand. 'I have known Adam for many years, Claire, he is like a brother to me, Thierry and Theo. We trust him with our lives,' Elodie explained. She spoke sincerely. 'He did not set out for any of this to happen. He just honestly didn't know how to tell you, how to say he knew your father. He wanted to tell you he worked for the family, but he was so worried about how you would take it.' Elodie continued. 'Losing you was not an option. He was so happy, Claire, he loved your company. He had fallen in love with you. The longer it went on, the harder it was for him to tell you,' She explained. 'Now he knows he should have done it from the beginning, not lived a lie. It has broken his heart. He wants nothing more than to make this up to you.' Elodie looked at Claire for a reaction.

Claire sat staring at the dying flames in the small fireplace. 'I just don't know any more, Elodie. I just don't feel I can trust in him; I feel used. He just wanted to be with me to find out more to tell Mathieu.' Claire turned her gaze from the fire to look at Elodie.

'What do you want to do from here, Claire?' Elodie asked quietly.

Claire shrugged her shoulders. 'I don't know, I honestly don't know.' It was all she could say. It was enough for one day. Looking at the clock she saw it was almost midnight; they had been talking all evening, they were both exhausted. The two cousins stood up and Elodie embraced Claire. It was comforting to feel Elodie's arms around her. Claire so needed a hug right now. They stood for a few minutes together in silence, then drew apart.

'We can talk more tomorrow, Elodie, but I really need to sleep. I think I am going to have a bath. Do you want to use the bathroom first? I'll go after you,' Claire said as she pulled the lock over on the front door.

Half an hour later, Elodie away to bed, Claire lay in the steamy bubbles of the bath. Lighting a lavender candle, she lay in its glow, the hot water caressing her. Claire desperately wanted the water to wash away how she felt right now. She missed Adam terribly; she wasn't ready to admit that to anyone yet. He had had no right to keep something so important from her. Claire could, however, see why he hadn't known what to say. Later, as she switched off her little bedside light, pulling the hot water bottle to her, she felt sleep overcoming her. Closing her eyes, she just needed to forget it all. Tomorrow would be another day.

Elodie departed the next morning. They had agreed to keep in touch. She had invited Claire to come to the chateau the following weekend. Claire said she needed time to think about it. The prospect of seeing Adam again filled her with dread. She knew it would have to happen at some point. They needed to talk if they wanted a future together.

For now, Claire couldn't see that far. She didn't know what that future would be. Not only did she need time to think about Adam, but Claire also needed time to think about Mathieu. How would she feel about meeting him face to face? Only a few months ago, she didn't know who or where he was. So much had changed since then. In fact, it was only just under a year since her mother had died, even less time since she had made this life-changing discovery. She kept herself very busy for the next few days. There were no more missed calls from Adam. Claire guessed that Elodie had something to do with that. She would have told Adam to bide his time. Staring out of the window, her laptop open on the table, she couldn't write. Her mind really wasn't on work. This was very unlike her.

Claire hated to admit that she was lonely without Adam. The evenings were quiet, very lonely, in fact. Finally, with this in mind, she made a call to Elodie. She told her she had decided that she would like to come to the chateau at the weekend. Claire also asked Elodie if she would arrange for her to see Adam. She needed to hear what he had to say. Elodie, of course, had been delighted; she knew how much this would mean to Adam. However, Claire also pointed out, it would be on the provision that Mathieu wasn't told of her being there. Claire wasn't ready for that yet. Elodie promised. Putting down her phone, Claire felt a little relief. It felt like a step in the right direction.

Chapter 28

Claire sighed. There was still that feeling that her insides had been wrenched open. The whole situation still felt raw. She also knew that she needed to move on with this, close the wounds, give them time to heal. How she was going to feel where Adam was concerned, she wasn't sure. Claire guessed that wouldn't hit her until she saw him again. Fighting with her conscience, she wondered what she would have done in the same situation? The thought kept going round and round in her head.

Sitting by the fire, hands around her mug of tea, Claire closed her eyes. What a long way she had come in less than a year. Splitting up with Sean, losing her mum, meeting Adam. Then, to top it all off, finding out the man she had known as Dad for most of her life wasn't her real father. Maurice would always be Dad to her, Claire was sure of that.

Looking at the clock, it was almost midnight. She had sat

there for well over three hours, enjoying the silence, watching the embers of the fire and nursing her inner thoughts. She would visit Elodie. It certainly wasn't under the circumstances she had imagined when she first met her. Claire really hoped she could put some of this dilemma to bed. Standing up, pulling her cardigan around her, she placed her mug by the kitchen sink, yawning. It was time for bed.

It was now the beginning of December, and little signs that Christmas was on the way were appearing on TV, in the supermarkets. The village street was having its Christmas lights put up. Claire didn't know what would happen tomorrow, let alone Christmas. She didn't relish the thought of being alone. Actually, that wasn't exactly true: Claire knew what would happen tomorrow. Tomorrow would be the day she would meet with Elodie at Chateau Chenosay. This should have been a moment to relish, to be excited about, to celebrate that she had a cousin. Now, instead, it almost filled her with dread. She couldn't get Adam out of her mind no matter how hard she tried. It was almost as if they had been destined to meet. So many coincidences. Maybe she had to give him a chance, but she had vowed to herself that no one would ever hurt her again in the way Sean had. Adam was a different man though and she couldn't help thinking she owed him the chance. She would have to see how she felt when she saw him. Then she would know.

Saturday morning dawned, crisp and bright. There was definitely a chill in the air. Claire, on pulling back the curtains, saw the ground had a light covering of frost. The pond at the end of the lane was frozen over. A lone duck sat on top, preening its feathers. Scanning her wardrobe, she didn't want to overdress; something sophisticated but plain would work. Opting for a pair of black trousers and a red polo jumper, she laid them on the bed, then went to get washed.

An hour later, showered, hair brushed, makeup on. Claire took a last glance in the mirror. It was almost a stranger staring back at her. France had treated her well, her skin still had a slight hue of a tan from the summer, her hair hung long and wavy with shafts of sun-kissed blonde framing her face. She had decided not to straighten it today. She wanted to feel as natural as she could. There had been days recently where she just felt totally drained from all the emotion. It was just under a two-hour drive to the chateau and the drive never failed to leave Claire in awe.

Each season had its own merits. A couple of deer were grazing in the field as she pulled up at the entrance to Chateau Chenonsay. Claire had to stop the engine for a few minutes, staring out at the stunning grandeur of her cousin's home. Claire almost let out a gasp. Not as big as Le Grand Fontaine, but the condition was a million times better. The black iron gates hung proudly with the grass either side neatly trimmed. The gold crest on each side of the gates gleamed in the morning sun. Slowly, she drove up the long gravel driveway. There were two turrets at each end of the chateau. There was a huge frozen lake, the chateau mirroring itself on the solid waters. The front door was incredible; double-fronted, large oak doors. They were at least a double-decker bus in height. To the right of the front door stood the most amazing Christmas tree, Claire would love to see that lit up at night-time. She pulled her little Fiat in next to Elodie's elegant red Evoque. Gripping the steering wheel tightly, Claire let out a long breath. Before she had any further time to think, Elodie came gracefully down the steps to greet her.

Claire smiled, waving from the car. Reaching for her handbag, she opened the door. Elodie was at her side in seconds, embracing her, kissing both cheeks, then exclaiming, 'Claire, you look wonderful.' Claire thanked her. Elodie squeezed her hand as if to let her know she was there for her.

Claire, of course, hadn't yet met Theo, Elodie's husband, so she had that all to go through too. Elodie, sensing this was all going to be difficult for Claire, gave her a hug.

'It will all be good, Claire, you will see.'

Claire attempted a smile. It certainly wasn't feeling alright just now!

'Theo and Adam are out hunting this morning,' Elodie informed her. 'So I have time to show you around the chateau. We can take some coffee by the fire in the drawing room. How does that sound?' The thought of this perked Claire up. 'Elodie, perfect,' she said, squeezing Elodie's hand, still lodged in hers. 'Thank you, I couldn't do this without you.'

Elodie showed Claire into the large marble hallway. A fire

burned brightly in the ornate grate. Above the fireplace was also the biggest stag's head Claire had ever seen. This was going to be a weekend of firsts all round, thought Claire to herself.

Elodie was pleased to see her cousin was smiling. They spent the morning doing a tour of the chateau. When finished, they enjoyed morning coffee in the large drawing room; beautifully decorated, but more contemporary than she would have expected. Claire knew that must be Elodie's impeccable taste; she obviously had an eye for decoration.

Claire told her so as they sat and chatted. Adam was not mentioned. The Victorian clock on the mantlepiece chimed twelve. 'Why don't I show you to your room, Claire. It will give you time to freshen up,' Elodie suggested.

'Thank you, that would be nice,' replied Claire. They walked out of the drawing room onto the large gallery landing area, as Claire shivered. Such a contrast to the cosiness of the drawing room. Elodie laughed; she had grown up in this large draughty chateau, she was used to the chill. The gallery landing had some beautiful paintings adorning the walls. As they walked along, Elodie pointed out to Claire who the people were. Elodie explained that this chateau had belonged to her grandmother on her father's side. It had been left to Elodie when she was very young as her brother Thierry didn't want the responsibility of it. Elodie explained that Thierry had taken himself off to New Zealand to establish a wine business in Marlborough. He was happy there with his wife Sophia. They also had two children Pierre and Isabella, Elodie explained.

The centrepiece of the paintings was of an absolutely stunning woman. She was wearing a gold dress encrusted with tiny diamonds. The artist had captured every detail. Claire stood in silence for a moment, then Elodie speaking first said, 'This is my mother, Liselle Le Fontaine. Your mother worked for her.'

Claire couldn't help but notice her own resemblance to this woman, a woman that she had never met.

Elodie, sensing this, said, 'You are quite like her, Claire.'

Claire laughed. 'If only I was that beautiful, you're very kind though.'

The two women hugged, each sensing the other's pain, Claire for an aunt she would never know, mixed in with her mother's pain. Elodie's pain for the mother she had lost.

'Come, let me show you your room,' Elodie said, lightening the mood.

Claire was looking forward to this. Elodie opened the door to the bedroom and Claire was certainly not disappointed. The room was decorated in peaches and corals, beautiful drapes adorned the stunning curved bay window and a terracotta chaise longue filled the space in the bay. Turning to the right, Claire took in the oak four poster, beautifully carved with rambling roses trailing up the posts. Its coral velvet curtains were draped elegantly at each corner. The bed looked sumptuous. Even before Claire had laid on it, the chance to sleep on it was very appealing.

Elodie looked on with delight as Claire took in her surroundings. 'This used to be my grandmother's room, Claire,' smiled Elodie. 'I only let special people stay in here.'

Claire smiled at Elodie. 'Wow, that is all I can say, Elodie. Words fail me, it is just beautiful.' Claire was suddenly feeling incredibly emotional and her eyes filled with tears.

Elodie pulled her close, holding her tight. Then she told Claire to get herself settled in. 'The men will be back for lunch soon. Maybe it would be a good idea if you and Adam were to meet before lunch,' suggested Elodie.

Claire felt herself tense a little. She knew she had to do this. Turning to Elodie, she said, 'If you could arrange for him to be in the drawing room at 12.30, I will see him there.'

Elodie agreed. It would be a good idea for Adam to meet her there; they would have a little privacy. Claire also knew it would be much better for everyone if they talked before lunch. However, if any of them thought that an hour would solve their problems, it couldn't be further from the truth. They would have to talk together long after lunch if they were going to make this work.

Elodie left Claire. There was half an hour before she was to meet Adam. It gave Claire time to unpack her bag. Touching up her lipstick, she took a last look in the mirror. The red roll neck was just her colour. Claire made her way down to the drawing room. Pushing open the oak-studded door, she walked in. She was, for now, alone. Looking around the room, Claire walked over to the large bay window. She stood, looking out across the magnificent grounds of the chateau. How beautiful, even now. It would look even more amazing in the summer, she thought.

Turning towards the sound of the drawing-room door being pushed open. Claire took a deep breath. There, framed in the doorway, was Adam. He looked pale, tired, but still incredibly handsome. Claire was slightly surprised by the flip feeling in her stomach. She hadn't expected to feel that. Neither of them spoke for what seemed like minutes. It was probably only seconds.

Then Adam, clearing his throat, said, 'Hello, it is so good to see you. I am so pleased you decided to come.' He looked directly at her, his voice full of emotion.

Claire wished she could turn away, hide. She spoke, rather formerly. 'Adam, thank you for coming.'

There was a slight awkwardness to him as he walked into the room. They took seats at opposite sides of the fireplace.

'Claire, please listen to me. You have to know I wanted none of this to happen,' Adam said with such sadness in his voice.

Claire almost felt sorry for him. Only almost! Clearing her throat, she spoke, 'You destroyed all my trust, Adam. You knew what I had been through, yet you deceived me,' Claire said, trying to maintain composure in her voice. 'You made me feel cheap, like I was a pawn in your game; tracking me down then luring me in, just so you could satisfy your employer.' Claire fought back tears as she spoke.

Adam shifted uncomfortably in his seat. 'I understand how it looks, Claire,' he replied, tapping his foot on the floor as he spoke. He was nervous. 'Understand me, please, meeting you in Cheshire, then bumping into you in France was fated. I had absolutely no idea who you were.'

Claire was quiet. Fate had certainly dealt them both a cruel hand, or had it? Maybe fate had made it happen for a reason. Adam got up off his seat. Slowly, he made his way to Claire's armchair. Claire could feel herself become even more tense. Adam, sensing this, dropped onto his knees, a foot from the armchair. He wanted to hold her, tell her he loved her. But he knew he couldn't push her. There he sat, hunkered down in front of her. Claire could almost feel his warmth. Looking across at him, she felt a tear slid down her cheek. She knew then, despite everything, that she loved him more than anything.

Adam, reaching out his arm, placed his hand on her hand. 'Claire, please, please don't cry, we can work this out, we can get through this.'

Claire felt exhausted. Feeling his hand on hers, she wanted him to hold her in his arms, to tell her it would all be OK. 'Adam, I-I...' Claire struggled as he placed his arms on her shoulders. This was too much for her; she couldn't fight it any longer. Her body melted into his embrace and tears streamed down her cheeks. His breath was warm on her face and Claire felt his tears mingle with her tears. They stayed like this for some minutes before Claire pulled away. Adam, losing his balance, toppled backwards. Claire couldn't help it. She had to laugh. Adam, feigning injury, looked dejected before laughing, too.

Elodie, who had just arrived to tell them lunch would be served in ten minutes, stood delightedly on the other side of the door. She could hear laughter from them both. Hesitantly, she knocked on the door. She hoped she wasn't spoiling the moment. It all sounded hopeful. Entering the room, she saw Claire extending a hand to Adam as she helped him up off the floor. Elodie looked alarmed for a moment; had Claire punched him?

Claire and Adam turned to look at Elodie. They saw the look on her face. Laughing, they explained what had happened. They asked Elodie to give them another ten minutes, they would then come straight to the dining room.

'Where do we go from here now, Claire,' Adam asked tentatively. 'And don't say, "To the dining room"', Adam quipped. Claire smiled. She loved his sense of humour more than anything.

Exhaling a deep breath, Claire spoke. 'We still have lots to work through. I have missed you so much, but you hurt me. That's difficult to forget. We need honesty in our relationship if we are to go on, not lies.'

Adam, nodding, replied. 'Claire, I know. Believe me, if I could turn back the clock I would, but I can't,' he said sadly. 'I will forever hate myself for the pain that I have caused you.'

He hung his head.

Taking a step towards him, Claire placed her hands on his waist. Slowly, Adam looked up. They looked each other in the eye. Claire placed her body against his, feeling the warmth, the familiar comfort she loved. Slowly reaching up, she placed a delicate kiss on his lips. Adam pulled her into an embrace. They stood silently, each feeling complete in the other's arms. Claire knew she had to let him back into her life. She had to give him a chance.

Chapter 29

Agreeing for now, to put their problems aside. Adam and Claire made their way to the dining room. They both knew they weren't through the woods yet. There would still be lots to talk about. Of course, Adam knew that Claire still had the hurdle of meeting her father. Adam still wasn't sure what Claire's thoughts were on this and, as yet, Adam, despite Mathieu's continuous phone calls, still hadn't told the old man he had found Claire. For now, though, they were both going to enjoy lunch with the wonderful company of Elodie and Theo.

Adam took Claire's hand at the dining-room door. 'Whatever happens from here, Claire,' he said, looking into her eyes, 'whatever happens, we are in this together.' Claire knew Adam meant this.

She was very grateful to have him by her side, although he had caused a lot of this mess! Although her mother must take the blame for some of it. Claire smiled. 'That means a lot, Adam, thank you.'

Adam pushed open the door to the dining room, another stunning room, yet another fire blazing in the grate. Claire wasn't used to such grandeur. It made her feel overwhelmingly small. Sensing this, Adam squeezed her hand a little tighter. Claire smiled at him.

'Claire, how lovely to meet you, I'm Theo.' Claire was taken a little by surprise. She hadn't spotted Theo sitting in the armchair with a glass of red wine. He stood up, striding over to her.

'Such a pleasure to meet you, Elodie has told me so much about you.' Theo embraced Claire, kissing her on each cheek.

The dining room door opened, in breezed Elodie, smiling at seeing her husband, her friend and her cousin all assembled in the dining room together. 'So, Claire, you have met my worst half then,' laughed Elodie, reaching up and kissing Theo on the cheek.

'I have indeed.' Claire smiled. 'It is so lovely to meet you, to be invited to such a beautiful place too.' Then, turning to Elodie, 'Elodie, thank you, thank you for making this happen.' Claire felt a little choked. Elodie hugged her. 'You are my family, Claire, we help each other.'

Lunch was superb. It was going to take her some time to come to terms that this was her family. To Claire, it all seemed like another world. Life had always been simple for her; comfortable, but simple. Elodie was used to things on a much grander scale. That said, Claire was surprised at just how relaxed lunch was. Theo, Elodie, and Adam were all easy company. The four chatted like they had known each other for years. It was funny how when you meet a member of the family for the first time, it can often feel you have known each other for ever. Claire had never really known much family; her grandparents had all died whilst young. Maurice had no brother or sisters, neither had her mother Gloria, so no cousins, aunts or uncles. When Maurice had died, then Gloria, Claire was really left with no one. On top of all that, she had also had to contend with a marriage breakdown. Looking round her now, Claire smiled. Here was her family, a cousin she never knew she had. Then, glancing at Adam, she felt overwhelming love. This man had changed her world. It hadn't all been done the right way, but it had happened.

After lunch, Claire and Adam decided to take a walk. Adam wanted to show her around the grounds. Elodie wanted the children to help her put the Christmas tree up in the drawing room. Claire said she would like to help too. She agreed with Elodie that she would come in after the walk. Adam and Claire wrapped up warmly; Claire borrowed some socks and wellies from Elodie. They then stepped outside. Adam really wanted to show her around the grounds, he knew she would love them. He wasn't wrong. The gardens stretched as far as the eye could see. Adam told her that Elodie did most of her own gardening; she was very hands on around the chateau despite the way she had been raised. Elodie didn't rely on servants. They walked hand in hand in the late afternoon sunshine; the lake looked stunning, like fondant on a cake. Right at the end of the lake, Claire could see a little boathouse; she persuaded Adam to take her to it. There they sat, huddled together, looking out at the view and the magnificent chateau that dominated the background.

Claire rested her head on Adam's shoulder for a few minutes. Then, turning to him, Claire said, 'Adam, I know I need to meet Mathieu, until I have done that I can't move on. I need to do this, but I need you by my side. Will you be there for me?' Claire looked at him, waiting for his reply.

Adam pulled her to him. 'Always, Claire, always from this day onwards, I will be there for you. We will do this together, I promise you.' Claire could see the sincerity in his eyes. Adam knew that Mathieu probably only had a few months left; he was keen to move this on, but knew he had to be delicate about it. 'Claire,' Adam asked, 'How would you feel about meeting him tomorrow, while you are here?' Adam was very hesitant, not wanting to spoil anything between them.

Claire was quiet for a moment. Her stomach knotted, deep in thought. Turning her face towards Adam, squeezing his hand, Claire replied. 'Yes, OK, I know I have to do this. I can't move on until I do.' She sighed. 'Can you set up the meeting for me?'

Adam nodded. Holding her close. 'It's the right thing, Claire, albeit the hardest.' Adam knew it would not be easy for either Claire or Mathieu.

'Whilst we are being honest,' said Adam slowly. 'You know that Mathieu has cancer.'

Claire nodded and Adam continued. 'The doctors now only think it will only be nine to twelve months. He is very frail, Claire, seeing you will be just the boost he needs.' Claire nodded again. Fate was cruel sometimes, but at least she had the chance to meet him. To hear his side of the story, to understand why.

Claire wasn't sure if she was going to like it, but she knew she had to hear it. So much had happened in such a short time. Claire knew that you had to forgive things in life, to move on. Some things were harder than others, though. And meeting her father was one of them. It was agreed then that Adam would set up the meeting for tomorrow afternoon in the drawing room at Elodie's.

They made their way back across the grounds, hand in hand, both lost in their own thoughts. As they walked into the hallway, the peace was short-lived. They could hear the children arguing over the Christmas tree in the drawing room as they took off their wellies. Claire suddenly felt very excited. There was nothing like decorating a Christmas tree. She needed this to cheer her up, to distract her thoughts. She would bet this would be a tree to beat all trees.

Joining the children and Elodie in the drawing room, they could see the tree decoration was well under way! The children were fighting about who would go up the ladder the highest. Elodie rolled her eyes as Claire and Adam entered the room.

The children, hearing the door opened, turned. Delightedly, they called out, 'Uncle Adam! 'Look at me, Uncle Adam, I am the highest!' shouted Pierre. 'I have been higher than that,' replied Lucille indignantly.

Adam laughed. The children looked at Claire. 'Children, this is my cousin Claire,' said Elodie.

'Hi, Claire,' they called in unison.

'Do you like decorating trees?' Lucille asked, waving a bit of tinsel in the air.

Claire laughed. 'Yes I do, where are the baubles? Let me help.'

Claire, turning to the large box by Elodie, began helping the children with the decorations. Behind her, Elodie looked at Adam and smiled. He returned the smile. Elodie, relieved, quietly clapped her hands in glee: this was going to be a lovely family Christmas. Not that Claire knew it yet of course, mused Elodie, but they would all be spending Christmas here together, she would see to that.

The afternoon was great fun. It finally came to the time to put the fairy on the top of the tree. The children were arguing who would do it and Elodie stepped in. 'Neither of you will put the fairy on the tree,' she said firmly.

'Awww!' they both said in unison. 'This year our special guest will put up the fairy.' Elodie turned, handing the fairy to Claire.

Claire looked surprised. 'Me, you want me to do it?'

'Yes, Claire. It would be an honour if you would do this for me,' Elodie said, eyes glistening. Claire stepped forward, taking the fairy from Elodie. She turned it gently in her hands. Such a beautiful white lace dress. Such detail to the face, the tiara, the wand. It was magical. Claire loved it.

Placing her foot on the first step of the ladder, Adam appeared by her side. 'I'll hold the ladder for you.'

Claire smiled. She could feel his protectiveness of her. Making her way up the ladder to the top, she glanced down. Claire took in her newfound family below. Such a strange feeling. Then, leaning forward, she placed the fairy on the top of the tree. 'For you, Mum,' she whispered.

Claire and Adam agreed they wouldn't spend the night together. They knew they both still had to talk. There was still tomorrow to get through yet. Adam knew meeting Mathieu would be an ordeal for her. They could have left it; she could have come back next week. Adam had discussed that with Claire. However, her decision had been made. She couldn't stand another week of not knowing. The emotion would be too much to bear. Elodie, Adam and Theo had agreed they wouldn't say anything to Mathieu until tomorrow morning. It would be too much for the old man. They had a wonderful evening, though. Another sumptuous meal was served. Claire hoped they didn't live like this the whole time. It had to be because they had company, surely? She would be as fat as a house if she stayed any longer than a weekend. After dinner they played charades in the lounge, with great hilarity. It was what they all needed just now. Later, sitting by the fire, they finished the evening with a brandy.

Claire yawned. 'I think I am ready for bed.'

Elodie agreed. Claire thanked both Elodie and Theo for a good night, kissing them both on the cheek. Adam offered to walk her to her room and Claire nodded. Stopping at the bedroom door they stood awkwardly for a moment before Adam broke the silence. 'Thank you for talking to me today, for hearing me out. Thank you for allowing me another chance.'

Claire touched his face, leaning forward to kiss him goodnight. No words were needed. Pushing open her bedroom door, she turned and smiled. 'Goodnight, Adam. Sleep well.' Adam blew her a kiss, then walked away. Claire closed the bedroom door. Leaning with her back against the door, she looked around the room. The bedside lights glowed, warming the room. Crisp white cotton sheets had been turned back. The velvet drapes at the window were drawn, it all looked so restful. Claire wondered what Elodie's grandmother had been like. It also made Claire wonder who else had frequented it over the last three hundred years.

Removing her clothes, Claire went to the bathroom. She put on her cosy PJs that she had left warming on the radiator, pleased with herself for thinking to do that. Pulling the brush through her long hair, she thought of tomorrow. That feeling of nervousness was creeping over her again. She longed to feel Adam's arms around her. She was feeling a little unnerved in this huge room all by herself. She knew she was being silly. Her emotions were all over the place just now. Claire pulled her dressing gown around her. Opening the bedroom door, she walked out on to the cold landing. It was dimly lit with wall lights. A long corridor stretched between her and Adam. Pulling the door too, she bravely started off down the corridor. Adam's door was not too far away. Claire quickened her step. How stupid did she feel? She didn't believe in ghosts, or did she? Hesitantly, she tapped on Adam's door. She was trying to be quiet so as not to wake anyone else.

Adam was sat reading in bed; at first he thought he was hearing things. Then the tapping came again. Placing the book on the bedside table, he climbed out, walking across the cold wooden floorboards to open the door. Adam was quite surprised to see Claire standing there, her long blonde hair spilling over her shoulders.

'Adam, can I come in?' said Claire, shyly. Feeling rather stupid at leaving her stood in the doorway, Adam opened the door wider.

'Claire, sorry, of course, I am just a little surprised to see you standing there.' He laughed.

Claire stepped inside the room and Adam quietly shut the door behind them. His room was much more masculine than Claire's. It still had the same feeling of grandeur, though. 'I needed to see you. Can I stay with you tonight?' Claire blushed as she spoke.

No further words were needed. Adam took her hand, leading her to his bed. They lay in each other's arms and drifted off into a deep and restful sleep.

Chapter 30

Claire woke to hear Adam in the bathroom; she could hear his electric toothbrush whirring. Glints of the morning light filtered through the heavy navy damask curtains with the gold tassel finish. Claire, curious to see the view, climbed out of bed and pulled them open. Light flooded the room; a crisp December morning, the lake once again glazed over with ice. The sky, however, was an azure blue. Glancing at the window ledge, Claire couldn't help but notice a little red robin sitting quietly, taking in the same view as Claire. Claire recalled her mother's friend saying that if you saw a robin after a death, then important news was on the way. Well, she needed no more news. There had been enough of that over the last year. Today was incredibly important. It was probably about to change her life for ever. Adam walked out of the bathroom; a towel tied around his waist. Claire smiled as he joined her by the large bay window.

'Stunning, isn't it?' he whispered into her ear. Claire could feel his breath against her cheek. Minty toothpaste, bringing with it a familiarity that she loved.

They stood, his arms around her, looking at the view together. Then Adam realised he had to get to Mathieu early, to prepare him. Taking hold of Claire's hand, he said, 'Claire, I am going to have to go to see Mathieu this morning. I need to tell him I have found you. Are you still willing to meet with him? Is this OK still?' Adam held his breath, waiting for the reply. Claire nodded. No words, just a nod. Going off to get dressed, Adam also felt nervous. He didn't know how today would work out. He knew, however, that it would be an emotional one. There was no doubt about that.

Adam, now dressed, knocked on the bathroom door.

'Claire, love, I am off. Will I see you at breakfast in say about an hour?'

'OK,' Claire called back.

Adam left and Claire, returning to her bedroom, got herself dressed. She wasn't sure she could handle breakfast. Her stomach churned. She was feeling sick again.

Adam, taking a deep breath, knocked on the wooden door of what was the housekeeper's cottage at Chateau Le Grand Fontaine. He could hear Mathieu shuffling towards the door.

This was going to be a shock to the old man.

'Adam, Adam!' Mathieu greeted him in delight. 'Lovely to see you, I wasn't expecting you today, I thought it was the nurse calling in with my injection.' He grinned. 'Nice little nurse she is, too,' he chuckled. With wispy grey hair he looked a bit ruffled, but he was still, as always, impeccably dressed. A smart checked shirt, ochre waistcoat. His dark-brown cords were neatly pressed with a crease down the middle. His shoes, obviously of quality, shone so much so that you could almost see your face in them.

The old man, although he chose to live in the cottage, was incredibly wealthy: Claire didn't know the half of it, Adam guessed neither did he.

'Come in, young man, come in.' Mathieu stood back, opening the door for Adam to enter.

'You're looking good, Mathieu.' He really was looking better than Adam had expected, which was good to see. 'Now, young man, have you been avoiding my calls?' Mathieu asked, looking a little perplexed.

Adam, feeling a little awkward, replied, 'No, not all. I am sorry, I have been extremely busy. We have the wine fair in January, remember. That doesn't get put together on its own, now does it.' Adam tried to sound light-hearted.

Gesturing to the armchair, Mathieu asked, 'Would you like some coffee?'

Adam agreed to a coffee as he settled himself in the armchair. It might help settle his nerves a little. Once the coffee was poured, the two men sat facing each other.

'Well, to what do I owe the honour of this visit?'

Adam fidgeted in his seat for a moment. Clearing his throat, he took a deep breath. 'Mathieu, I have some news for you.' Adam looked the old man in the eyes. 'I have found your daughter.'

Mathieu's teacup shook in his hand. The rattling rang around the room, penetrating the silence. The old man looked pale as he placed the cup down on the little side table. 'You have?' he replied, his voice almost a whisper.

Adam nodded, then told Mathieu the story of how he had met Claire. He didn't go into the detail of how Claire had found out or about how hurt she had been by Adam's deceit. Mathieu sat quietly, listening, taking it all in. Adam was worried about the shock. This might be too much for Mathieu. Continuing to sit in silence, Mathieu listened whilst Adam continued with the story.

Then, wiping a tear from his eye, Mathieu asked, 'Where is Claire now, Adam? Does she want to meet me?' Mathieu was afraid of the answer. His heart was heavy but elated at the same time. This question could destroy any hope he had held. Gripping his fingers on the edge of the armchair, he looked at Adam. Mathieu knew he certainly didn't deserve her acceptance. Yet he hoped it would be the answer he wanted to hear.

Adam didn't keep him waiting. 'Yes, Mathieu, Claire wants to meet you. In fact, at this moment, Claire is with Elodie at the chateau.' Adam observed the old man, scared of what the information might do to him.

Mathieu shook, tears flowing down his face. It broke Adam's heart to see this strong man crumble before him. Mathieu fumbled for a handkerchief in his top pocket. He never went without a hanky. Pulling it out, he blew his nose rather loudly.

Adam, getting up off his chair, squatted on the stool next to Mathieu. 'Claire would like to see you this afternoon. Do you think you are up to it?' he asked. 'I am more than happy to take you over to the chateau. What do you think, Mathieu?'

Mathieu sat in silence, taking it all in, trying to speak, but the words wouldn't come. His daughter, Claire, was here. She wanted to see him. His hands shaking, he turned to Adam. 'I would very much like that, Adam, please can you arrange it.'

Adam was relieved. However, there was no guarantee that it would all run smoothly. Claire was still very protective of her mother. How she would react, seeing the man who had slept with her mother, then left her, pregnant. A man who had left her mother devastated. It wouldn't be easy on either of them, but it had to be done. Adam had to admit that he was ever so slightly worried.

Adam agreed with Mathieu that he would come back for him at 3pm; he would drive him over to Elodie and Theo's. There, he and Claire could meet and talk in private. Adam would be there, as would Elodie and Theo. The children were away at a friends for the day so there would be no interruptions. It was just what everyone needed.

Arriving back at Chateau Chenosay, Adam parked his car next to Claire's Fiat. He sat for a moment, head resting on the car headrest. He felt quite drained. This morning's encounter had been hard. His heart ached for Mathieu. Adam knew he wasn't a bad man. Leaving the car and entering the chateau, Adam made his way down the long corridor, he could hear Elodie and Claire laughing in the breakfast room.

Claire was sat at the breakfast table. Knowing that Adam wouldn't yet be back, she was enjoying some time alone with Elodie. The two women had talked about her meeting with Adam. They both agreed that a good start had been made on building bridges.

Elodie knew today would be an extremely hard day for both Claire and Mathieu, in fact, for all of them. Elodie really loved Claire's company. Such a shame they had not had the opportunity to grow up together. It would have been great fun.

Both women turned as they heard the door open. 'Ah, there you are,' said Claire, walking up to Adam and kissing him. Elodie greeted Adam with a kiss on each cheek. They all sat down at the breakfast table. There was an awkward silence; they were all treading on eggshells.

Claire spoke first. She realised that everyone was probably waiting for her. 'How did it go, Adam, how did Mathieu take the news?' she asked hesitantly.

Adam told both of them how he had got on with Mathieu

this morning. Missing none of the details, Adam thought it was important that Claire knew that Mathieu was only human, despite what Claire may think of him.

Claire was reserving her judgement. She listened carefully to what Adam had to say. She knew she had to do this.

'It will be OK, you will see,' said Elodie. Then, turning the conversation away from Mathieu to ease the tension in the room, Elodie said, 'Claire, what are your plans for Christmas?'

Claire looked pensive for a moment. 'Do you know, Elodie, I haven't really thought much about it with everything that has been going on.'

Turning to look at Adam, she then said, 'I had hoped that I could at least spend it with Adam.'

Adam was delighted. It was more than he could have hoped for. Smiling, he slipped his arm around Claire's shoulders on the chair next to him, kissing her on the cheek before replying, 'That would mean the world to me.'

Elodie was grinning. 'Listen, you two,' she clapped her hands as she spoke. 'It would mean more than anything to me to have you both here at the chateau this Christmas, what do you think?'

Adam and Claire both looked at each other, trying to judge each other's response. Claire spoke first. 'Well, if Adam would like to, then I could think of nothing better. If you're happy to have me, that is?'

Elodie, jumping up from her chair, threw her arms around them both. 'It would make my Christmas!' She grinned, giving them both a hug.

'Just one thing,' Claire said quietly. 'It will all depend on what happens today.'

Elodie nodded, she understood. However, she was quietly confident that it would all work out. Mathieu and Claire were alike; but Claire wouldn't see that yet. Elodie hoped that wounds could be healed. *Fingers crossed*, she thought to herself.

'Adam, can I borrow Claire for a little while, I'd love to show her around my garden and vegetable plot,' Elodie asked, her dark-brown eyes looking soulfully at Adam.

What a woman, thought Adam. *How did Theo ever say no to her!* 'Of course! I have some work I can get on with, plus it would be nice for the two of you to spend some time together.' Then he added, 'I have arranged to pick Mathieu up at three, Claire, so we should be back here by 3.15. Can you be in the drawing room for then?' Adam tried to sound matter of fact about it all.

Claire nodded, replying, 'Yes, Adam, that will be fine.'

Elodie, not wanting the conversation to drift back, tugged at Claire's arm. 'Come on, you, let's go get some wellies and bobble hats on. We can go on a tour.'

Out in the garden, Claire was so impressed with what Elodie had created. 'You should be very proud of what you have achieved.'

Elodie glowed in the winter sunshine. In fact, both of them did. The fresh air was good for the soul. Walking back with arms linked, Elodie chatted away. They both knew time was getting on. Elodie thought that Claire probably needed some time to herself before meeting Mathieu. Once back in the house, Elodie turned to Claire. 'Why don't you go and rest for a while. Get your thoughts together,' suggested Elodie. Claire agreed and said she would see her cousin later. They were all going to take afternoon tea together after the meeting. Claire climbed the stairs to her room.

Once inside, taking off her jeans and jumper, she thought she would have soak in the bath. It would give her time to relax a little. Looking out of the window, Claire again noticed the robin sitting on the windowsill again. How strange. Maybe it was her mother; a sign for Claire that she was with her. It gave Claire some comfort.

Laying in the bath, the hot water was soothing. She closed her eyes. The aroma of lavender was relaxing her tired mind. Lying there in the hot water, it felt perfect after the coldness of the garden. Claire had so much to take in but tiredness overtook her as she dozed. Suddenly, realising the time, she jumped quickly out of the bath, throwing a towel around herself. Fifteen minutes to be dressed and ready. Standing there, ready, in front of the mirror, Claire knew the time had come. It was time to face her father.

Chapter 31

Standing by the drawing room door, Claire felt her hand tremble a little. She couldn't quite bring herself to touch it. That would mean exposing herself, her emotions, her feelings. Then, feeling someone behind her, she turned, finding herself face to face with Adam. He took her hand. 'Mathieu is in there, Claire, he wants to meet you,' Adam whispered. 'You can do this,' he said, squeezing her hand. 'Would you like me to come in with you?'

Claire shook her head. 'I have to do this alone, Adam, but thank you.'

Adam kissed her cheek. Claire stepped forward, once again, placing her hand on the cold brass handle. Taking a deep breath, she stepped into the room, slowly closing the oak door behind her. There was no turning back now.

In front of the fire, in the large gold velvet armchair, Claire could see an old man. Older than she had expected him to be. Claire stood, rooted to the spot.

Mathieu tried to lever himself up in the chair, his hands shaking. Claire saw this and she spoke softly. 'Please sit, you don't need to get up.' The emotion was choking her throat as she took another couple of steps. Claire, resting her hand on the back of the large Victorian sofa, needed to regain her balance.

Mathieu looked at her, his heart pounding. This was his daughter. How like Gloria she looked. The hair, the eyes, it brought all the memories flooding back to him. He couldn't help himself. He wiped away a tear.

Claire walked closer to him. Once again Mathieu tried to lift himself up out of the chair. He was too weak; his legs didn't want to work, damn them, he thought.

Claire, realising he was struggling, sat down next to him on the old leather pouffe. Instinctively, her hand reached out to touch his. Tears were now streaming down her face. The emotions for both of them were more than each could bear. No words were said as Claire embraced her father for the first time. He felt frail and weak, but somehow, she found comfort in his embrace. Neither of them could speak. Claire had run this scenario over and over in her mind for the last few hours, but here, now, in the reality, nothing seemed to matter other than they had found each other. She couldn't find anger or hate. Maybe she was forgiving too easily? To her though it was time to let go. Nothing would bring her mum back.

Claire wasn't sure how long they stayed like that. It felt

like hours, yet probably only ten minutes had passed. They slowly opened up to each other, talking, explaining, listening. Claire heard his side of the story. Mathieu was honest with her. Claire, in return, was honest with him. There was a lot of ground to cover. Mathieu was sincere in how he spoke. Claire tried hard to understand the background that Mathieu had come from: the pressure of title and nobility in France. A different world, very different from her upbringing. Claire knew her mum had been happy and certainly well cared for by Maurice.

On the other side, Mathieu had lived in grandeur, yet with regret for all of his life. Surely now he was owed some happiness, some forgiveness, she thought. She wondered if she could give him that small gift. They could not go back and change what had happened. They needed to look forward. Surely her mum would want her to make the most of the time that Mathieu had left. Writing that letter to her gave her the impression that her mother wanted her to find him. The minutes passed into a couple of hours. Eventually, with a knock on the door, Adam appeared, his head poking round. Relieved to see them sitting and chatting, he entered the room.

Claire got to her feet, helping Mathieu to his. Both hugged Adam. The next to appear was Elodie, not wanting to be left out. She too was embraced by them all. It was a comforting scene for anyone to see; a family reunited, the fire burning bright in the hearth, the lights of the Christmas tree twinkling in the background. They were complete.

Over the next week, Claire was feeling a little under the weather. It had been a lot to deal with. Elodie, Mathieu and Adam had all been urging her to stay on. So, keeping the peace, Claire had agreed to move into the chateau, at least until New Year. Claire knew she would need to go back to her cottage at some point. There would be things to sort out, not least the fact that the six months' tenancy was almost up and the rental car to return. None of this seemed pressing just now. She was confident it would be OK with Claude to continue renting the cottage. That was the least of her worries. Claire had decided she was just going to enjoy time getting to know her new family. It would be a lovely lead up to Christmas day. Adam had been away early this morning, was due back by lunchtime. They had agreed to have lunch together.

Claire, feeling exhausted, had had a lie-in. Outside in the chateau grounds the dogs were barking. It didn't disturb her. It was a good two hours before Claire came too again. This emotional roller coaster that she had been on must have taken its toll on her far more than she realised, thought Claire, sitting herself up in bed.

Claire really didn't feel too good; a little queasy. Climbing out of bed, she went to the bathroom, pushing open the large door. Claire stepped onto the cold marble tiles. Suddenly, feeling very sick, Claire lurched forward to the toilet, just making it in time. Just at that moment, Adam had walked through the door, hearing her in the bathroom. Frowning and slightly concerned, he sat down on the bed. A few minutes later, Claire appeared back into the bedroom, looking rather pale.

She pulled her dressing gown belt around her middle. She grimaced weakly at Adam who got off the bed, taking her hand and making her sit down in the large armchair by the window.

Claire felt a little better. Adam, though, was very concerned. He asked Claire if he should call the doctor.

'No, I'll be fine. It is probably something I ate.' She smiled feebly at him. Adam was not convinced at all. 'You have to stay here and rest then.'

Claire agreed. There was a knock on the bedroom door. It was Elsa from the kitchen with a large tray. Adam had arranged for them to have lunch in their room together. Taking the tray from her, Adam thanked her, setting it down on the large cherry table in the bay window. Claire, perking up a little, tucked into the ham sandwiches. The colour had come back to her cheeks. Adam was relieved to see this; she had given him quite a fright.

After lunch, Adam said he had some paperwork to do. He would do it at the table, insisting that Claire went back to bed for an hour. She didn't need any encouragement; an afternoon nap would do her good. When she woke, Adam was still working at the table. He looked up and smiled.

'How are you feeling now?'

Claire pulled herself up in bed. 'A little better, I think the last few days have taken it out of me.'

Adam sat down on the bed next to her. 'I'm not surprised, it has been very emotional. I think you should stay here for the rest of the day.'

Claire had to agree. But it was only two days before Christmas now and she hadn't been able to get Adam a present yet. She didn't know what to buy him. Turning to him, she asked, 'Do you have much on tomorrow?' Lying on the bed next to her he replied, 'No, is there something you want to do?'

'Yes,' said Claire. 'I haven't been able to do any Christmas shopping yet, do you think you could come with me and help me? You know everyone well so you can help me choose some presents.'

Adam pulled her to him. 'I couldn't think of anything better than taking you Christmas shopping, it's a date.' He smiled. Claire snuggled into him, closing her eyes. What a difference compared to this time last year. Her mother had just died. She was about to discover her husband was having an affair. Now here she lay, in the arms of a man she loved. Claire didn't care that they hadn't known each other long. She was going to take this chance of happiness; she deserved it.

The next morning, Claire was relieved to be feeling much better. Adam commented on how well she looked. He kissed the tip of her nose. 'Your chauffeur awaits, madame.'

Claire laughed. She was looking forward to this trip. Adam said he would go to fetch the car. Claire needed the toilet again. 'I'll meet you outside in five,' she called as she headed back to her bedroom.

As she stood washing her hands, a thought suddenly crossed Claire's mind. Walking back to the bedroom, she picked her handbag up off the bed, looking for her diary. Flicking back through the pages, she found the date of her last period. Claire sat down on the bed in shock. According to her calculations it was at least seven weeks ago. That couldn't be right, she thought, re-counting the days. It was. Claire always wrote in her diary the first day of her period. It was a habit from when she was undergoing her fertility treatment. A habit she had never got out of. What should she do now? Oh, goodness, what would Adam say? Then the overwhelming feeling of knowing that a test could be negative, just like all those other times. Then there was Adam. What if he didn't want children. They had never discussed it. He would think she had trapped him. They had been together no time at all. Claire couldn't get pregnant. She sat on the bed, then got up, then sat back down again.

Trying to stay calm, she decided she would buy a pregnancy test in town. Like all the others, it would be negative. The thought of sitting there again, waiting for the blue lines, filled her with fear. Claire made her way out to Adam. She was going to try not to think about it for now. They would just enjoy the day out. He smiled as she climbed into the car.

'Are you ready?'

Claire smiled back. 'Yes, let's hit the town.'

The centre of Moulin was busy. Fairy lights adorned the build-ings around the marketplace. 'Have you ever been to Cafe Bourgogne?' Claire asked Adam as they walked along the street. 'I have indeed, it's one of my favourites. Would you like to go for lunch?' he asked.

'Why not?'

They walked along, looking at all the lovely shops. People were coming in and out, laden with parcels. The atmosphere was very festive. They stopped near Cafe Bourgogne. 'Would you mind if I deserted you for half an hour?' Adam asked.

'I certainly wouldn't,' she smiled. 'I have some shopping to do myself, anyway.'

Adam pulled her in, kissing her tenderly on the lips.

'OK, thirty minutes, then see you back here.'

Claire watched him walk away up the road. Up ahead she could see a neon green pharmacy sign flashing. She couldn't believe she was doing this. She felt numb. Over the years of fertility treatment she had only learned to be anxious, never excited. Claire popped the test in her handbag and walked back on to the street. She still had twenty minutes until she was to meet Adam, so she went looking for a present for him. It was a fruitless search. A lovely jumper and a wool scarf were the best she could do. It wasn't very exciting, she thought to herself. As she got back to the restaurant, Adam was nowhere to be seen. Five minutes passed. Claire was relieved to see him coming running round the corner. 'I thought you had deserted me,' she laughed.

Kissing her, he replied, 'Never.'

The restaurant was busy inside. Everyone was in the festive spirit. There was a beautiful tree in the corner and all the serving staff were wearing Santa hats. Each table had a red candle decorated with holly. 'Isn't this lovely!' exclaimed Claire, drinking in the ambiance of it all. Adam loved to see her happy. He hoped he could make her happy for the rest of their lives. They enjoyed a delicious meal comfortable in each other's company. Later they laughed as they went around the shops picking up presents for the whole family. Her new family. This would be a Christmas Claire would never forget!

Chapter 32

Christmas Eve dawned. Claire woke and looked at the clock. Adam was already up and about. She went through to the bathroom, then, remembering about the pregnancy test, she went back to the bedroom to look for her handbag. Just as she was about to pull it out, Adam walked in.

'You're up then, lazy daisy,' he jested. 'I hope you don't mind but there are a few things I still need to do this morning. I am going to head out. Will you be OK?' he asked.

'Of course I will. Have you bought presents for the children yet?'

'No, that was what I was planning to do this morning,' he replied, picking up his wallet from the dressing table. 'Would you mind if we shared the presents?' asked Claire. She hoped that wasn't cheeky.

'That's a great idea,' agreed Adam. 'Elodie has made some suggestions, so how about I just chose from those. We can wrap them together tonight.'

Claire thought that would be a lovely idea. It would give her time today to wrap the presents she had bought for Adam yesterday; plus the ones she had bought for Elodie and Theo. Claire had never had a Christmas like this with so many people. It filled her with excitement. Adam kissed her goodbye.

Alone again in the room, she picked up her handbag and pulled out the paper bag. Pulling the pregnancy test from the box, she sat staring at it. There was probably no point in doing this, she thought. Part of her wanted to put it back in the box. Then, reminding herself she was the new assertive Claire, she picked up the test. I can do this, she thought, taking the test through to the bathroom. Two minutes later, sitting on the edge of the bath, Claire gripped the stick. Memories of all the times she had sat there in the past waiting for the results came flooding back to her. The anxiety, the pain, the disappointment. Keeping the stick in her hand, she walked back to the bedroom. She didn't want to be reminded of sitting on a bathroom floor crying. Looking at her watch, there was still another minute to go.

Claire stood looking out of the bedroom window. Snow had fallen. Just a light dusting, but enough to leave a cover on the ground. To her surprise, a little robin landed on the window ledge. Claire smiled. She was sure this was her mother watching over her. Why else would a robin keep popping up?

It was time to look. Slowly, Claire turned the stick over in her hand. There, outlined on the stark white stick were two blue lines. She sat staring. Two blue lines, two blue lines. Her heartbeat to the same rhythm. 'Oh, my goodness, I AM pregnant.'

Then the tears came, the salty water running down her face. The sickness, the tiredness. She was pregnant. Then she was laughing. As the robin flew away, Claire whispered,

'Thank you, Mum.' Suddenly the reality of it all hit home.'

Adam, she thought. How am I going to tell Adam? We have only known each other five months. Does he actually want children? What if he is angry? What if he accuses me of getting pregnant deliberately? Claire sat down on the bed. What if I end up like my mother? The elation was slipping away. Claire was now worried. She put the pregnancy stick back in her handbag. Zipping it shut, just in case. She needed to think this through.

Reaching for the wrapping paper she had brought yesterday, she started wrapping the gifts. It would take her mind off things for a while. Claire needed to work out just how she was going to tell him. The presents wrapped; Claire went looking for Elodie.

It was lunchtime and she suddenly felt ravenous. Theo was just coming through the front door as Claire came down the stairs. 'Hi, Claire, everything OK,' he asked as he hung his coat up.

'Yes, I am fine thanks. Is Elodie around?'

I think she will probably be in the dining room. Are you going to join us for lunch?' asked Theo.

'If you don't mind.'

'Of course we don't mind. Come on, let's find her.' He smiled, leading the way. Claire enjoyed her lunch with them. Elodie was certainly relieved to see her looking much better. Claire asked if there was anything she could do to help with the preparations for Christmas day. Elodie insisted she would be fine. 'Why don't you have a lie down? I want you to be in top condition tomorrow for your first family Christmas. It's going to be a busy day.'

Claire certainly felt like she could have a nap 'If you're sure, Elodie.'

'I am.' She laughed.

Claire left them to it and went back up to the room. Outside, a little more snow had fallen. Adam would be back soon. Claire needed to think how she was going to tell him about the results. Did she really want to spoil Christmas? Or maybe it would make his day. Claire hoped the latter, but she wasn't sure.

Adam arrived back about 5pm. Sticking his head quietly around the bedroom door, he looked to see what Claire was doing. She was in bed, fast asleep. He tiptoed into the room. Removing his coat and shoes, he went into the bathroom. He didn't want to wake her. Today had been a busy day, so he wondered if Elodie would mind if they ate in their room tonight. It would give them both time with the children to enjoy Christmas Eve as a family. Deep down, Adam was still worried about Claire being under the weather. He tiptoed back out again. Claire didn't stir. He made his way down to find Elodie. There was something he wanted to discuss with her, anyway.

Claire woke. The light had gone; the room was dark. Leaning over, she switched on the little table lamp. Pulling herself up in bed, she looked at the clock. Almost 6pm. She wondered where Adam had got to. As she got out of bed, she noticed his coat and shoes over by the window. He must be home, she thought. Claire went to the bathroom to run a bath. It would make her feel better. Just as she switched on the taps, Adam appeared in the room.

'So, you're up, are you, sleepy. Come here,' he said, opening his arms to her. Claire snuggled in. 'I have just spoken to Elodie,' he said, caressing her back. 'We are going to have dinner in our room tonight. Are you OK with that?'

Claire pulled back from Adam to look at him. 'That would be lovely but won't Elodie mind with it being Christmas Eve?' she asked hesitantly.

'Actually, she thought it was an excellent idea. Mathieu is staying at the cottage tonight. He wanted to be in his own place. It will give them time alone with the children.'

Claire nodded; she understood. Adam was looking at her. She still looked tired. He was a little worried; it certainly wasn't like Claire. Reaching for her hand, he asked, 'Are you sure you are OK?'

Claire nodded again. 'I was just going to have a bath,' she said, pulling her hand from his. She kissed his cheek. Adam watched her walk to the bathroom. Something wasn't quite right. He wanted to make tonight special for her. Their first Christmas Eve together. The meal had been organised, so he would get the table set. Elodie said she would leave some bits by the bedroom door so as not to disturb them.

Opening the door, Adam looked. Elodie, true to her word, had left a small box by the door. Adam looked inside. Candles, napkins, even a couple of roses. He would set it up whilst Claire bathed. Slipping into the heavenly bubbles, Claire sighed. She knew she had to speak to Adam. It would be hypocritical of her not to. Especially after the way she had been when she had found out that Adam knew her father. They had promised each other no more secrets. Meeting her father was life changing. So was this.

Slipping further down, the warm water enveloped her. Lavender infused her thoughts. Running her hand over her still-flat stomach, she thought of the baby. She realised as she did so, it was the first time, she had let herself think she was actually carrying a baby. So many years of disappointment, negative tests, all the stress. Claire knew she needed to enjoy every moment. It terrified her to think about Adam and how he would feel. Claire lay in the bath for a good twenty minutes.

Adam knocked on the door, 'Are you OK, sweetheart,' he asked, his voice full of concern. 'I'm fine, I'll be out in a minute,' she replied. Claire climbed out of the bath, wrapping her dressing gown around her. Pulling her damp hair back, she fastened it into a low bun at the back. Taking a pot of moisturiser from the shelf, she carefully worked the cream into her face. She looked tired. Taking a deep breath, she walked into the bedroom.

Adam stood by the window. Beautifully set out on the table were candles, flickering in the dimmed bedroom lights. Roses filled a small vase. The table was complete with Christmas napkins. Claire was speechless. As she walked towards him, the tears came spilling down her cheeks. They wouldn't stop. Adam, looking alarmed, quickly went to her, pulling her into his arms. 'Claire, what is it? Please tell me. I know something isn't right,' he said, gently stroking her hair. He led her to the armchair in the bay window, helping her to sit. Kneeling at her side, he handed her some tissues.

Claire looked at him. 'Adam, there is something I need to tell you.'

Adam was worried now. Was she going to split up with him? Had she not forgiven him about Mathieu? Did she not trust him?

Claire looked at his concerned face, taking his hand, she knew she had to tell him. 'I'm pregnant,' she whispered. Adam just looked at her, her pretty face, her beautiful eyes.

Claire suddenly felt alarmed. He didn't want a baby; she knew it. Before she had the chance to say anything, Adam was holding her. 'Oh, Claire, oh, Claire. I can't believe it.

That is fantastic news.'

Claire pulled back a little and through her tears she said, 'Is it?'

Adam pulled her back to him. 'I couldn't think of anything better; it's a wonderful Christmas present.' He too had tears in his eyes now. 'I never thought I would get to be a father.'

Claire smiled. 'Well, you are now.'

He held her tight, 'How pregnant?'

'I don't know exactly, but I think about eight weeks.' He beamed. 'This is wonderful news.' Claire thought he looked elated and it made her smile. They sat in the light of the candles. Adam ran his hand across Claire's tummy. 'Hello, little one. Your mummy and daddy can't wait to meet you.'

Claire felt a huge sense of relief wash over her. They had been together for such little time, but it all felt so right. From the day they had bumped into each other again in France, Claire had been falling in love with him. Sometimes she worried it was too quick. Did they really know each other? Yet she felt she had known him for years. In her mind it was right. That was all that mattered. Her father had always said if it felt right, then it was right. Thinking of her mum for a moment, Claire smiled. She would have been so happy to be a granny. It had only been a year since she had said goodbye to her. She couldn't help feeling her mum had had a hand in all this.

Adam smiled at her from across the table. 'Penny for your thoughts,' he asked, taking her hand.

'I was just thinking of my mum and how happy she would

have been to know she would be a granny.'

Adam understood how she felt. It made him think of his own mother. 'Our two mums will keep an eye on us,' he laughed.

Looking at Claire, he asked, 'What happens from here then?' He was so excited.

'Well, I will need to see a doctor as soon as we can after Christmas. Then, after that, I'm not sure. I've never been pregnant before!' Adam remembered Claire telling him about all her failed IVF attempts. For a moment he wished she had told him before she did the test. He could have supported her. What if it had been negative, how would she have coped? Claire was a strong woman, he knew that, but he was going to be there for her every step of the way. Looking at her now, he took her hand.

'Claire, I love you more than anything. Thank you for making my Christmas.'

'I love you too, Adam,' she whispered back.

Adam got up from his seat, walking round to Claire's side of the table. Taking her hand, he pulled her up. 'Come, look out of the window,' he said. Claire stood up and Adam pulled back the heavy curtains. The snow lay thick on the ground, the garden lanterns cast a glow across the gardens. It looked absolutely stunning, the perfect winter scene. They stood, together, looking out across the grounds. They knew this was the first of many Christmases to come.

Chapter 33

Claire woke on Christmas morning feeling joyful. Yes, joyful, that was the only way she could describe it. The past two weeks that Claire had spent at the chateau had felt such a blessing. Here she was, waking up on Christmas morning, with a man she loved and this wonderful new family. Not only that, but she was finally going to be a mum. Turning over in the large four-poster bed, she grinned at Adam, who was just waking up beside her. He grinned sleepily back at her. Kissing him, Claire said, 'Happy Christmas, sweetheart.' Adam pulled her towards him.

'Happy Christmas to you too, darling.'

Their first Christmas together. Claire felt so content. A Christmas with her newfound family. She was so excited about Christmas Day. Elodie and Theo, the children and Mathieu, would all be with them in the grand dining room downstairs. The chateau would ring with the sounds of family, as any home should on Christmas Day. Nobody would be alone. 'Adam,' said Claire, sitting up in bed. 'Can we keep our news to ourselves for now?'

Adam, yawning, sat up next to Claire. 'Of course we can,' he said.

'I just want to make sure it's all confirmed before we say anything,' Claire said, as Adam snuggled up to her.

'I understand,' he replied. He kissed her tenderly.

Claire responded. 'Come on, we need to get up,' she laughed, we can't lay here all day.

Adam reluctantly got out of bed. Walking to the window, he pulled open the curtains. There had been more snow overnight. It was all looking perfect for his plan. He just hoped Elodie had done everything in time. Claire said she would go to the bathroom first, far too excited to stay in bed any longer. She grabbed her fluffy dressing gown and headed off. Adam then took his turn in the bathroom. Soon, they were both ready and dressed for Christmas morning.

'Claire,' said Adam, 'before we go for breakfast, would you like a walk with me outside?'

'That would be lovely,' said Claire.

'But before we go, I have a gift for you,' smiled Adam. Reaching under the bed, he pulled out a large, wrapped box and handed it to her. Claire beamed. She loved presents, she loved Christmas. Excitedly she tore open the paper with Adam sitting, watching. The big box had Aigre written on it, a well-known outdoor range of clothing. Claire was in-

trigued as she lifted off the lid. There, wrapped inside, Adam
had bought Claire her own pair of wellies.

Claire laughed. 'My own wellies, I don't have to borrow
Elodie's anymore.' Inside each boot was a pair of long, thick
socks. 'They are to keep your pretty little toes warm,' Adam
laughed.

All wrapped up and ready to go, they set off together down
the path. They walked through the rose garden, now dormant,
turning in the lake's direction. They walked quietly, side by
side, alongside the lake, hand in hand. Claire felt in perfect
harmony with Adam. There were a couple of ducks sat on the
ice. All the trees looked like they had been sugar-coated with
frost. Adam looked at Claire's flushed face. He kissed the tip
of her nose; it was icy cold. Wrapping his arms around her,
they stood for a moment, looking out across the sheet of ice.
Behind them the chateau looked majestic, snow covering
the roof. Lights shone out from the mullioned windows. The
huge Christmas tree at the front, adorned with fairy lights.

Ahead was the little boathouse. It had become a special
place for them when out on their walks. It was where they
had both sat that day, trying to piece back together a shattered relationship. As they got closer, Claire could see little lights twinkling in the window. Bemused, she looked at
Adam, who only smiled and held her hand tighter. He loved
how Claire looked today, radiant, flushed cheeks, sparkling
eyes. Adam knew he loved her more than anything. Reaching the boathouse door, he opened it wide. There, inside, lit

by hundreds of fairy lights, was a table set for breakfast for two. Claire gasped in amazement. 'Adam, this is beautiful. When did you do all this?'

Adam laughed. 'I had a little help from your cousin,' he confessed, kissing her tenderly. The two of them took their seat at the little table. A flask of fresh coffee stood on the side, a basket of croissants and fresh orange juice. He wrapped the mohair rug around her knees to keep her warm, kissing her softly on the lips as he did so. Claire thought for a moment that Adam looked slightly uncomfortable.

Adam reached out and took Claire's hand. Slowly, he dropped to one knee. Claire was laughing, thinking he was fooling around. Then, realising he was being serious, Claire gasped.

Adam spoke. 'Claire, will you do me the honour of becoming my wife.'

Claire just stared at him. Adam, for a moment, albeit a brief one, thought Claire was going to say no. Then Claire, breaking the silence, said, 'Adam, I would love to be your wife.'

Fumbling in his pocket, Adam pulled out a little box, opening the lid as he did so. Inside, gleaming back at her, sat a stunning ring of sapphire and diamonds. Claire couldn't help herself gasping again. 'This was Mathieu's mother's engagement ring, Claire, he wanted you to have it when I sought his permission to ask for your hand in marriage.'

Claire couldn't believe what she was seeing: there were at least six stunning diamonds circled around a large dark-blue sapphire. Incidentally, sapphires were her favourite, not that she owned any.

Adam, taking the ring from the box, slipped the ring onto Claire's finger. It fitted perfectly. Adam sighed with relief. They kissed, laughed, kissed, then laughed again, Claire flashing her ring in front of him on the table. Adam thought his now wife-to-be was glowing beautifully.

'I promise I will be there for you always,' said Adam, placing his hand softly on her tummy, 'for our baby too.'

Later, as they made their way back up to the chateau, Adam laughed, pointing ahead. 'Look, Claire!'

Claire, shielding her eyes from the sunshine, looked up to the chateau. There at the front door was Elodie, Theo, the children and Mathieu, all standing, waiting. Elodie, not being able to contain herself, ran forward. 'Well?' she gasped.

'Well, what did she say?'

Claire, laughing, said, 'I said yes, of course.'

'You did!' exclaimed Elodie.

'Yes!' Claire shouted, then again she repeated, 'I said yes.' Everyone laughed and clapped hands.

Christmas Day was an amazing day of celebration, presents, champagne, more champagne. It just flowed. Claire had just the one glass, discreetly trying not to let anyone realise she wasn't drinking. Adam caught her eye across the table. He smiled at her. Looking round, Claire couldn't quite believe that she had this amazing family. She couldn't wait to tell Elodie and Theo the baby news. Claire knew they would be over the moon for them both.

Lunch was superb. Roasted goose with all the Christmas trimmings. The dining room had a Christmas tree almost as spectacular as the drawing room. Late afternoon, they all lazed around in the drawing room; Mathieu snoozing in the chair, the children on their phones, Elodie laying contentedly with Theo on the large sofa. Adam was curled up with Claire next to him, her head on his shoulder. Carefully pulling away from Claire, Adam stood up with his glass. 'I'd like to say something, if I may.'

The children looked up from their mobile phones and Elodie smiled, 'Of course you can.'

Adam cleared his throat. 'Elodie, Theo and children, over the past twenty years that we have all known each other, you have become like family to me. The family that I have never really had.' Elodie smiled at him. Reaching out, she squeezed his hand. 'Mathieu, you have been the most cantankerous, stubborn, annoying boss I have ever had, but you are like my father.'

Mathieu coughed, looking a little embarrassed. It was true, though, this man was like his own son.

Adam continued, 'Now I am the luckiest man alive to have this beautiful woman by my side who has crazily agreed to be my wife.' With this, Adam pulled Claire to her feet. Laughing, she stood by his side. 'Why you have agreed to marry me I will never know,' laughed Adam, kissing her cheek. 'I want to raise a toast to you all, to family.' He smiled, raising his glass in the air.

They stood and toasted 'To Family'. Slowly, behind them all, Mathieu pulled himself to his feet, walking towards Claire. No words were said as he hugged her. Then, slowly, looking quite emotional, he said, 'You have made me the proudest man on earth. We have only a short time together, but you have made this old man so happy to know that you have Adam to care for you.' Mathieu shook a little as he spoke.

Claire, with a tear sliding down her cheek, took Mathieu's hand as she smiled at him. 'Will you walk me down the aisle?' All Mathieu could do was nod.

Claire had forgiven him. It would be what her mother wanted.

Later that night, as Claire and Adam lay in bed, Adam looked at Claire, stroking her face. 'That was a wonderful thing you did today,' he said, 'asking Mathieu to walk you down the aisle.'

Claire smiled, 'It just seemed the right thing to do.' Adam nodded.

Claire went on. 'There is no point in resentment. It won't

change anything. Mum had a happy life with Maurice and I believe she truly loved him. I know though that a part of Mathieu stayed in her heart. I honestly believe she wanted me to find him.'

Adam pulled her to him. 'You're such a kind person, Claire, I am such a lucky man to have you.'

Claire kissed him. 'I am lucky to have you too,' she sighed. Within minutes, she was asleep. Adam lay looking at her in the light from the moon. Claire had found forgiveness where many people hadn't. She had been through such a lot in the last year. Adam was determined no one would ever hurt her.

He would always protect her.

Chapter 34

Two days later, Adam and Claire sat in the car in Moulin. They had just visited the doctor, who confirmed that Claire was indeed pregnant. A date for a first scan had been arranged for the new year and she would meet the midwife in due course.

Claire still couldn't quite believe it. She smiled at Adam. 'Are you happy?' he asked.

'I have never been happier in my life,' she said, squeezing his hand. 'Shall we tell the family on New Year's Eve then?'

Adam smiled. 'That would be a great time to tell them. Good idea,' he said. 'Come on, let's get back home. I want you to rest this afternoon.'

Back at the house, they sneaked upstairs. They didn't want Elodie asking where they had been. The two of them just wanted to enjoy this time to themselves. Adam was off work for the rest of the week so he was going to make sure Claire was pampered. There would be time soon enough for the family to join in their celebration. Claire sat in the armchair by the window. She was fiddling with the ring on her finger. She had never owned such a stunning piece of jewellery and to think it had been her grandmother's. Claire couldn't help wondering that this might have been her mother's if things had turned out differently. As she turned the ring in the sunlight, prisms of colour splashed on to the walls. It sparkled with every turn. Adam laughed, watching her. 'It's beautiful, isn't it? You don't mind that it was given to me rather than me buying you one,' he asked hesitantly. 'I'd happily take you and buy you a new one.'

'It's perfect.'

Adam sat down with her. 'Do you wish things had been different for your mother?' he asked.

Claire sat, thinking for a moment. 'If she had spent her life being unhappy, maybe. But I know she and Dad had a wonderful life together. They loved each other dearly. They doted on me.'

Adam thought how much he would have liked to have met them. 'Maybe a little of Mum carried something for Mathieu, but she put Maurice and my happiness over everything. I honestly believe she wanted me to find out. I think she knew Mathieu had suffered through his life. She would have wanted him to have closure. She had me, which is something he never had. Knowing Mum, she would also have felt a little guilty for not telling Mathieu about me that night. She has allowed me to forgive him for her.'

Adam took her hand. 'That's a lovely way of looking at it,' he said. 'You're a very special lady, Claire.'

New Year's Eve arrived. Elodie was throwing a small party to celebrate their engagement. Little did she know that there would be baby news, too. Claire was excited. She was bubbling over trying to keep the news to herself. Claire had spent the last couple of afternoons with Mathieu. Slowly they were trying to build a father and daughter relationship. They both knew it would take time; however, Mathieu also knew that his time was limited. Every step they took, was a step in the right direction.

On this morning, Mathieu had asked Claire if she would walk with him a little. He had asked her if she could come to his cottage, saying he would like to show her the chateau. Of course she had agreed. It would give Adam time to help Theo sort the wines and champagne for the party tonight. This would be time for her to spend with her 'father'. Claire still wasn't used to saying this word in connection with Mathieu. As each day had passed, it had become a little easier. Claire had arrived spot on 10am. There was Mathieu, waiting by the door of the cottage, looking rather dapper, more dapper than usual, Claire had thought. Mathieu was pleased to see Claire, kissing her tenderly on each cheek. They walked together,

Mathieu's arm resting on hers, his walking stick in the other.

As they walked, Mathieu pointed out various things around the garden and grounds. Then, turning the corner at the side of the chateau, they looked over the vast expanse of garden which sadly, over the last ten years, had fallen into neglect. Mathieu could close his eyes and picture the gardens back in the days when they had been cared for. He tried his hardest to explain to Claire how it had all once looked. 'Your mother loved the gardens,' he told her.

Then, moving on, they followed the path that led to the grand front door of the chateau. The doors were huge, with iron studs. They loomed above them. A huge brass knocker, now rather tarnished, sat untouched after many years of neglect. Claire stood on the doorstep for a moment, taking it all in. In the distance by the trees she could she just the cottage where her mother had lived. Then beyond that there were still rows and rows of vines. 'Claire,' said Mathieu, fumbling in his pocket. 'My days of living in the chateau are done; it's too vast, too cold for my old bones.' Sighing, he went on, 'However it would give me nothing but pleasure and pride to hand this beautiful building over to you, my only daughter.' With that, Mathieu took the old key from his pocket and handed it to Claire. Claire was stunned. Silently she shook her head, not quite believing what Mathieu had just said. Mathieu, sensing her hesitance, pressed the key tighter into her palm. 'Please,' he said, looking at her. 'Take it, it is yours to do with as you wish.' The old man's eyes glazed over. Suddenly Claire too was overcome with emotion.

Turning to him, all Claire could say was, 'Thank you, thank you, Dad'. Mathieu's heart missed a beat and he hugged her. She had finally said the word. Mathieu would remember that moment for as long as he had left. As the pair stood, by the large oak doors, looking out across the vast gardens of the chateau, a little robin chirped happily on the branch of the old oak tree in front of them.

That evening, the night of the party, Claire put on a blue silk dress that she had picked up on the shopping trip with Elodie. Claire felt like a princess, the soft fabric clinging to her body, falling into a fish tail at the bottom. Elodie had said the blue brought out the colour of her eyes. Adam looked extremely handsome in his tuxedo and bow tie. The pair of them made quite a stunning couple. Elodie had lent her a magnificent sapphire and diamond necklace to match her ring, one of the family heirlooms. They had half an hour before they needed to be downstairs, so Claire took Adam's hand, leading him to the window. They looked out over the flood-lit chateau gardens.

Claire turned to him, smiling. 'Isn't this all so beautiful.'

Adam nodded in agreement 'And so are you.'

They had arranged to meet with Elodie, Theo and Mathieu before the party. This was when they were going to deliver their news. Adam held Claire's hand as they walked towards the drawing room. Claire couldn't stop grinning. Pushing open the door, they walked into the room. Mathieu was already there, sat in his favourite armchair. He was wearing a burgundy velvet dinner jacket with matching bow tie. 'Don't you look dashing,' Claire said, bending to kiss his cheek.

'You, my dear, look absolutely stunning.' Mathieu could have almost mistaken her for Gloria. The drawing room door opened again and Elodie and Theo came breezing in. Elodie looked stunning in a gold silk gown.

Claire, suddenly realising, asked, 'Is that your mother's dress?'

'It is,' smiled Elodie, giving a twirl to her onlookers.

'It's beautiful, Elodie. You look amazing,' said Claire, as she walked over to hug her.

'So do you, Claire. The dress looks beautiful on you. I am so glad I made you buy it.'

Theo kissed Claire on both cheeks, then shook hands with Adam before walking over to open a bottle of champagne left on the table. He poured out five glasses, handing them around the room, as he did. With glasses in their hands,

Adam spoke, 'Would you mind if I said something?'

'Again!' laughed Elodie.

'I know, but it is important,' he said in all earnest.

Elodie laughed, 'I am only teasing, please go on.'

Adam came to stand next to Claire, placing an arm around her shoulder. She looked up at him and smiled. 'Ready?' She just nodded. 'Well, as you know, this beautiful woman at my side has agreed to be my wife. You would have thought this would have made me the happiest man alive. You would think there wasn't anything that could have made me happier.'

All eyes on the room were on him as he continued. 'However, not only has Claire agreed to be my wife but we have also found out that we are expecting our first child.' Adam couldn't have been prouder as he spoke these words.

Elodie, Theo, Mathieu all looked quite shocked. Then Elodie sprang to her feet, throwing her arms around them both. 'Oh my goodness, oh my goodness, Claire, you kept that from me.' Elodie was screaming in delight.

Theo took Adam's hand, pumping it warmly. 'Well done, you two!' Then he took Claire in his arms and hugged her. 'Fantastic news, so delighted for you both!' He beamed.

Mathieu, for the second time in a week, was totally overcome with emotion. Claire knelt at his side. She knew he found it difficult to get up. He held her hand in his, shaking his head in disbelief. 'Not only do I find a daughter but now I am to be a grandfather. I never thought this would happen to me, thank you,' he whispered, 'Thank you so much.' Claire squeezed his hand, then stood to join the others.

'Please, can we keep this between family for now?' she asked, 'Just until I have had my scan.'

'Of course,' said Elodie, 'Mum's the word'. They all laughed.

The party was fantastic. It was just a handful of Elodie and Theo's closest friends. They enjoyed a fantastic meal together and the laughter could be heard echoing around the chateau. Mathieu had made his excuses after dinner. Waiting until midnight was too long for him, he tired easily. Theo had organised for him to be taken home by their housekeeper.

Claire had stood at the chateau door, waving him off. Adam had appeared by her side. It was almost midnight. Claire took Adam's hand, leading him on to the chateau's terrace that looked out over the floodlit gardens. Elodie had seen them from the window and had been about to call them in, then thought better of it. Maybe they wanted to see the New Year in, alone, together.

Claire turned to Adam, smiling. 'I have something else to tell you, Adam,' whispered Claire. Adam looked at her. 'Another surprise, I don't think I can take many more.' They both laughed.

'As you know, I had a walk with Mathieu again this morning. He took me to the chateau to have a look.'

'What did you think?' asked Adam. Claire shivered a little. Adam removed his jacket, placing it around her shoulders.

'Well,' said Claire. 'It's absolutely beautiful or should I say it could be with a little work. Mathieu gave me a gift today. It is one that I want to share with you.' She smiled, kissing him. 'It is with great delight that I can tell you that we are now the proud new owners of Chateau Le Grand Fontaine.'

Adam looked shocked. He shook his head in disbelief. Here

he was, stood with his wife-to-be, a child on the way, and now, they were the proud owners of a stunning chateau. They both stood, laughing, shaking their heads, overjoyed. As the clock struck twelve, Claire tucked herself against Adam.

Little snowflakes fluttered down on them. 'I am so proud of you, Claire, of all that you have overcome. The purpose you have given to my life, the family you are giving me,' Adam said emotionally. He touched her hair as he spoke.

'And me you, Adam. I love you more than anything,' Claire whispered. Smiling at her, Adam said, 'I am so proud of you for forgiving Mathieu.'

Claire nodded. 'It's what my mum wanted; I am sure of that.'

Adam had to agree. He bent down and kissed her tenderly, 'Happy New Year, Claire.'

'Happy New Year, Adam.' Claire cuddled into him as the snow fell. It had been a journey, but Claire knew she had walked the path her mother's footsteps had once trod. She had the happy ending that they both so deserved.

Mathieu

On the 28th of June, five days late, Noah Mathieu Fontaine Johnson was born weighing in at 9lbs 8oz. Claire and Adam and all the family were over the moon, no one more so than Mathieu. He finally had a grandchild. Looking back now, Mathieu marvelled at how life had turned out over the last seven months. He was suddenly feeling elated with life; he had Claire, Adam, and now Noah. He hadn't felt this good for a long time. The mistake with Gloria had eaten away at his life. He had always wanted to apologise for the terrible choices he had made all those years ago. He knew Gloria had had a good life; she had brought up their daughter to be a beautiful woman. One who had found a place in her heart to forgive Mathieu on Gloria's behalf. Mathieu knew more than anyone it could have worked out so differently. Claire had amazing plans for the chateau. Sadly, Mathieu knew that he probably wouldn't be around to see her realise all her dreams. He felt comfort though that she had her family around her. He knew they would love and support her, like he would now, for as long as he could.

Today, 22nd of July, Mathieu was still marvelling at his new grandson who was now almost four weeks old. The relationship he had with Claire was going well. They were moving on slowly, father and daughter, enjoying their new life together. Today, as usual, he was taking his daily walk down by the river. Still now, after all these years, it was his favourite spot. This morning he even had a little spring in his step. The bird song was in full chorus as the river babbled over the rocks. It held so many memories for Mathieu, times spent with Gloria, swimming together, lying on a blanket, talking.

He found it a comfort to sit by the old oak tree, watching the birds swoop over the water, the occasional fish leap up. He could almost hear himself and Gloria splashing in the water, laughter rippling in the air. It had been here that he had given Gloria the beautiful necklace with the lily and rose engraved on it; their initials entwined on the back.

Mathieu had noticed Claire wearing it; she had the habit of rubbing it, especially when she was deep in thought. He prided himself on getting to know these little things about his daughter. Sitting on the old tree stump, he thought again of Claire and Adam. Never had two people meant to be together as much as those two. They were now complete with their son, Noah. Mathieu was enjoying their time together.

The past months had meant the world to him. The first day he had met Claire he could see Gloria in her, just as beautiful. Why had he not stood up to his family and their blasted roots and traditions all those years ago? He could have taken the woman he loved and their unborn child and made a life together. His one solace was that Claire had come to an understanding with him, a forgiveness. Mathieu felt that he no longer needed to torture himself over the past.

Now, with Claire, he had a relationship that he had never thought he would. One of the best parts of the last few months was seeing Claire take great delight in the chateau. This had surprised him, rekindling a new passion in the chateau in himself. Mathieu was on board with all her plans. He had every faith she would make it work. Claire talked of hosting weddings, accommodation, dinners, events. Mathieu smiled at her enthusiasm and courage. He loved just watching her. There were so many similarities between her and Gloria. He could also see a bit of himself in her, especially the stubbornness. This made him smile.

Today, by the river, he watched the water ripple. A little robin joined him on the tree stump. It was a beautiful day. His eyes strained in the bright sunlight. Was that a young woman he could see? He was conscious of his erratic heartbeat. 'Gloria,' he whispered 'Gloria, is that you?'

The woman reached out her hands to him. He steadied himself on the trunk. Standing, he took her hands in his.

Trembling as he felt the softness of her skin in his palms.

'Mathieu, I love you.' It was a whisper in the wind. Mathieu still couldn't make her out completely; the light was so bright. He stood with her, their hands linked, at the water's edge. Reaching out, he pulled Gloria to him. He wanted to take her in his arms. His eyes were misty. There was a little chill in the air, but he was conscious of the warm sun bathing their bodies. Mathieu's lips touched Gloria's. He could feel his breath catching in his throat, a pain in his chest. Mathieu slid down on to the grass bank, the gnarled oak tree supporting his back. He felt Gloria laying down next to him. He turned his face to her. She smiled. Mathieu could see her beautiful eyes in the fading sun. Tenderly, he touched her cheek. Then, smiling back at her, his eyes slowly closed.

It was Adam who found Mathieu. All life had left him. He was but a shell, but he was finally complete. Mathieu and Gloria were together at last.

Printed in Great Britain
by Amazon

66792609R00194